The

Shameless

M.A. Nichols

Flirt

Books by M.A. Nichols

Generations of Love Series

The Kingsleys

Flame and Ember
Hearts Entwined
A Stolen Kiss

The Ashbrooks

A True Gentleman
The Shameless Flirt
A Twist of Fate
The Honorable Choice

The Finches

The Jack of All Trades
Tempest and Sunshine
The Christmas Wish

The Leighs

An Accidental Courtship
Love in Disguise
His Mystery Lady
A Debt of Honor

Christmas Courtships

A Holiday Engagement
Beneath the Mistletoe

Standalone Romances

Honor and Redemption
A Tender Soul
A Passing Fancy
To Have and to Hold

Fantasy Novels

The Villainy Consultant Series

Geoffrey P. Ward's Guide to Villainy
Geoffrey P. Ward's Guide to Questing
Magic Slippers: A Novella

The Shadow Army Trilogy

Smoke and Shadow
Blood Magic
A Dark Destiny

Table of Contents

Prologue

Bristow, Essex
Summer 1810

The sun must shine when a lady gets engaged. If that were not possible, then the rain must pour from the heavens in great heaving buckets. There was something terribly romantic about a rainstorm, and Mary Hayward would be pleased with either option. However, sullen clouds on a dry afternoon would never do; gloomy weather was not permissible on the most important day in her life.

After three days of the most disappointing weather, the skies had cleared in honor of this momentous occasion, casting the world in a vibrant wash of colors. Golden sunshine shone from the clear sapphire sky, sparkling off the emerald fields that stretched around her. Standing in the middle of the country lane, Mary basked in this most beautiful of days. Even the birdsong was sweeter and the flowers were more fragrant, for the air was heady with the sounds and smells of nature.

Stopping at a patch of cornflowers, Mary removed her bonnet. The shabby thing had seen better days, but it was the best she had. Gathering a few of the blossoms, she threaded them through the worn holes in the woven straw, providing the drab thing with a bit of decoration that complemented her dark hair and brought a hint of blue to her gray eyes. Examining her work, Mary wanted to laugh at herself. As though those little flowers could do much to complement her plain features. She knew better than to hope for miracles, but she did wish to present her very best self to Mr. Henry Cavendish. A lady should feel beautiful on the day she gets engaged.

Securing the bonnet on her head, Mary walked down the lane, twirling a stray cornflower between her fingers, the spiky petals brushing across her skin. Though she was mere moments from her dreams becoming reality, her mind played through the possibilities of what was to come. Mary had seen illustrations of medieval knights kneeling before their lady loves, and she pictured her dear friend, Henry, in a similar pose, supplicating with all the earnestness of his heart. That made her laugh, for that was a tad much even for her fantastical notions.

But there would be a kiss. A lady did not get engaged without one, and the thought of it had Mary blushing as she touched her lips. Their first kiss had been on a day much like this one. A lazy afternoon, the skies clear and bright as they strolled the fields of Bristow. Those dreamy hours as they explored those routes so familiar that their feet required no prompting. And then Henry had pulled her into his arms and pressed his lips to hers.

Just the memory of it set her heart pounding. That kiss! For several glorious minutes, there had been nothing in the world but them. Herself and Henry sharing that most tender moment. Mary longed for another embrace, but in the weeks since, they'd not had time alone to do so, and she could hardly wait to see him.

And there would be a pledge of love. Mary was in no doubt of Henry's feelings, but she longed to hear them stated aloud. Not just the simple declarations they had shared so often throughout their childhood, but that of a gentleman baring his soul to the lady he loved. She could hear his voice speaking the words, and that alone was enough to bring tears to her eyes.

A picnic on a sunny afternoon that culminated in a proposal, a declaration, and a kiss. Mary could not think of a better day. Shaking herself from her thoughts, she hurried along. It would not do to make Henry wait.

Cresting the hill beside the Petersons' farm, Mary saw Henry standing beneath the large oak tree, surrounded by a mountain of food, blankets, and cushions fit for a dozen people. At the sight of her, he smiled, and her heart stopped. Oh, how she adored that smile. The way his handsome face lit up as though she were the very best thing in the world.

"Mary!" he called, hurrying to her and catching her up in a hug. "I had just about given up on you. I was worried you had not received my note."

"I had," she said, dipping her head in a manner that other girls used, smiling up at him with all the coyness she could muster. "But I am afraid I was waylaid by some rather lovely wildflowers."

Brushing his fingers across the blossoms, Henry's eyes sparkled as he examined the adornments. "Then the time was not wasted. You look lovely, my dear friend. Though I had wished for a bit more time before the others arrived."

"Others?"

"For the celebration," said Henry, offering up his arm so that he could escort her to the base of the tree.

Mary's eyes widened. She could hardly hold back the tears threatening to gather, but she would not allow them to overtake her because her skin had a tendency to redden in great splotches when she cried. It was bad enough that she could do nothing to erase the smattering of freckles along her cheeks; Mary need not add to those blemishes.

"You are my dearest friend and have been my entire life," said Henry, gathering her hands in his. "And I had to tell you the news first."

Mary thought that an odd way to word it, but she was not about to critique the manner in which her love declared his intentions.

"I am in love," he said. The emotion behind it softened his features, drawing her in, but Mary forced herself to stay put, for it would not do to act before the words were spoken. No matter how much she wished to get to the kissing.

"And I am going to be married," he said.

Mary stiffened. It may be certain that she would say yes, but she preferred his proposal to be expressed in more of a question than a definitive statement. But she waited, allowing him to continue his speech.

"No doubt you have noticed my marked attention these last few weeks," he said, and Mary felt her heart flutter at the thought of it. She and Henry had always shared a special bond, but since his return after Easter term, it was as though he were permanently attached to her side.

"She is the loveliest of women," he said, and Mary held her breath at the word that echoed his earlier compliment. "And she is kind and good—though I need not tell you how wonderful she is, as I am certain you are well aware of her virtues."

Clutching her hands, Henry looked ready to burst with joy. "I could not wait to tell you, and I knew I must say something before we announced it formally because you are so very dear to both of us."

The breath froze in Mary's lungs. She could not have heard him right. Blinking at him, Mary somehow found her voice. "Pardon?"

Henry cocked his head, his brows gathering together. "Have you not guessed how strongly I feel for Bess? I would have thought it obvious with how I have followed her around like the lovesick fool I am."

"Bess?" Mary's heart twisted in her chest, and the strength ebbed from her, leaving her shaky and weak. She had never fainted in her life, but she felt distinctly light-headed. "You are engaged to Bess?"

Mary pulled her hands from Henry's grip and turned to the trunk of the tree, leaning against it to keep herself from toppling over.

"Are you unwell? May I fetch you something?" asked Henry, touching her shoulder.

"No," she said, holding a hand to her stomach as though that could settle it. "I am just in shock."

"Is it truly that surprising?" asked Henry. "You two have become thick as thieves since she moved into the neighborhood last autumn, and I know you care greatly for her and see how fine a lady she is."

"Of course," she replied, her voice catching.

"Please, Mary," he said, stepping closer. "Tell me what is wrong."

Mary turned to stare at him, though her tears blurred his face. "Are you going to pretend you do not understand the source of my distress?"

His eyes widened, and Henry stared at her as though she had grown a second head. Mary's hand itched to strike his face; perhaps that might wipe away the confusion filling his expression. "I thought you would be happy for us. Your two closest friends have fallen in love. Though our marriage is bound to change some things, the three of us will continue on as we have, and you will be like an aunt to our children."

"Continue on as we have?" asked Mary. "You made me believe that you loved me."

"I do," he replied with a furrowed brow.

"I thought you asked me here to propose," she said. Just admitting it aloud made Mary's face blaze, but the fire fueling her words burned hotter than the calm voice in her head warning her to remain silent.

Henry's head cocked to the side, his eyes widening once again. "Whatever made you think that? I have shown admiration and brotherly affection but nothing more."

"A brother does not kiss his sister!"

At that, Henry scoffed, shaking his head at her with a shrug. "That was naught but a bit of fun. Just something to pass the time. You knew that."

Mary shook her head, her breath catching. She wiped at her

tears, the droplets wetting her gloves. "All these years...I thought..."

"That I would marry you?" Henry jumped backward, putting a firm distance between them. "I care deeply about you, Mary. I count you as my closest friend, but I have never felt anything more than that. I do apologize if you have misinterpreted my feelings, but I could never think of you as anything more than a chum."

Never had a word struck a girl's heart with such force. It was so much worse than a mere friend or companion. Chum was what one called the lads at school. It was lifeless. Empty. The farthest thing from romantic.

"But you wrote to me," said Mary, casting her thoughts to the stack of missives secreted in her room.

"As I would with any of my chums."

"You sent me flowers!"

"Because you care for them," said Henry with another accursed shrug. "You've often said how much you adore flowers, and you aren't likely to receive them from any other gentleman."

And that was when Mary's heart ceased beating altogether; she had thought the self-same words many a time, but she had never thought to hear them from Henry's lips.

"I apologize, Mary," he said, reaching for her hands again, but she tugged them away. "I do not mean to hurt your feelings. I never thought you believed my actions meant anything more than friendship, for I have never felt even an inkling of attraction for you. When a man marries, he wishes for something more than companionship, and your looks are not the type to entice a man towards matrimony—as you have said yourself on many an occasion."

Gritting her teeth against the sorrow washing over her, Mary looked down at her lanky frame that belonged to a "chum" and not a lover. Over the years, she had bemoaned her boyish figure, but never had she thought that Henry agreed with her assessment. The stark truth of the matter struck Mary, the despair of her situation shooting through her in a quick flash, but she refused to be dragged down by it, choosing instead to embrace the fury that followed on its heels.

"And you think you are—" But before Mary could finish her vicious thought, the sounds of a large party came from just over the hill, and Mary turned towards the tree trunk to collect herself. Henry's footsteps moved away from her as he greeted the other guests. Wringing the edge of her shawl, Mary's jaw ached as she choked back her words. Now was not the time for such a scene.

Facing the crowd, Mary steeled her heart against the sight of Bess taking Henry's arm, their smiles beaming as brightly as the sun above them. Family and friends gathered around as the couple made their grand announcement, and the people broke into cheers and applause.

"We were wondering if you would ever gather the courage, my boy," said Mrs. Drake. "You have been mooning over the girl for weeks now."

Bess blushed, dipping her face away from the crowd, and Henry rested his hand atop hers.

Others expressed similar sentiments, and Mary felt her eyes burn anew. She fought it back, though she could not disguise the vivid red tinge to her cheeks. Not a single person there was shocked or surprised by the announcement—not even her parents or sister. She had been the only fool to think that Henry's heart leaned a different direction. Only she had believed he loved her.

Though no one looked at her, Mary felt on display like the main attraction at a traveling carnival. She could not stand another moment of this humiliation, and she turned away, disappearing from the party as though she had never been a part of it.

Cutting through the fields, Mary felt the tears spilling down her hot cheeks. Her eyes burned, and her sleeve grew moist with each swipe of her wrist across her face. An utter fool.

"Mary!"

It was possibly the last person Mary wished to see, but no matter how she ignored it, the voice kept calling after her.

"Please stop," the voice begged. "Let me explain—"

Mary whipped around to glare at Bess. "Explain what exactly?"

"I am truly sorry," she said, a shine of tears in her brown eyes. "We never meant to hurt you."

"You knew that I loved him!" Mary's voice broke, and her hands flew to her mouth to hold in a sob. Bess stepped closer, but Mary pulled away. When she gained control, she spoke. "You were my friend and confidant. You even advised me on how to catch Henry's attention, and all the while you were courting him in secret!"

Bess's gaze dropped away, and a flush that had nothing to do with the warm summer sun filled the young lady's cheeks. "I did not wish to deceive you, but there was no way for me to tell you the truth. Henry does not love you as a man loves a woman, and I could not pass up an opportunity to secure my future."

"'Secure your future'?" Mary's fists clenched at her side, her shoulders stiffening.

Bess dropped her head, and Mary could no longer listen to the mercenary who had stolen away her love. Turning from the only two people whom Mary had ever counted as friends, she trudged through the field, her heart as dead as the dirt beneath her feet.

Chapter 1

Nine Years Later

Tapping his fingers along the arm of his chair, Ambrose watched his brother as he tugged at his sleeves and straightened his waistcoat. Again. Graham had already paced the parlor at great length and was now passing the time by staring out the window as he fidgeted. Ambrose had arrived at Avebury Park just the day before, yet it felt as though he had passed a month of Sundays here. With the final wedding preparations underway, the whole household was in a dither, and Ambrose wished he could have avoided the uproar.

"There's no need to be nervous," said Nicholas, leaning into his armchair with that calm, all-knowing air of his, as though being a few scant years older than Graham gave him a dash of omniscience.

"I am rushing her," said Graham, fiddling with the buttons on his waistcoat as he turned to face his brothers.

"Perhaps," said Nicholas, folding his arms. "But better to move hastily than chance losing her."

"And lose her heart instead because I pushed her into matrimony before she is ready?" asked Graham. "Tabby wanted a small, private ceremony, but I allowed Mina to push her into this monstrosity."

"Your sister was right in suggesting it," said Simon, coming to his wife's defense. Pushing away from the wall, he came to Graham's side and clapped a hand on his shoulder. "I know neither of you wished for it, but an elaborate affair will help establish your reputation in the neighborhood, which is a necessary evil if you wish to stay in Bristow."

"All because of a little gossip," grumbled Graham.

"A lot of gossip," corrected Simon.

The muscles in Graham's jaw twitched.

Giving a silent sigh, Ambrose watched the ensuing wreckage of a conversation. Nicholas rattled on as he always did when convinced he was right—which was more often than he actually was. Simon was no less forceful in his opinions, though his words gave insight into his own marriage and were not entirely applicable to Graham. All the while, the middle brother stood there, squirming under the onslaught of advice and wedding nerves.

"You need not worry, Graham," said Ambrose, piping up around the time Graham looked as disheveled as Ambrose had ever seen him. Which is to say that the man's brow furrowed and his jaw was close to snapping under the pressure of his clenching. "Any woman who throws herself so enthusiastically into your embrace as Tabby did last night is certain about her choice. She is likely to drag you to the altar, should you drag your feet."

Graham's eyes widened, and Ambrose nearly laughed at the tinge of a blush that came to his brother's cheeks. "You witnessed that?"

"I was not peeping if that is what you are thinking," said Ambrose. "But you should be more aware of your surroundings if you wish not to be spied in such a private moment. Though I doubt you would have noticed a circus parading beside you."

Yes, there was a definite redness creeping across Graham's face, and Ambrose did chuckle at that.

"Ambrose," Nicholas said through gritted teeth, "your

crude comments are unwelcome."

He shrugged. "But they are the truth, nonetheless."

"Ambrose," said Simon with a warning huff.

"I am simply pointing out that the lady has a clear...admiration for Graham," said Ambrose, allowing the significance in his pause to say that which the others were too priggish to hear. It was not as though Graham and his fiancée had done anything wrong. Ambrose heartily approved of kissing and thought that many a couple would be far happier if they indulged in such warm affection on a regular basis.

Another twitch of Graham's jaw, and he stared down at Ambrose. It was the self-same look his family often gave him that blended irritation and impatience into a perfectly scornful expression. Their low expectations and continual disapproval of him would do some good today as it was providing a suitable distraction for Graham.

"She is thoroughly besotted with you, dear brother," Ambrose said with a smile. "Though I have tried my hardest to steal her away, the lady is immune to my flattery. You need not worry that she has eyes for another."

"Ambrose!" Nicholas barked.

Holding his hands up in surrender, Ambrose allowed the topic to drop as the three turned away to chat about some business matter of which he had no part, effectively cutting him out of the conversation.

Pasting on a lazy smile, Ambrose watched his brothers and was left with the same frustration he usually felt when visiting his family. It made no sense that he could simultaneously despise such interactions and long for them when they were over. Perhaps he was a glutton for punishment, for Ambrose could not fathom abstaining from such an event even if he was bound to spend the entire visit as the unwanted outsider. They included him because they must, but he doubted that anyone cared whether he attended.

Except for Mina, of course.

Drumming the arm of the chair, Ambrose tried not to let it

bother him as the conversation shifted into foreign topics. Men of means and industry, his brothers stood about discussing their livelihoods. For Nicholas and Simon, it revolved around the work to be done at their estates. For Graham, it was his writing and lectures. Ambrose tried to follow the conversation, but it was useless. He would have nothing to add even if he could decipher what they were saying. Their lives were in such vastly different spheres that they might as well live on a different continent.

The door opened, and Tabby's boy slipped inside the parlor. Though Ambrose had seen Graham play the father figure to the lad before, it still surprised him to see how rapidly Graham was taking to the role.

"Phillip," Graham said with a grin, patting the boy on his shoulder, "you look quite handsome today."

The lad gave his soon-to-be father a gap-toothed smile. "Mama is ready."

"Then tell her I shall see her at the church," said Graham with a smile that perfectly conveyed his deep-seated joy at that prospect. It was good to see him so content with his life, for Ambrose had worried his brother might never recover from losing his beloved position in the navy. But it appeared that the injury that had stranded him ashore had turned into a blessing, for Graham was minutes away from becoming a husband and father.

Phillip nodded and headed to the door, but his smile disappeared once he spied Ambrose slouched in the armchair. Skirting around Ambrose's outstretched legs, he snuck out of the room.

"I do believe your boy does not care for me," said Ambrose, forcing a lighthearted tone into his words. Though his soon-to-be sister-in-law was more open in her disgust for Ambrose, her son's behavior felt far worse; there was something in the lad's furtive manners that felt like he expected Ambrose to lash out like some brute. "It is not as though I have given him any reason to dislike me."

"You have given him no reason to like you, either," said Graham. "And you bring up memories he would rather forget."

Ambrose sat upright at that. "Are you comparing me to his lout of a father?"

Graham grumbled something under his breath that Ambrose did not catch, though he felt the meaning behind it.

"I am nothing like him," said Ambrose. "Just because I spend my time in London and enjoy cards does not place me in the same category as that worthless worm who ruined his family—"

"Ambrose," said Nicholas, breaking off his tirade, "as delightful as it is to sit around stroking your ego, we have more pressing matters to attend to."

Ambrose fell silent. There was no point in arguing with his eldest brother. He had never won such battles before, and that was not bound to change. Snapping his mouth closed, he trailed after his brothers, feeling every bit the nuisance they thought him to be.

...

Looking out at the crowd, Ambrose struggled to keep from laughing out loud at the chaos that was his brother's wedding breakfast. Though he had not spent much time in Bristow, Ambrose guessed that anyone who was anyone was milling about Avebury Park's ballroom. Chuckling to himself, he took a sip of tea and scanned the room of toad-eaters. He would never have thought his soft-spoken sister would be so adept at maneuvering through society, but casting his eyes on what could only be deemed a success, it tickled him to see that Mina had found her place in the world.

Seeing Graham and his lovely bride together made this whole ordeal worthwhile. Ambrose would have put up with far more than a bit of discomfort to witness Graham's felicity. The man looked ready to burst as he glanced down at his bride in a manner that sent the more conservative guests into a dither. Lifting a mental glass to his brother, Ambrose toasted his good fortune.

Searching the crowd, Ambrose scoured the revelers for possible conversation. His brothers were clumped together with a few gentlemen from the neighborhood, but Ambrose had reached his fill of discussing estate finances and crop rotations.

And that was when his eyes rested on a chit that looked eager to provide some entertainment for the afternoon. She was not the loveliest in attendance, but Ambrose sensed she welcomed a bit of harmless flirtation. He had long ago developed a talent for differentiating between the innocent and the amiable ladies, and this one reeked of the latter. Her sparkling eyes called out to him, and Ambrose thought it might be a bit of sport to see if he could wheedle a kiss from her. Judging from the blatant manner in which she flirted from across the room, he doubted it would take more than twenty minutes before he could be much more pleasantly diverted.

"There you are," said his sister-in-law, and Ambrose downed his teacup, wishing for something stronger than steeped herbs.

"Good morning, Louisa-Margaretta," he said, pasting on a smile. Bowing over her hand, he said, "You are looking even lovelier than the last time we met."

She pursed her lips, shaking her head at his nonsense. "You do know how to spin a tale, Ambrose."

Clutching at his heart, he sighed. "It is no tale, my dear. You grow even more beautiful with each year. Though some ladies grow harried under the strain of motherhood, you grow more vibrant."

Louisa-Margaretta chuckled, tapping his arm with her fan. "Banbury tales indeed, sir."

"And how is life faring for Mrs. Nicholas Ashbrook?" asked Ambrose. "I hear I am to congratulate you on another forthcoming nephew."

Louisa-Margaretta gasped and then gaped. "Don't you dare

curse me with another boy, Ambrose! I do love my sons dearly, but I am desperate for a little girl." She touched a hand to the slight swell of her belly.

"Who would terrorize her dear papa," said Nicholas, sidling up to his wife and tucking her hand through his arm. "I can hardly keep up with my wife. I shudder to think of another girl in residence."

Louisa-Margaretta whacked Nicholas with a playful scowl. "No more boys!"

Ambrose placed his teacup down on an obliging side table and tried to ignore the niggling discomfort he felt at his brother's appearance; perhaps if he said nothing, the pair would forget he was there, and he could make his escape.

"And now there is only one Ashbrook bachelor left," said Nicholas; his words were like lead in Ambrose's stomach. "When are you going to settle down?"

"Why would I do that?" asked Ambrose, forcing an extra bit of joviality into his smile. "It appears as though one marries to improve one's life, and I am perfectly content as is."

"But surely you wish to do more than haunt London's gambling clubs forever," said Louisa-Margaretta, her delicate brow drawing together. There was too much genuine concern in her voice for Ambrose to feel offended at her intrusion into his life. However, his brother made it far easier.

"It is where Ambrose shines," said Nicholas. "He is never so comfortable as when he has a fist full of playing cards. It is the only thing he has ever shown an interest in."

"Now, that cannot be true," said Louisa-Margaretta, glancing over at her husband before returning her gaze to Ambrose. "Surely, you would like to settle down. You could buy a pretty piece of property out in the country—"

"To house my pretty little wife and fill to the rafters with children?" asked Ambrose with a chuckle. "I doubt a lady would have me."

"Nonsense," she said, thumping his arm with her fan once again.

Clasping his hands behind him—to protect them from Louisa-Margaretta, if nothing else—Ambrose smiled to himself. If only she knew how wrong she was. Many a woman might flirt with him, but there was a vast difference between that and binding oneself irrevocably to another. It would take trust and honesty, and Ambrose knew that if he ever admitted the truth, the lady would run screaming from her dunderhead of a beau.

Nicholas chuckled, and Ambrose's hackles rose before his brother even spoke. "Settling down with a wife is one thing, but Ambrose would go mad out in the country. Not to mention his contempt for running an estate."

"I seem to recall talking to you and Father once about helping out with our family's estate," said Ambrose. "And you both told me not to waste your time."

Nicholas's gaze fell away, his brow drawing down. "That is right...I had forgotten it completely." Nicholas laughed as he smiled over at his wife. "Ambrose got into Father's ledgers and tried to balance the books. They were an absolute mess, and it took us a good week to sort it out."

Ambrose gave a responding laugh as was expected, focusing on his performance to keep his cheeks from turning as bright as Mina's were wont to do.

Nicholas clapped Ambrose on the shoulder. "I am afraid you were rather hopeless at it," he said as though it were some grand joke between them.

Hopeless was the exact word that Nicholas and their father had used then, too, though with far less humor. Ambrose could still hear his father's voice shouting at him as he barred Ambrose from his study. It was his and Nicholas's domain, and Ambrose was no longer welcome.

"Hopeless," said Ambrose with that affected drawl of the bored gentleman he had perfected. "I have never had a head for accounts and estate work, and I doubt that is to change. I am afraid you are stuck with your bachelor brother for a long time."

Nicholas opened his mouth, but Ambrose excused himself. He had reached his limit for such conversation, and it would not do to continue in such a vein. "Addled" Ambrose was not one to sit around discussing such lofty matters. He was better served flattering the ladies and stealing a bit of affection where he could.

The eyes of the lady he had noticed before called to him, but Ambrose was in no fit state to pursue such things. Not at present. Veering towards the doors, he strolled into the garden and plopped down on a step that was out of the way and out of sight for a bit of peace and quiet.

But it wasn't to be.

Mina came to stand beside him, and Ambrose held in the sigh that wanted to come out. It appeared that their family drama would play out as it always did, and it was now Mina's turn. Looking up at her, he saw little Oliver on her hip, and she smiled down at him, extending her hand. Taking it, he helped her to sit beside him.

Oliver gave him a rascally smile before wriggling free of his mama to toddle off into the gardens. Mina called after him, but the boy was moving steadily ahead. She sighed but left it to the boy's nursemaid to give chase.

"I am glad this is over," said Mina. "I find myself terribly exhausted of late and cannot muster the energy to keep up."

She was making a decent attempt at nonchalance, but Ambrose was not fooled. He squinted up at the morning sky. "Is this the point in the conversation where you tell me that Nicholas means well?"

Mina smiled as she watched her son. "Are my intentions that conspicuous?"

"They are certainly consistent," he replied. "Whenever Nicholas and I quarrel, you step in to calm the ruffled feathers and lecture me on letting go of my anger."

"If it makes you feel better, I give Nicholas a much more strident earful," said Mina.

"And yet, it is left to me to do all the forgiving," grumbled Ambrose.

Mina threaded her arm through his, tucking him closer to

her side. "I understand. Believe me, I do. Nicholas is not mean-spirited, but he is positively convinced of his infallibility."

Ambrose chuckled.

"I learned long ago that you cannot change him," said Mina. "You have to accept his flaws and shortcomings—just as he has to accept yours."

"Not that he ever does so."

"Which is exactly the lecture I shall give him when I find him alone," said Mina. "But he is right occasionally. If Nicholas hadn't been so pigheaded, I would have missed out on the greatest happiness in my life."

Ambrose met Mina's eyes. "What do you mean?"

But she waved the question away. "That is a long story for another day, but if it weren't for Nicholas's infernal interference I would be living alone at Rosewood Cottage without my beautiful boy or adoring husband."

Their conversation lapsed into silence as Ambrose thought over that revelation and Mina gathered her courage. From the corner of his eye, he saw her hands clench together and recognized the sign of her internal struggle.

"And?" he prompted. He knew she wished to say something further, and she was not about to leave the conversation without having said her fill, so there was no point in avoiding it.

"And what?" she said, straightening and pulling her arm free of his.

"You did not come out here solely to tell me to be patient with Nicholas."

Mina stared at her hands, and she relaxed them for a brief moment. "I worry about you, Ambrose."

"You have my entire life," he replied with a flippant smile.

Upon seeing that, Mina scowled. "You know my meaning. I worry about the life you are leading. I don't believe you are happy, and it pains me to see you idling your life away."

"I happen to be one of the premier card players in London," said Ambrose, waggling his eyebrows at her. "A reputation that has taken a fair bit of work and skill to gain, so I would not say that I idle away anything."

Mina's shoulders fell, and she turned her gaze to her son. "I hate how you hide behind your smiles and flippant words whenever I try to speak seriously to you. No matter how you behave in public, I know you are not as much of a fribble as you pretend to be."

Ambrose leaned back and smiled. "Ah, but you should know better. It was you who received the countless letters and accounts from my schoolmasters. 'Addled' Ambrose isn't much good for—"

Shooting to her feet, Mina glared at him, her hands on her hips as she blurted out over his words. "Don't you dare speak such things! You are not a halfwit or 'addled' or any of those other horrid things they said you were. And I will not allow you to say such things about yourself or use that horrid nickname."

Ambrose's eyebrows rose, and he could not help but be impressed by her vehemence, even if he knew it was misplaced. The fierceness looked good on her, and it made him respect Simon all the more for bringing it out in his sister. For too many years she had shrunk into herself, and Ambrose was eternally grateful to the gentleman who had drawn her out.

"Sit, Mina. I promise to behave if you promise not to shout again," he said, offering her a hand to sit once again.

"Only if you do not say such hurtful things about my dear brother," she said. Weaving her arm through his, she held it, gazing at him with a tenderness that would melt the hardest of hearts. "You are not those things. You are so much better than you give yourself credit for, and I hate seeing you sink to the opinions of others and blind yourself to your true value. You are worth so much more than this aimless bachelor life."

Ambrose ducked his head and gave a huff. "So we have reached the point of the lecture where you prod me to marry."

Mina sighed and pulled free of Ambrose, her shoulders drooping. Her gaze turned to her son, who was swatting near a bush of purple blossoms. "I just wish for you to find the happiness I have found. To find someone who sees your value, even when you do not. Someone who inspires you to be better and supports you when you fall short. I wish for you to find purpose and happiness in living for someone other than yourself, Ambrose."

Her passionate words served as a stark contrast to his milk-and-water existence, awakening a familiar sentiment that seemed to have been an ever-constant companion over the years. He wasn't entirely certain how to categorize it, though he had tried on many an occasion. Not dissatisfaction precisely, but a sort of restless boredom that painted his life in dull tones. It was not melancholia, for he was not unhappy in his lot, but more that he was fixed in a place between joy and misery—a bland middle ground.

Ambrose did not know what he needed in his life, but he doubted that shackling himself to a lady would be the magical cure-all Mina claimed. Of course, he also doubted he could find a lady willing to bind herself to a gentleman such as himself; though Mina may not wish to acknowledge it, there was a reason he had been christened "addled" by his classmates.

"That is assuming I could ever find a lady worth marrying," said Ambrose, pasting a smile on his face. As he continued, he threaded a touch of lasciviousness into his words. "In my *vast* experience with the fairer sex, those are a scarce commodity."

"Perhaps that has something to do with the company you keep. But it appears we have reached the point in the conversation where you don your armor and fake an air of levity so that you might drive the conversation into more comfortable waters," said Mina, turning a knowing eye on him.

Ambrose clutched his heart with a melodramatic shake of his head. "You pain me, sister."

But she did not smile as he had intended. Mina watched him for several quiet moments, the sounds of Oliver squealing and the buzz of the wedding breakfast filling the background. Reaching over, she squeezed his arm and stood, calling to her son.

"I know you think I do not understand or that I am wrong

about you," she said, giving Ambrose one final look. He hated that there was such sadness coloring it. "But I understand more than you think. I just wish for you to be happy, and it is clear that you are not."

Oliver came running over, and Mina knelt to scoop him up. The babe's arms wrapped around her neck, pulling free a lock of her hair, and Mina kissed his cheeks, eliciting another giggle from her son.

"I nearly gave up on finding happiness," said Mina, giving Ambrose one final look, "and I would have lost so much if I had."

The nursemaid trailed behind Mina as they returned to the party, and Ambrose reveled in his newly found solitude. He could not wait to return to London. As much as he loved his family, every visit simply reiterated what Ambrose had long ago discovered. He did not belong in the Ashbrook family.

Chapter 2

Mary wished for a quiet corner in which to hide; the swell of revelers was stifling, and she desired nothing more than a bit of peace and quiet. But it was not to be. As the Kingsleys were one of the premier families in Bristow, their ballroom was packed, and her mama would never pass up an opportunity to "see and be seen", as they say.

Staring up at the high ceilings, Mary marveled at the plaster designs decorating them. This was not her first visit to the room, but those other occasions had been in the evening. With the shutters thrown open and the daylight shining through, Mary could appreciate the intricate details that had been lost in the candlelight.

Taking a sip from her teacup, Mary watched her mama chatter animatedly to Mrs. Ingalls about the topic that was ever-present on her lips—London. Or rather, the London Season. Or more precisely, Lydia's chances of finding a good match during the London Season. Mama had talked of little else since it had been decided that this was the year in which the youngest Hayward daughter would be launched into society.

Mary's attention drifted as her mama recited the details of dresses and balls that had been recounted on numerous other occasions. She had heard it so often that she could predict word for word what her mama would say next. Years of planning had culminated in this most important year for their family, and Mary was heartily sick of it. The money they were wasting on such extravagance was disgusting. Though many treated the London Season as a trifling jaunt to Town, there was nothing insignificant about the bills her family was accumulating in the hopes that Lydia would make a splendid match.

The only saving grace was that gambling on Lydia's future was not much of a risk. She had been receiving offers of marriage since her first foray into society, and Mary had no doubt that her little sister would do well in London's grand social scene.

Watching her younger sister flit about the room, Mary mused about providence's perverse sense of humor in giving herself plain features and a boyish figure while blessing Lydia with an equal portion of loveliness; it was as though every ounce of grace, poise, and beauty that had avoided Mary at birth had been bestowed on her younger sister. From the top of her golden locks to the tips of her delicate toes, Miss Lydia Hayward was everything a gentleman wanted in a wife; if not for the fact that her heart matched her angelic looks, Mary might resent her sister's good fortune.

"Mary."

At her mother's prompting, Mary shook free of her thoughts. "Yes, Mama?"

"Would you be a dear and fetch me another cup of tea?" she asked, handing over her empty cup.

With a nod, Mary strode to the side tables. The wedding breakfast had been cleared long ago, but as none of the guests were in a hurry to quit Avebury Park, more refreshments had been laid out as they chatted. Popping a bit of biscuit into her mouth, Mary poured a fresh cup of tea and placed a selection of treats on the accompanying dish.

The noise in the room was overwhelming, and if she had

any propensity towards headaches, Mary was certain the cacophony would bring one about. But amid the din, a sound caught her ear. A warm laugh drew her eyes, and Mary saw Sally Hensen batting her eyelashes at a gentleman.

His grin broadened as he gazed upon Miss Hensen, and Mary's heart gave a quick stutter. His smile was enticing. Magnetic. And with just the right dash of confidence. She could not point to the precise quality that made his expression so alluring, but the gentleman ensnared Mary's fancy as easily as he did Miss Hensen. Mary's cheeks blazed as she pictured herself in Miss Hensen's slippers and receiving such unabashed adoration. To be complimented and courted. Fawned over. Loved.

What nonsense! Mary wrenched herself out of such ridiculous musings. It was nothing but a heaping pile of balderdash! Mary Hayward was not Sally Hensen and never would be. Besides, gentlemen were a fickle lot and not worth pining over. They thought nothing of raising a girl's hopes just to dash them when something—or someone—more appealing arrived.

The gentleman let out another laugh, and Mary's eyes narrowed. Though unable to make out Miss Hensen's words, Mary knew the girl was not terribly witty nor likely to say anything to elicit such a hearty response; no doubt, the gentleman had other intentions for poor Miss Hensen than empty conversation. His expression never faltered, but the more Mary watched him, the more she sensed the falseness lurking beneath the warm glow in his eyes. Sally may be a silly girl, but she did not deserve to be toyed with, and Mary doubted the fellow harbored serious intentions; no honorable gentleman would stand so scandalously close in public.

Mary glanced to Mrs. Hensen, but the lady seemed unaware that her eldest daughter looked ready to sneak into the garden with the mysterious man. Part of her felt that she should do something to prevent it, but then again, it was none of Mary's concern. Besides, if she was not mistaken, the man in question was Mrs. Kingsley's brother, and Mary doubted that anyone in attendance would stop the well-connected gentleman from seeking his pleasure where he chose—as gentlemen were wont to do.

And it wasn't as though Sally had a pristine reputation. The girl had done her fair share of breaking hearts.

Turning away from the scene, Mary decided the pair deserved each other and returned to her mother's side where she could count the minutes until she was free to escape this horrendous party.

"...no doubt she will make a good match, and how comforting it will be for you to have your Lydia married off," said Mrs. Ingalls. "Though it must be an awful burden to know that Mary has no such hopes."

Those words froze Mary in place, out of sight of the two ladies but close enough to hear every sordid detail of their conversation.

Her mama straightened. "Whatever do you mean?"

"An unmarried lady is such a strain on her family," said Mrs. Ingalls with a piteous shake of her head. "What point does a woman have if she does not marry and have children? As is, Mary will be nothing more than a drain on your finances for the rest of her life."

Mary's hands shook, a bit of tea slopping over the edge of the cup. The wise course would be to allow the ladies to know she was there, but Mary could not force her feet forward as she clung to every awful word Mrs. Ingalls spoke.

"My daughter is anything but a burden," said her mama, squaring her shoulders. "I have never understood why people believe spinsters to be such a hardship. They are a blessing!"

Having never heard her mother say such a thing, Mary was shocked to know that she felt that way as Mrs. Ingalls' way of thinking was the prevailing attitude (a fact that others grew bolder in pointing out the closer Mary drew to spinsterhood). Though twenty-eight was a tad young to be labeled a spinster, no one who looked at Mary's dull features and bony frame would think her capable of avoiding that fate.

"Nonsense," said Mrs. Ingalls with a huff.

"It is true. In the first place, Mary is a great help at home," said Mama. "She is more capable than any housekeeper I have ever seen and manages everything so brilliantly that I never have to worry about the household. Mary is positively indispensable."

Mrs. Ingalls gave a hesitant nod.

"And furthermore," said her mama, "I always knew that Lydia would leave me eventually. And as a mother of five married daughters, I am certain you understand just how painful it is when your children leave home. Mary never shall, and I will always have one of my children close by. In my way of thinking, every family should hope for a spinster."

Hearing her mother's assessment of the situation left Mary perplexed. Should she be affronted that her greatest value was doing the work her mother despised? Or grateful that her mama longed to keep her nearby? Pleased that her efforts to care for the family were recognized and appreciated? Or hurt that her mother had no hopes that she would ever marry?

Regardless, Mary knew the time for eavesdropping had passed, and she stepped forward to make herself known by handing the cup and saucer to her mother. The lady praised Mary's foresight at bringing the extra treats, but neither she nor her companion seemed the least bit disturbed by the possibility that Mary might have overheard their conversation. And why should they? In Mary's experience, few concerned themselves with a spinster's feelings.

Standing beside her mama once again, Mary silently stewed as the two ladies prattled on. Eventually, Mrs. Ingalls left in search of new companions and conversation, and Mama quietly nibbled on a bit of cake and sipped her tea, quite pleased with the world and her place in it.

"Do you truly believe what you said about me?" asked Mary.

Mama's eyebrows rose. "Whatever do you mean?" But before Mary could clarify, the lady answered her own question. "About you being a blessing? Of course, dearest."

"The blessing of an ugly daughter who cannot attract a husband," said Mary, unable to keep the bitterness from her tone.

Her mama put the teacup aside and faced Mary. "Looks are not everything, and dwelling on what you lack does no good."

"Spoken by someone who has never lacked such things."

Her mama's lips pinched together for a brief moment. "I suppose you are right. I have no idea where your freckles came from as neither your father nor I have ever had such things. And it is a shame that you inherited your father's features. And his frame..." The words trailed off as her mother cast a glance at Mary's bony body. But the look of sadness faded as she met her daughter's eyes again. "It does no good to dwell on that which we cannot change, Mary. I am simply grateful that we have you, freckles and all."

"Freckles?" asked Lydia, sidling up to Mary. "I love your freckles."

"I believe you may be the only one who does," said Mary. She attempted a light tone but knew it was a failure.

"That is nonsense," said Lydia as she turned to a couple who were passing by—a couple that Mary had been studiously ignoring. "You two must talk some sense into Mary, for she will not believe me."

It should not bother her to see Henry and Bess. It really should not. With the Cavendishes being such good friends to the Haywards, it had been impossible to sever all ties—especially when only the three of them knew what had transpired all those years ago. Though Mary had made an effort to avoid their company, it was not always possible, and one would think that such moments would train her to remain unaffected by their presence. Yet still, she found her heart thumping erratically and her breath coming in quick bursts while her muscles tightened until she was as rigid and immovable as stone.

"And what sense does Mary need?" asked Henry Cavendish, bestowing her with that smile of his. Where once it had filled Mary with glee, it now only served to remind her of what a great fool she had been.

"I told her that I adore her freckles, and she thinks that no one else does," said Lydia, smiling over at Mary. With her face turned away from Henry, the girl did not notice the awkward manner in which Henry cleared his throat and glanced around as though anxious for an escape.

"I always believed that your freckles were quite becoming on you," said Bess, matching Lydia's grin.

Mary's eyes narrowed a fraction, her jaw tensing as she fought to keep her voice even. "I do believe Henry said the same thing many years ago."

Henry coughed again.

"Several times, in fact," said Mary, staring at Henry, though he avoided her gaze.

Bess stepped closer to her husband, gripping his arm, though her smile never faltered. "Yes, my Henry is quite the kindest of gentlemen."

"I understand you are bound for London, young miss," said Henry, turning his dazzling smile towards Mary's younger sister.

"I am quite overcome with the excitement of it all," said Lydia, and Mary's heart softened at the sight of her sister's giddy grin. "Though I fear that something shall go wrong," she admitted with a delicately furrowed brow.

"Nonsense," said Bess, reaching forward to squeeze Lydia's arm. "You are such a sweet and lovely creature that you are certain to be a great success and far exceed everyone's expectations. I just hope you will be as happy in your match as I have been in mine."

Bess clung to Henry's arm, gazing at him with unrestrained adoration, though it faltered when she caught sight of Mary's cold stare. Though no one else might notice, Mary saw a hint of a blush creeping into the lady's cheeks, and Mary felt a flash of victory. Bess may act as though the past had not happened, but Mary could not forget so easily.

"I understand that we are to congratulate you two," said

Mama. "Your mothers both mentioned that another little Cavendish is soon to make an appearance."

Bess smiled, running a hand along the swell that Mary had not noticed. "Henry wishes for another boy, but I am determined it shall be a girl. Thomasina is desperate for a little sister, and it would not do for the two of us to be so thoroughly outnumbered in the household."

"As though you two do not hold the whip hand over us," said Henry with a chuckle. "The boys and I need another ally if we are ever to come out victors in any disagreement."

Mary stared at the sign of their growing family and then at their radiant expressions, her heart dropping as she witnessed it.

In the ensuing years since Henry had broken her heart, Mary had come to understand that she was lucky to have escaped being shackled to such a selfish husband; her foolish heart had blinded her to his true nature, and Mary did not wish to be tied to such a person. However, that did not stop her from feeling a twinge of bitter jealousy—not over losing Henry, but for losing the bright fantasy she had envisioned. A loving husband and growing brood of children.

"I should return home," said Mary, stepping away from the group. "There is still much to be done before we leave for London tomorrow."

But Lydia waved the words away. "Nonsense. You already have everything in hand."

Mary gave a quick curtsy and turned to the door. "I have stayed too long as is. I must go," she said before fleeing Avebury Park.

Chapter 3

"Place that over here," said Mary, directing the footman whose name she could not remember. With a whole regiment of new servants bustling about the townhouse, Mary could not keep them straight at present; a few more days and she would come to know each one. The footman placed the last empty trunk in the cupboard and returned to his usual work after Mary dismissed him.

It was finished. They were moved into their London townhouse. Normally, such an accomplishment would've left Mary feeling elated or pleased with herself on some level, but standing there in the far-too-fine building, she felt decidedly out of place. Brushing at her worn dress, she felt more like a servant than one of the family—though that was not entirely true, either, for the servants were more turned out than she.

The hallway was cavernous, and Mary missed the pokey halls of her family home. The Haywards did not belong here. Spying a particularly fine vase decorating one of the many side tables along the wall, Mary was certain it was worth more than all the furnishings in Buckthorn Manor's parlor. The place even smelled expensive, if such a smell existed; it was a mixture of freshly waxed furniture and polished floors with a floral under-tone. Mary suspected the previous tenants were in a better financial position to keep the multitude of vases filled with bouquets.

What were her parents thinking when they took on such a place? Mary had no idea what it cost, but it was clearly more than her family could afford. But that wasn't her concern. Or at least Mary had told herself that many times. She was not in control of the family finances, so it was not her business to worry about them, though she did regardless. No doubt Papa had been saving for many years for this Season. It seemed extravagant to Mary, but if it helped secure Lydia a good match, Mary knew it would be worth it. Her dear sister deserved to find a wonderful husband.

Heading down the hall, Mary went in search of her next chore, but she paused at the sounds of music coming from the parlor. With a quick glance inside, she saw Lydia in the midst of her dancing lessons. Though Mary had every intention of continuing on her way, Mama waved to her, calling her over to observe the goings-on.

Taking a seat, Mary watched her sister glide across the parquet, twirling and dipping with a grace that bordered on the preternatural. Having often witnessed such scenes, there was no envy in Mary's gaze or heart, though she felt a twinge of longing as she wondered how it would feel to be swept up in a dance with a gentleman of her own. Not some clumsy jig that was more about frivolity, but an elegant sliding across the ballroom with lingering gazes and coquettish banter.

"I am certain we have waited too long," said her mama. It had become a familiar refrain over the past few weeks, and one that Mary was tired of discussing.

"Mama, if we cannot stay for the entire Season, then it is better that we arrive later in order to ensure that everyone has arrived in Town," said Mary.

"But what if the most eligible bachelors have already been snatched up?"

"With one look at Lydia, they are likely to throw over their fiancées and fawn at her feet," said Mary with a smile. "The solicitors of London will be thanking us for the business they will drum up with all the breach of contract suits that will flood the courts."

"Mary! To say such a thing," she replied with a gasp, her mouth gaping—though there was a hint of smug agreement underlying the shock. But that expression faded as Mama's gaze turned back to her youngest. She watched Lydia dance for several moments, her brow furrowing with each beat of the music. "She is so lovely. Surely, she will marry well."

"It sounds as though she already has an overabundance of admirers."

"Until the marriage contract is signed, there is no such thing as an 'overabundance of admirers,'" replied Mama. "If we can only find her a good match, then I shall rest easy knowing that we have secured our future."

Mama's tone sent a discomforting skitter down Mary's spine. It was not as though her parents had been secretive concerning their mercenary motives for this trip. The Haywards had little prospects, and Lydia's marriage could improve them. That was a matrimonial fact, but they rarely expressed it in such bald terms.

"And *her* happiness," added Mary.

Her mama raised her eyebrows, casting her eyes from Lydia to Mary. "Of course, dearest. Money and financial security are happiness."

"But they are not love."

Mama gave a low laugh. "A love match. Such a modern, fanciful thing. Love is well and good, but it does not put clothes on your back nor a roof over your head."

Another prickle ran along her spine at that. There was truth to that sentiment, but Mary would not want her sister's future sacrificed for the sake of money. Sending out a silent prayer, she pleaded for Lydia to find a good man of good fortune who would please both her heart and her pocketbook.

Returning her attention to the makeshift ballroom, Mama let the conversation lapse into silence. Watching Lydia and her dance instructor move through the steps, Mary studied their movements. Though she held her upper half still, her feet moved unseen beneath her skirts as she tried to mimic them. Not that there was any need for her to learn such a frivolous thing, but Mary could not stop herself from trying.

"Lydia did meet a few good prospects at the Westins' ball," said Mama, and Mary held in a sigh as she returned her attention to the conversation she wished would end.

"So I was told," said Mary, hoping that acknowledging the statement in such a noncommittal manner would be enough to show that she was listening without encouraging further discussion. Mary had not accompanied them to the ball because she had nothing suitable to wear, but in her naiveté, Mary had hoped that meant she would avoid the hours of boredom that accompanied such a gathering. However, she had forgotten just how many hours could be spent recounting the evening, and Mary had been made to suffer through each agonizing detail.

"Sir Duncan Whiting was quite attentive," said Mama. "Insisted on an introduction and looked crushed when his set was over, and Lydia's hand was claimed for the next."

Mary nodded and glanced over at the dancers, her feet secretly moving through the steps while her mind dredged up fantasies of being led about the dancefloor by a love-struck gentleman.

"To think our Lydia might snag herself a baronet," said Mama.

"I have everything unpacked and settled for the coming weeks," blurted Mary, hoping for any subject that might divert this present conversation.

Her mama smiled and patted Mary's knee. "You are such a good, steady girl. And so very kind to your dear mama."

"Yes, she is," said Lydia, dabbing at her brow with a handkerchief as she joined them.

"Are your lessons over so soon?" asked Mary, glancing at

the ormolu clock over the fireplace to find that the morning was long gone and the afternoon was chasing quickly after it.

"Not soon, Mary," said Lydia. "You've been running yourself ragged and lost track of time."

"Not ragged," she retorted. "But it is a fair bit of work to get everything settled so that we might enjoy the Season. I have been most anxious to visit the museum, especially the Egyptian exhibit. And I have heard of an exhibition full of mechanical creations that are said to do the most incredible things—"

"We are not here to see the sights," said Mama with a frown. "We do not have time for such things. I already have a long list of morning calls to make, and then there will be balls and parties and all sorts of affairs in the evening."

Mary nodded, trying to hide her disappointment. She had known that much of their time would be dedicated to Lydia's Season, but she had hoped for some freedom to explore the city. "Perhaps I might find some time between those things to sneak away and see the city."

Mama's head cocked to the side. "But dear heart, your carriage for Bristow leaves tomorrow morning, so there shan't be time for it."

"What?" exclaimed both girls.

Their mama glanced between them. "We have spoken of this before."

"Clearly not, Mama, or Mary and I would not be so shocked," said Lydia, her hands falling to her sides. "You cannot mean to send Mary home without having experienced London."

Mama waved that away. "Mary has no need to stay as she is not suited for society."

"That is harsh," said Lydia with a frown.

Their mother patted Mary's hand with a smile. "My dear, you have many talents, but being at ease in society is not among them. Would you truly be comfortable at a ball when we know you are a hopeless dancer? Or spending hours visiting ladies and speaking of the weather and the latest fashions and gossip?"

Mary shook her head. In truth, it sounded dreadful, but that did not ease the pain at being summarily dismissed by her family.

"Your work is done here," said Mama, squeezing Mary's hand. "And you have done an admirable job of it, but you are no longer needed, and it is best if you return home."

"Mama!" said Lydia.

Again, the lady waved away her daughter's shock. "I do not mean that we do not need her. Mary is my help and comfort in life, but this is not a grand tour or house party. We are here to find you a husband, and our focus must be on that. I do not want her to leave and shall miss her dearly, but it is for the best."

Mary swallowed past the lump in her throat. "I understand, but I shan't be a bother. I can spend my days on my own."

Lydia slid into the chair next to Mama, clutching her hands in her lap. "We might be occupied, but that does not mean Mary cannot go exploring while we are gone. Perhaps we could hire her a companion and escort so she may do as she pleases during the day."

"Do you girls not understand how precarious our situation is?" asked Mama with a scowl. "Our family's only hope is that Lydia marries well, and we must put our limited resources into securing that. We have not the funds for Mary to traipse about London when Lydia is in need of a new wardrobe."

"But that will cost a mint," said Mary, her eyebrows shooting up. "And I thought you commissioned an entirely new wardrobe before we left."

"We did," she said, her lips pursing. "But it was made clear last night that our country fashions are not up to Town standards. I shan't have her looking like a pauper or bumpkin to be laughed at and overlooked."

Mama's eyes trailed down Mary's worn frock. "We cannot afford to outfit the entire family, and Mary has no need of such things. And we cannot afford for it to be known that we are in such dire straits. Being seen about town with Mary's wardrobe in such disarray would make our situation clear to everyone. As is, only the servants have met Mary, and if she returns home now, London will be none the wiser."

Lydia's expression fell with each word, and their arguments died away. There was no point in trying. Mama had made her decree, and there was no other course than to accept it. For the good of her family, Mary would return to Bristow.

With a slow nod, she rose to her feet. "It appears I need to pack. Please, excuse me." And Mary made her escape.

Chapter 4

O nly a fool relies on chance in a card game, and regardless of what anyone else thought him, Ambrose was no fool when it came to gambling. He could not comprehend why anyone would rest their hopes on luck's fickleness, for it was a universal truth that luck rarely performed on command. Any time Ambrose needed a good dose of it, the cards never obliged, only to shower him with an overabundance of good fortune when he wished for a poor hand. Either way, it was skill alone that got him out of messes such as this.

The air in the dim room was heavy with tobacco smoke. Having long ago acclimated to the stench, it hardly bothered him anymore, even if he did not indulge in the disgusting habit himself. Needing no more than a quick glance at his hand, he left his cards on the table. Braying laughter echoed off the wooden walls, but Ambrose ignored it to study the players surrounding the table. After all, those pieces of paper had little to do with the outcome of the game; it was the players who held the power.

Not to mention that it flustered his opponents when he gave the cards no more than a cursory glance. Why anyone would grace the gaming tables without a decent memory was a mystery to him; if they could not recall the cards they held and those which had been played, they relied far too heavily on capricious chance. Though that would explain why so many gentlemen in the room were losing great fistfuls of money.

Though none of that mattered at present.

The question before him wasn't whether or not to win the game, but whether or not to throw it. There was only so much money he could win before the other patrons complained too loudly and his membership would be summarily revoked, and Ambrose was in no mood to find a new club. His wager amounted to no more than sixty-eight pounds, after all.

With a rueful smile, he raised the bet. Losing a few more pounds would hardly dent his earnings for the night, but it would earn him a bit of goodwill with the players and those who ran this gaming establishment. Adding a few more empty bets, Ambrose bowed out of the hand to allow the others to crow over their victory.

Taking a swig from his glass, Ambrose stood and wandered the room, wondering what he should do with himself. Instinct told him there was no more money to win tonight, and Ambrose had no interest in losing any more of his earnings.

"Have you heard about Lord Maybury?" asked Coles, nudging Ambrose before shoving a newspaper in front of his nose. "Of course, I heard about it from Mademoiselle Cécile, who had it straight from Lady Maybury's maid."

Ambrose glanced at the words before him, but they shifted and moved about the page like a cloud of mosquitoes. Racking his brain to decipher the symbols, Ambrose picked out "Maybury", but that was due to context and not his ability to read the mysterious words.

Shoving the paper at Coles, Ambrose sent his friend a bored look. "I've been far too busy with other matters to be bothered with such things."

"That is right," said Coles, tossing the newspaper aside. "You just returned from the country for some family thing. A funeral?"

"Wedding, actually."

Coles snorted. "That amounts to the same thing."

"Lord Maybury, eh?" added Barnaby from his slouched position in the armchair opposite. "I hear he got himself into quite a scrape with his wife..."

But Ambrose tuned out the conversation. He need not hear the details to know what was being said. Most lurid tales revolve around the same things, and Ambrose had heard enough of them to fill a lifetime. The whole situation made him miss Burke. And Charles. And Wentworth. And all the others who had provided a bit of sensible conversation in the past.

However, there was no point pining over his friends who had been lured into the country by their wives. Beggars cannot be choosers (as they are wont to say), and when it came to unattached gentlemen who Ambrose could count as friends, he was most certainly in the position of a beggar. Each year saw more and more of his set disappearing into matrimony.

Ambrose took another swig and realized that was not entirely true, for Coles had married just last year. Perhaps it wasn't so much that his set was disappearing, but rather, the ones worth knowing were.

Coles and Barnaby let out lascivious laughs, and Ambrose took his cue and followed suit, feigning the interest the fellows expected.

"And what of you, Ambrose?" asked Coles. "I hear that you have gotten quite close to that pretty bit of muslin posing as a prim and proper widow."

Having no idea who the gentleman was speaking of, Ambrose merely lifted his eyebrows in a manner that conveyed a wealth of meanings, allowing the chap to interpret it as he wished.

"Mrs. Greene?" said Barnaby with a guffaw and a solid clap on Ambrose's shoulder. "You rascal!"

Ambrose nearly choked on his drink but covered it with a vague grunt. The woman had certainly made it clear that she was available in whatever capacity he desired, but other than a few bored kisses, it had progressed no further than that. And never would. She was a comely woman, but Ambrose had no interest in dalliances—especially with a partner whose bed had been warmed by countless others.

But Ambrose had no interest in explaining his actions to his companions, for they would not understand. Rather, he chose a vague expression that neither confirmed nor denied their assertions. Let them make of his silence what they would. Their opinion was of no consequence.

The conversation around him shifted to the usual topics. Horses, betting, women, all interspersed with drink and raucous laughter. Anyone watching the exchange would never guess that Ambrose felt not a lick of enjoyment, for he played his part to perfection. The gadabout was in high form tonight.

Staring out at the card room that was identical to any number he had frequented over the years, Ambrose wondered at the stagnant life he lived. This evening was much the same as the ones that had preceded it and nothing but a foreshadowing of all those that were to follow. A never-ending chain of nothingness.

"After a week in the country, it seems that I have not the stamina for London hours, gentlemen," said Ambrose, setting his drink on the side table. "I fear I must turn in early tonight."

Coles scoffed. "But it is not yet midnight. You know as well as I that the best rounds do not start until at least two."

Barnaby offered some other similarly insipid remark, but Ambrose begged off, making his way to the exit. Just as he was about to don his hat, delicate hands ran along Ambrose's back. Turning, he was greeted by Sally Owen, who plastered herself to his front.

"Going so soon, Ambrose?" she said, her voice a velvet purr. "I was hoping for some time alone with you."

"Is that true, Sally?" he asked, donning his most enticing smile. Honestly, he never understood why it set the ladies aflutter, but he wasn't about to question its efficacy.

"Absolutely," she said, her lips drawing closer to his.

"That is difficult to believe when Thomas Endicott escorted you here tonight and has been your benefactor for a good year now."

Sally gave a coy pout. "But I have been so anxious to make your better acquaintance."

The art with which she used proper words to convey all sorts of improper ideas was quite impressive. The woman was lovely, and Ambrose certainly felt a resounding attraction to her allures, but the whole affair was wasted on him. If his friends ever knew his true reputation with the ladies, they would dub him a prude, but no matter how enticing the situation, Ambrose could not forget the lesson his father had taught him: A man does not share a bed with anyone other than his wife.

"I cannot imagine why you would care about the youngest son of a modest family," he said, adding a dash of self-deprecation to his grin.

"Do not underestimate your appeal," she said before leaning in to whisper into his ear, all subtlety abandoned. "I need you."

Ambrose extricated himself with a laugh. "Mademoiselle, what you need is someone who will make your protector jealous and remind him how coveted you are, and any number of fellows will gladly fill that role."

Her face pulled into a frown, or rather, the pretty approximation of a frown that was as sincere as her affections.

With an elegant bow, Ambrose leaned over her hand and gave it a kiss befitting an elegant lady. "Your charms are beyond enticing, mademoiselle, but I fear that I am not the best of companions at present. You deserve far better than to waste your time on me."

The irritation faded from Sally's eyes, and a true blush colored her cheeks. Ambrose had not thought her capable of such an authentic display, and the sight of it brought a tinge of sorrow to his heart for it was clear that the woman was unused to such gallantry. In her line of work, he doubted she was often treated with such respect, so he gave her another of his popular smiles and bowed low over her hand before giving his farewell and stepping out into the night.

Strolling along the street, Ambrose felt unsettled. There was no particular reason why he should feel so, and he had no idea how to dispel it. He desired solitude yet did not wish to be alone with his thoughts. Shaking his head at himself, he realized it was nothing more than a byproduct of visiting his family. It always left him out of sorts, and this visit had been particularly disquieting, for Mina's words haunted him.

She believed he had a grand future ahead of him, but Ambrose knew he did not. This was his life, and this was how it would continue. He just wished that thought didn't fill him with such melancholy.

Nodding to a passing gentleman, Ambrose turned his thoughts away from such morose contemplation as he made his way through the streets of London. A distraction was what he needed, and his latest project was just the thing. The pivots were worn and needed restoration before he could replace them in the clock. He had cleaned the grit out of the gears, but they were still not catching as they ought. It would take time to get the thing properly cleaned and pieced together, but he was certain he could do so.

Caught up in those plans, Ambrose entered Wintersmith Court, nodding at the various gentlemen coming to and from their lodgings. He exchanged a few quick comments and quickly escaped up the stairs to his rooms, grateful for a quiet evening at home with his hobby.

But such thoughts evaporated when he spied a bundle lying on his doorstep.

Standing over it, Ambrose looked down at a sleeping baby nestled in a thick blanket. He stared at the infant for a good minute before he nudged open his front door.

"Turner!" he hollered.

Mere moments later, his valet stood opposite Ambrose in a similarly shocked stance.

"Sir?" he asked.

"There is an infant on my doorstep," said Ambrose, his eyes fixed on the babe.

"I can see that, sir," replied Turner.

"How did it get there?"

"It crawled?"

Ambrose glanced at the valet. "Crawled? While wrapped in a blanket? And then plunked itself down on my doorstep?"

Turner shrugged.

The bundle stirred and the babe squawked, its face pulling into a frown. It gave a short cry, and Ambrose scooped it up as its eyes opened, staring into his. Its lips twitched, and Ambrose bounced the babe a few times, as he had seen others do. The sour expression cleared, and its tiny lips pulled into a toothless grin.

"The child seems taken with you," said Turner with a raised brow, his eyes darting between Ambrose and the bundle. "Is there something you wish to tell me?"

Ambrose scowled at the valet, stepping past the man. "Unless the rules of nature have changed drastically, there is no way I fathered this child."

"Sir," said Turner, and Ambrose turned to see the valet retrieve a slip of paper that was lying on the doorstep. Unfolding it, Turner read aloud. "'This is your daughter. Please take care of her.' It's addressed to Mr. St. Claire," he added.

"St. Claire?" asked Ambrose, looking down at the little girl in his arms. Her brown eyes were so dark that there was scant difference between the iris and pupil, but it made them all the more entrancing. Especially when she smiled and two deep dimples appeared in her chubby cheeks. A matching grin rose on Ambrose's face as the babe began to flirt quite outrageously with him. "Is there nothing more than that?"

Turner shook his head, and Ambrose wondered about the girl's mother and the circumstances leading to this abandonment. The whole situation seemed like a scene from one of those terrible gothic novels that were all the rage.

"Must have mistaken our doors," said Ambrose, rocking the

girl as she cooed at him.

"Would you like me to take the child to Mr. St. Claire?"

"No, Turner. I'd best explain things," said Ambrose, retrieving the note and turning to the hallway. "As it so happens, I saw him staggering home when I arrived."

With that, Ambrose walked to his nearest neighbor's door.

"I'm afraid my master is busy, sir," said the manservant when he answered Ambrose's knock.

"I'm certain he is," said Ambrose, knowing full well how the fellow was occupied. "But nonetheless, I've come to see him and shan't be turned away."

The servant gave Ambrose a dark look. "One moment, sir." And then he shut the door.

There were muffled sounds and a raised voice. A few footsteps and the door opened again.

"He is not at home," was the repeated message.

"Tell your master that I insist he receive me," said Ambrose. Though he was loath to hold the baby so precariously in only one arm, he freed his left hand and pushed at the door.

"Insist nothing, Ashbrook!" came the bellowing response from behind the servant. "I am occupied!"

Careful to keep the girl from being jostled, Ambrose shouldered past the servant and saw the man's master sitting on the sofa in the parlor beside a buxom and barely covered woman. Though St. Claire gave a decent show of straightening his open shirt, he was betrayed by the woman's lip color smeared across his lips, cheeks, and neck. His companion giggled; her décolletage hung so dangerously low that Ambrose darted his eyes away before she put herself on full display.

"This shan't wait. There has been a mistake."

"I would say so," said St. Claire, gaping at the babe in Ambrose's arms. "Got yourself in a bit of hot water, have you?"

"No," said Ambrose, stepping forward to place the child in her father's arms. "You have. Someone left her on my doorstep by mistake."

St. Claire leapt backward, pulling out of reach before Ambrose released his hold on the child. "I have no children."

"According to the note, you do," said Ambrose, struggling to keep his hold on the infant while extending the crumpled piece of paper. But the gentleman would have none of it.

"Out!" said St. Claire. "As you see, I am occupied, and I have no time for such nonsense."

The valet came forward, stepping in front of Ambrose, who was forced to step backward or risk the babe being crushed between them.

"I don't know if it is true or not," said Ambrose, "but you were identified as the child's father. It is your responsibility—"

"That child is not mine," said St. Claire, and though Ambrose tried to step around the valet, the manservant maneuvered into Ambrose's path and forced him back another step. With the babe in his arms, he had little choice but to allow the servant to herd him to the front door.

"You cannot be serious. Can you not take a few moments to consider it?" asked Ambrose, nodding at the child. "She is the mirror image of you."

"Nothing like," said St. Claire, refusing to even look at her. Waving Ambrose off, the libertine took his place on the sofa beside his bit of muslin.

"And what do you suggest I do with her?" asked Ambrose.

"Toss it in the gutter," came the reply as the door swung shut on him.

Chapter 5

Ambrose gaped at the door. He was by no means naive and knew that many of his set felt no responsibility towards their ill-begotten offspring, but never had he thought to witness such heartlessness. St. Claire had had his fun and now could not be bothered to give a passing glance at the consequences.

The child squirmed, and Ambrose cast his eyes to the bundle in his arms. Her brows pinched together, her dark eyes worrying as though she understood how dire her circumstances were.

"I shan't toss you in the gutter," he said. He knew she did not understand, but he felt the need to reassure her. As that altered nothing in her expression, Ambrose simply smiled at her, and in a trice, her mood shifted and her brows rose, pulling her lips into another dimpled smile.

"You are a shameless flirt, little miss," Ambrose said to the babe, rocking her as he returned to his rooms.

Turner stared at him when he pushed open his front door, but there was nothing to say. The child's father had refused his responsibility, but Ambrose could not.

"And what are you going to do with it?" asked Turner.

"Her," he corrected. "I know of a foundling home that Mina visits when she is in Town, and I shall go there in the morning."

The babe kicked and pushed at the blanket, her face pulling into a grimace before she let out a cry. Ambrose bounced her in his arms, but she did not settle. He tried smiling at her and cooing, but neither did any good. Turner had the good sense not to say a word, but his expression took on that pinched look that said he was holding his tongue.

"It is only a few hours until morning," said Ambrose. "There is no reason the two of us cannot care for an infant during that short time. You are a father, after all. Certainly, you must know what to do with her."

The man's eyebrows shot upwards. "Forgive me, sir, but it has been many years since my children were that size, and caring for them is women's work. My wife handled that nonsense."

"Nonsense?"

"You know what I mean," he said, his brow furrowing as he looked at the infant. "Besides, I lived under my master's roof. I only saw them on my evenings off."

"Come on, sweetheart," said Ambrose, bouncing the babe. "What is wrong?"

"She is either tired, in need of a clean napkin, or hungry," said Turner with a sigh. "It is nearly always one of those three things."

"But which is it?" asked Ambrose.

"If it were changing, you'd know without asking. Beyond that..." Turner gave a shrug.

Her cries weren't shrill, but they were so sorrowful that they tugged at Ambrose's heart. "Is there any milk?"

Turner puffed his cheeks, letting out a loud sigh as he headed to the kitchen. Walking the babe to the dining room, Ambrose stepped to the table but found the surface filled with gears and springs from the clock he had been disassembling. Shifting the child, he freed a hand and cleared a space. Sitting beside the table, he unwrapped the infant. Her arms and legs kicked and waved, her chin trembling as she stared at him with great teardrops hanging from her eyelashes. The whole expression was so tragic that Ambrose thought a man must be made of stone to remain unmoved by such heartbreak.

Turner returned, carrying a pitcher of milk, and Ambrose tucked the girl into the crook of his arm. She arched her back, but he kept her in place and tipped the pitcher to her mouth. It came out faster than anticipated and sloshed into her face, making her cough.

"Apologies!" he said, shoving away the pitcher and hollering for Turner to get him a towel. Milk ran down her cheeks, and she glowered at him as she cried. Moments later, they had her face dried off, though both their clothes were beyond hope.

Having never fed a child before, Ambrose had never given it much thought, but as he tried various manners of getting the liquid into her without causing her to choke, he realized it was more of an ordeal than he had anticipated. By the end, the pair of them and most of the rug below were soaked through, but it was worth the mess to see the babe lapping up the milk like a hungry kitten.

In many ways, it reminded him of rebuilding that broken friction machine the Bentleys had tossed away. The silly thing hadn't been worth repairing as it was nothing but a bit of entertainment for parties, but he had not been able to let it go. The machinery fascinated him. Piece by piece, he had examined it, trying various combinations to get the gears to work. An adjustment here. A tweak there. Hours of experimentation before it was finally restored. Not that the infant in his arms was a machine, but puzzling out how to care for her was as much of a mystery. And just as interesting.

She yawned, and her eyelids drooped, though she gave him a satisfied smile that made her dimples wink at him. Ambrose chuckled at her. A shameless flirt, indeed. She snuggled up against him, her body going slack. Though he had nephews in abundance, he had rarely been given the opportunity to hold them at such a young age, and Ambrose wondered if it were because he had avoided it or if his siblings assumed he would not want to. Holding this sweet bundle in his arms, he could not understand why anyone would not, though he had never felt such an inclination before.

...

The child laughed as they bounced along the cobblestones, which set Ambrose chuckling. The carriage bumped and rocked through the city, and the little girl reached out to grab at anything within reach, cooing and babbling at the world around her. She was such a sweet thing, and Ambrose was swept up in her charms. His siblings claimed that caring for children was a difficult endeavor, but Ambrose thought it a lark. The past few hours had been trying at times, but that was solely due to his ignorance; as long as the child had her needs met, she was an angel.

The carriage pulled to a stop, and the driver called out to him. Alighting from the cab, Ambrose stared at the forlorn building before him. The window trims had not seen fresh paint in many a year, and the bricks were crumbling at the edges. Though the walls were straight, something about the structure seemed to sag in on itself. There was no indication that it was a foundling home, but as the driver assured him it was, Ambrose forged ahead. Giving a rap on the worn door, he waited as the infant stared at him with her big brown eyes.

A maid answered the door, though the girl was more child than woman, and Ambrose was duly ushered into the house, which did not improve upon closer inspection. Though clean and adequately maintained, the rooms were stark. Where Ambrose expected to find children and toys underfoot, there was nothing. He heard young voices and small footsteps, but they were subdued.

The maid led him into a parlor, and Ambrose rocked the child to calm his unease.

"May I help you, sir?" asked an older lady as she entered.

Her face was taut, her mouth pinched, and Ambrose's smile broadened on instinct.

"I hate to bother you, but I have a child that is in need of a home."

"We are full, sir," she replied, motioning to the door. "I am sorry you wasted your time, but there is no place for the child here."

"Is there no way you could reconsider?" he asked, giving her his most winning smile. "I have no other options—"

"I can provide you with a list of other homes that might have room," said the matron, turning to leave, "but we do not."

"But my sister has spoken so highly of your establishment. I would hate to entrust the babe to just anyone."

The matron froze and turned back to look at him. "Your sister?"

"Mrs. Simon Kingsley," he said, and the frigid woman melted into a smile that was filled with such genuine warmth that Ambrose's grew in response.

"Dear Mrs. Kingsley! It is a shame she is not able to visit more often, though she is still very generous to us." She examined Ambrose and nodded. "You must be her youngest brother."

"Mr. Ambrose Ashbrook," he said with as much of a proper bow as he could manage with a babe in his arms. "And I would be forever grateful for whatever assistance you can offer, Mrs...?"

"Mrs. Follet," she said, offering up a sketch of a curtsy. "Is there no possibility for you to provide for the child yourself?"

Ambrose blinked at the woman, taking several seconds before he comprehended the implication. It should not have surprised him that she would assume he was the father, but for some reason, he had not expected it.

"I am not equipped to care for her," said Ambrose before launching into the tale of how the child entered his life. As he spoke, the woman drew closer to smile at the infant.

"Has she a name?" she asked.

"None that was indicated in the note. Though I have been thinking of her as Dottie on account of her dimples." At that, the babe graced the pair of them with a smile that displayed that particular feature.

Mrs. Follet chuckled. "Oh, she is a dear thing. Unusual coloring, though."

"She takes after her father," said Ambrose, fighting the urge to curse the man's name. "His mother is a Greek *émigré*, I believe, which gave him a darker complexion. But the crux of the matter is that he will not take responsibility, and I cannot abandon the babe to the elements."

"Of course not," she said, offering a finger to Dottie, who latched onto it. "But I am afraid we are not in a position to assist you. I was not lying when I said we do not have room."

Pulling free of the babe's grip, she led Ambrose through the foundling home. There were scores of children stashed in every room, and though they were dressed, fed, and obviously cared for by the matron and her staff, there was a sadness that haunted their eyes.

"Through donations from generous people, such as your sister, we are able to care for many children," she said, showing him the classrooms and bedrooms, each too cramped and too sparse for Ambrose's liking. "But we have to turn away far more than we are able to help."

Finally, she led him into the nursery where a single woman sat among a dozen infants. The sight of them crammed together in the scant bassinets was enough to break Ambrose's heart, but their unnatural stillness crushed it.

"Why are they so quiet?" he asked, though he knew he would not like the answer.

Mrs. Follet's brow wrinkled, and she stepped to the nearest one, reaching down to touch each of the babes, who stirred at the contact. "We do not have the staff to give them the attention they need. We try our best, but there is only so much we can do."

Clutching Dottie tighter to him, Ambrose's heart fell at the thought of her spirit and joy being slowly leached away in this place.

"The poor orphans," he mumbled.

But Mrs. Follet shook her head, giving the infants a pitying smile. "Not orphans. Not this lot, at any rate. Most that come to us as infants are simply unwanted, like Miss Dottie." Standing, she turned to face Ambrose again. "If I were to give you any advice, sir, I would say you are better served taking her to Mrs. Kingsley in the country. In the city, there are too many abandoned children. We train them for gainful employment, but at best, she will find work as a scullery maid. Far too many of our girls end up in unsavory situations when they leave us. And then their children often end up here."

Mrs. Follet paused, blinking at the babes lined up together, and Ambrose allowed her a silent moment to compose herself. Ambrose looked down at Dottie, her eyes pensive, and he felt sick at the thought of that happening. His mind turned to the various women of ill-repute that his friends frequented. How many had started their lives in such a place? How many of his friends' by-blows had ended up here? It was so utterly depressing that Ambrose struggled for self-control as despair washed over him.

Mrs. Follet cleared her throat and returned her gaze to Ambrose. "Dottie will have a much better chance in the country. There is bound to be someone who would take her in and give her a chance at something better than a life on the streets. She is such a sweet child, and with Mrs. Kingsley's connections and good heart, she will be able to find the babe a home in no time."

The band that had been constricting Ambrose's heart eased, allowing him a bit of relief. It was a plan and a fine one at that. Mina would know what to do with Dottie. A good home. A family to love her. Giving Dottie a little bounce, Ambrose knew he could do no less for her. Just a quick jaunt to Bristow, and Dottie's future would be secure.

Chapter 6

"**M**other, you cannot be serious," said Mary, keeping her tone subdued to avoid attracting the attention of the other passengers gathering at the coaching inn.

"It is an easy journey to Bristow, and even if we could spare a footman for two days as he journeys there and back, it would be wasteful to pay for three tickets when we only need one."

"But Mama..." Mary did not know why she bothered to argue. Once her mother's mind was made up, there was little hope in changing it, but to journey for hours unaccompanied was mortifying. Mary had not thought she had much pride, but apparently, she had some.

"I know, dear." Her mama took Mary's hands in hers. "I wish it could be different, but we all must make sacrifices. As is, we spent far more than intended to secure you a seat inside the coach. You shall be far more comfortable than up-top."

That was something, though nowhere near enough to heal the injury to Mary's ego.

"Not another word, young miss," she said, giving her daughter a kiss on the cheek. "You are such a good girl, I know I have nothing to fear from leaving you alone for a few hours.

You shall be home before dark, so there is no need to worry yourself so."

"I am not afraid—" But her mother stepped into their family's carriage, and Mary's protestations faded away into silence while Lydia stood there, staring after her mother with the same wide-eyed astonishment that Mary felt.

"I am terribly sorry," said Lydia, giving her sister a hug. "I had no idea Mama and Papa would do this to you."

Mary accepted the gesture for the kind, sisterly thing it was and tried to ignore the burning in her chest. Though she wished to dismiss the thought, Mary knew that their parents would not send Lydia alone by stagecoach.

"Please write when you arrive home," said Lydia. "I shall worry if you do not."

"And you would be the only one who would," said Mary, stepping away.

"You mustn't think that. We all love you dearly—"

But now it was Mary's turn to end the conversation prematurely.

"I must be going or the coach shall leave without me, and Mama is calling for you," she said, waving to her sister and hiding away the mixture of embarrassment, pain, and despair she felt at her exile—but when Lydia's expression fell, Mary knew she had not succeeded.

Lydia was ushered into the family's vehicle by a footman, and Mary was left alone to approach her coach. She lifted her foot to the step up and paused when a hand came into view. She realized the gesture was meant to be an offer of assistance, but it was not attached to a servant. Mary glanced at the gentleman and found an infant staring at her from the crook of his arm. Seeing a man carting about a child was strange enough, but when Mary met his gaze, she was doubly shocked to see that the gentleman was none other than Mrs. Kingsley's brother.

He smiled at her, though Mary detected no hint that he recognized her as easily as she did him. She supposed he had no reason to, for she would not have remembered seeing him if he had not made such a spectacle of himself by flirting with any female who crossed his path.

"May I?" he asked, nodding at his hand as though his original intent had not been clear. And then he grinned at her with that same smile he had used on every lady at the wedding breakfast. Mary sighed, accepting his assistance because she felt she must, and settled herself into the coach.

A gray-haired lady and gentleman sat in the front facing seats, and Mary gave them a nod just as Mrs. Kingsley's brother climbed in beside her.

"We are bound to have quite a pleasant journey with such lovely ladies to keep us company," the scoundrel said to the older gentleman opposite. It was such a ridiculous thing to say, yet the other lady—who was old enough to know better—blushed and tittered. Mary sighed and rolled her eyes at the window. This was going to be a long journey if she had to listen to such tripe.

"You, sir, are a lucky man to have secured such a wife," he said, shifting the child in his arms to give the other gentleman a hearty handshake. "I am Mr. Ashbrook."

"Mr. Young," said the other before nodding at the lady at his side as he tucked her arm in his. "And Mrs. Young."

"And who is this sweet lady?" the rogue asked, turning to Mary. She stared at the window, wishing for nothing but a bit of peace and quiet. She was in no mood for inane chatter with people who would ignore her if they were in less confined circumstances. But Mr. Ashbrook was persistent.

"I promise I am well behaved," he said with a chuckle. "You need not fear that I bite, Miss...?"

"You seek an acquaintance with no proper introduction?" she snapped. Did no one think that she deserved to be treated with the dignity and manners that would be afforded a lady such as Lydia?

His eyebrows raised. "It's going to be a long day if we have to sit here and pretend we are not in such close proximity. I see no reason to stand on ceremony in such a situation."

"I am certain you do not—now or in any situation," said Mary under her breath.

"Pardon?" he asked with a touch of a smile that made her wonder if he had, in fact, heard. Not that it mattered to her; he was nothing more than a pleasure-seeking libertine. Even if he had rich brown eyes that glimmered in the darkened confines of the coach.

Smoothing her skirts, Mary straightened her spine. "As much as I am loath to curb your amusement," she said in a tone that clearly stated the opposite, "I have nothing to say that might entertain you, sir, so there is no need for you to know my name."

Mr. Ashbrook leaned towards her, and his smile shifted into a decidedly wicked manner, his brown eyes sparkling with mirth, and Mary understood why so many ladies fell into his arms. For one brief moment, she wished to do so herself. But that was quickly extinguished by the sheer self-loathing that accompanied the realization that she was just another of those silly females taken in by a beguiling man.

"I am certain you have lots of interesting things to say, Miss...?" He drew the sentence out, and Mary knew he expected her to provide her name, but she refused to be toyed with.

Another gentleman stepped through the door and slipped in beside Mr. Ashbrook, nudging the bounder closer to her. The two of them were pressed together, shoulder to knee, and Mary tugged her cloak tighter around her as though it offered any protection from the cad.

"Quite cozy," Mr. Ashbrook murmured, his voice coming so close to Mary's ear that his breath tickled the wisps of hair at her neck.

Looking at the slight space beside Mrs. Young, Mary thought being crushed next to her was far more desirable, but she was fairly certain she would not fit. The seat was intended for two, and the Youngs were too stout to accommodate even Mary's lithe frame. The couple looked at each other, and then at Mary. A silent agreement passed between the couple, and they spread, filling every last space on their side of the coach. They studiously avoided Mary's glares as she resigned herself to her fate. No aid would be coming from that quarter. She had no choice but to suffer through the intimate seating arrangement.

Mr. Ashbrook took it upon himself to make the introductions to the new gentleman, Mr. Bennett, and he paused at Mary with a smirk as though that would force her to supply that which she was determined not to give. She may be traveling as no decent lady ought, but that did not mean she needed to surrender all her dignity.

The coach lurched and despite being wedged in as she was, Mary was jerked forward. Before she could right herself, Mr. Ashbrook's hand was there, holding her in her seat.

"Careful there," he said in a low whisper.

It was impossible to shake free of his touch, but she would not subject herself to further conversation. With a bit of careful maneuvering, she pulled a book from her reticule and hid behind it, dismissing him as clearly as if she had verbally rebuffed him. Or so she thought, for the gentleman spoke once more.

"That does look a stodgy tome, Miss Pert," he said.

Mary snapped her gaze to his, only to find the gentleman's eyes laughing at her. "Miss Pert?"

"You refuse to give me your name, and I must call you something," he said with another of his ridiculous smiles, bouncing the infant in his arms.

"You need not speak to me at all," said Mary, returning to her book. "I prefer to improve my mind and not fill the air with idiotic nonsense."

A frigid silence filled the coach. Mary had not meant to shift the mood so thoroughly, but she was not overly upset at the prospect of finding solace from the gentleman's relentless mockery. He would not leave her be, so her harsh words were on his head.

"We are having fine weather, are we not?" said Mr. Young.

Mary ignored the comment, as she could not think of a single person who would call a dreary, overcast day fine. But Mrs.

Young grasped that inane topic and picked it apart, as well-bred personages were wont to do. Mary could not see the final passenger, Mr. Bennett, from her seat, but the nasal sounds of sleep told her he had promptly drifted off.

Opening to her bookmark, Mary stared at the page, though she did not read a single word. It was too cramped in the coach, and the past day had provided far too many disappointments for Mary to be so easily distracted. The words blurred on the page, and Mary blinked away the tears that had snuck up on her. Though her eyes darted to the window, she forced them back to the book. There was no point in gaping at the sights of the city like some country simpleton when she would not be allowed to explore them for herself; it would only torture her further.

"What a pretty child," said Mrs. Young, leaning forward for a better look. "Though I do hope she will behave during the trip."

Mary pretended not to witness the exchange, but she sensed Mr. Ashbrook's mood lighten at the shift in subject, and she was appreciative to the others for distracting the cad beside her.

"Dottie is a darling," said Mr. Ashbrook with more warmth than Mary would have expected from a gentleman like him. "She is not much for crying and shall not trouble you one jot."

"Dottie," said Mr. Young. "That is quite fitting with her dimples. Is that short for Dorothy or Dorothea?"

There was a brief pause before Mr. Ashbrook responded, "Dorothy."

"And where are you and your papa traveling to?" the lady cooed.

"She is my niece," corrected Mr. Ashbrook. "I am bringing her to her family in Bristow."

Mary fought to keep from snorting at the blatant lie. Now that she was no longer the center of attention, it would not do to draw it back to her. Neither the Kingsleys nor the Ashbrooks had a daughter, but even if Mary were not privy to such knowledge, she could never imagine any scenario in which a mother would leave her child in the care of her irresponsible bachelor brother.

Sending a covert glance at the bag resting at Mr. Ashbrook's feet, Mary was fairly certain such a small thing could not contain the mountains of supplies needed to properly care for an infant. Whatever Mr. Ashbrook's game, the child was not his niece, and in a trice, her mind supplied a sordid tale of the babe's parentage. No doubt, Mr. Ashbrook was trying to foist off his by-blow onto his sister. For shame.

Yet another reason why Mary despised his flattery. The Youngs were so taken in by his performance that they did not see the fraud beneath the polished veneer. But Mary would not allow herself to be so deceived.

It did not matter. Let the others coo and babble over the child and her kind "uncle." Mary had more important things to do with her time. Turning her attention away from the trio's conversations about Dottie and the Youngs' children and grandchildren, Mary concentrated on the words before her as she delved into the legendary beginning of Rome.

...

Where had his sweet girl gone? Ambrose's ears rang as the babe wailed. Dottie paused for a breath, but it was only a brief respite before she let out another cry. Leaning her against his shoulder, he patted at her back. When that did not work, he shifted her to his knee in order to bounce her upon it. Then he shifted her to the crook of his arm, but she arched her back, struggling against it. He tried everything he'd seen mothers and nursemaids do to calm a squalling infant, yet nothing worked. If he could only understand her sudden shift in mood, perhaps he could remedy it, but between one breath and the next, she had gone from docile to distraught.

The camaraderie he had shared with the Youngs over the

past two hours was quickly fading as they frowned at him. Even Mr. Bennett awoke from his slumber, and Ambrose felt the heat of his glare. It was clear they expected him to do something, but Ambrose had no idea what Dottie needed, for she was fed, clean, and had napped not long ago.

Miss Pert shut her book, and Ambrose was in no mood to deal with the sour-faced spinster. He had never been so rebuffed by a lady, and Ambrose could only imagine her mood was worsening because of Dottie; even he was heartily sick of the noise.

Dottie's cries grew shriller, and great teardrops ran down her cheeks. Ambrose wanted to beg her to tell him what was amiss so that he might right it, but there was nothing to be done with the overwrought infant.

Miss Pert opened her mouth, and Ambrose steeled himself for sharp words, but she smiled. Not at him, of course, but at Dottie.

"It is a bit rough in a coach, isn't it?" she cooed. "All the jostling is enough to make any of us irritable." It did not calm the child in the slightest, but it did wonders for Ambrose. Just knowing that one of their companions was not wishing him to Hades was a blessing.

The lady shifted, bumping and elbowing him as she pulled a silver bracelet from her wrist and offered it to Dottie. The babe gave a few shuddering breaths, but her cries dwindled. Giving the bauble a watery smile, Dottie reached for it, and Ambrose was overtaken by an urge to hug Miss Pert. Once Dottie had it in her tiny fists, she shoved it right into her mouth, covering it in drool.

"Dottie," said Ambrose, reaching for it, but Miss Pert stayed his hand.

"I knew what she would do with it," said the lady. "A little gumming shan't hurt it."

"Infernal racket," grumbled Mr. Bennett before settling in for another nap.

"The same could be said of your snores," snapped Miss

Pert.

Mr. Bennett muttered something that Ambrose was grateful the lady could not hear and returned to his nap.

"My deepest gratitude, miss," said Ambrose. "I was at my wit's end."

"It was nothing. Traveling with a child is difficult enough and is not made any easier when your companions do nothing but scowl at you." At that, the lady gave the Youngs a disapproving glare, who gaped at the cheeky chit.

"I do not count it as nothing," he said, giving Miss Pert a warm smile. Her posture stiffened, and she frowned before she turned her attention to her book, leaving Ambrose to wonder what he had said in those few words to offend the odd lady.

Chapter 7

It was pointless to pretend she was reading. Though Mary had hidden behind her book for nearly three hours, she had yet to read a single page. Her eyes passed over the words, but they did not sink into her consciousness. Especially not while Mr. Ashbrook played with Dottie.

The little girl's arms jerked as she waved the bracelet, and it connected with Mr. Ashbrook's nose when he leaned in close to her. At that, she let out a peal of laughter as he rubbed it. The babe had spent much of the past quarter hour entertaining herself by pummeling her caretaker, yet he continued to play the game with her. Mr. Ashbrook may be a ridiculous man, but he clearly cared for that little girl.

With a flick, Dottie sent the bracelet flying, and it landed on Mary's lap. Picking it up, she offered it to Mr. Ashbrook, who promptly handed it to Dottie. The child gnawed at it before smacking Mr. Ashbrook once again with a laugh. Another few minutes and the bracelet was hurled once more but landed on the floor next to Mr. Young, who looked as displeased with the game as he had been with the crying.

Mary gave the older gentleman a scowl. It was one thing for

an unattached gentleman such as Mr. Bennett to have no patience for such things, but it was quite shocking how put-out the Youngs were with Dottie. She was only a child, and there was no need for them to be so ill-tempered; as they were parents, she expected more compassion from them, but she could see the blaring disapproval in the angry pull of their features.

Watching Mr. Ashbrook play with the babe made Mary wish to join them. Not that she wished for closer acquaintance with the gentleman, but she longed to cuddle the sweet infant. Though Mary was not enamored with children as many women were, Dottie was the type that begged to be kissed and cuddled.

But as much as Mary wished to join in the fun, she would not be so forward as to ask a stranger if she might hold his child. After all, she would never approach Mr. Ashbrook and ask to hold his bag or billfold, and a babe was far more precious. Besides, she had no desire to be painted as the desperate, infant-crazed spinster. Mary had seen others in her situation who pounced on every child, and she shuddered at the thought of being like them. People pitied women who did not marry, and showing even the slightest desire for a family increased that pity tenfold. It was better to feign stoicism.

So, it was no good thinking about how much she wished to pinch Dottie's round cheeks or kiss on her sweet neck.

Turning her attention back to the pages in front of her, Mary forced herself to put the heartwarming scene out of her mind, which would have been easier if a pungent smell had not filled the coach.

"Do you mind, sir?" barked Mr. Young as Mrs. Young clutched a handkerchief to her nose.

"My apologies," said Ambrose, holding back the nausea threatening to toss his breakfast over the rest of the passengers. He tried breathing through his mouth, but he swore he could taste the foul odor. "I had not thought that..." Ambrose stuttered, his face heating under the burning glares of the Youngs.

For the first time during their trip, he counted himself lucky that Mr. Bennett, with his rumbling snores, was fast asleep.

"This is beyond the pale!" said Mr. Young. "My wife has a delicate constitution and should not be subjected to such effrontery."

Ambrose searched for any solution, but the window would not open, leaving the door as the only source of fresh air; he would not risk their safety by opening it while the coach was lumbering along. Dottie gnawed on Miss Pert's bracelet and smiled as though she were having a good laugh at his expense.

"I—" But before Ambrose could offer up any more apologies, Miss Pert spoke up.

"Oh, good heavens, you two are insufferable!" she said, glaring at the pair opposite. "Neither Mr. Ashbrook nor the child has any control over the situation, and snapping at them is not helpful."

"Now see here." Mr. Young straightened, puffing his chest like an aging peacock. "We paid good money for this coach, and we do not need to be assaulted by such odors or your impertinent words!"

At the harsh voices, Dottie screwed up her expression and looked ready to cry anew, and Ambrose bounced her, waving the bracelet before her eyes, but her lungs hitched. Leaning forward, Miss Pert cooed at Dottie, which seemed to calm her. But then the lady turned her harsh gaze back to the Youngs, and Ambrose was quite grateful that Miss Pert was on his side at present.

"*I* am impertinent? When you are the ones acting like children?" she replied. "It is not pleasant, I grant you, but nothing we cannot withstand. The next stop cannot be more than a quarter of an hour from here. Surely, you can survive a few more minutes, for there is nothing to be done in the meantime. Barking at Mr. Ashbrook will not resolve the issue any quicker!"

Ambrose leaned down to open his bag in search of the few supplies Mrs. Follet at the foundling home had kindly given him, but Dottie slipped. Balancing the child in one arm, he struggled to reach the bag without dropping her. Shifting Dottie once more, he leaned to the side and cracked his head against something quite solid. Miss Pert grunted, and they both sat upright, rubbing the place where they had collided.

"My apologies," he said, getting frightfully tired of those two words.

"No, it was my fault, sir," she said with a wince. "You looked to be in need of assistance with your bag."

Glancing at the lady, Ambrose felt as though the whole situation had knocked something loose in his head for he could not understand why Miss Pert was being so solicitous.

"My thanks," he said. "I find I have my hands quite full of late."

She retrieved the bag, but there was no space for both it and Dottie on his lap. He juggled the two for a moment before he glanced over at Miss Pert.

"I hate to be more of a bother, but would you mind holding Dottie?" he asked. "I would never think to ask a thing when she is in such a state, but I am in need of another set of arms."

Miss Pert's expression softened, and the sight of it surprised Ambrose. Though Dottie had received a generous amount of sweetness and smiles, he had not thought her capable of being civil to him. Yet there she sat, looking quite pleased, and it had a pleasant effect on her features. Miss Pert would never be deemed pretty, but the expression softened her sharp features.

Reaching forward, Ambrose placed Dottie in Miss Pert's arms, but just as he was about to set the bag on his lap, he saw a brown smear across his greatcoat where Dottie had been resting. Looking at the babe in Miss Pert's arms, he could already see a growing stain along the lady's cloak. His head ached from the collision, his lungs choked on the stench, yet having to admit to Miss Pert that he had ruined her cloak was the most painful thing about his present situation. She was being rather kind, but he suspected it would not last with that revelation.

"Did you find what you need?" she asked.

"I am terribly sorry, but I fear I might have ruined your cloak," he said. Reaching into his bag, he retrieved a napkin and used it to dab at the mess.

Miss Pert's brows drew together, and she glanced down at it. He braced himself for the inevitable outrage, but she gave a shrug and waved him away. "What's done is done; there is no use trying to salvage things now. But we can wrap another napkin around her to keep it from spreading."

Snatching a fresh napkin from Ambrose, Miss Pert wrapped the old around the new with a few easy movements. It still stank like the River Thames on a hot summer's day inside the coach, but at least the mess was contained. And despite everything, Miss Pert remained kind to the babe who had caused it all.

Though there was no sign of further damage to the lady's clothes, Ambrose was unwilling to risk it and retrieved Dottie with a smile that conveyed the depth of his appreciation. But Miss Pert's eyes narrowed at it.

"I am already assisting you, so you need not waste such looks on me," she said, that pinched expression returning to her face.

"What looks?" he asked, settling Dottie in the crook of his arm; the babe gave a wide yawn, and Ambrose prayed she would nap.

"The looks you use to entrance ladies. The type that makes them fall straight into your embrace," she said, though her face flushed when the words left her mouth.

Ambrose had no idea why his behavior offended her so, but in his experience, there were not many who could withstand a dose of good-natured teasing and flirtation. "And are you likely to fall into my embrace?"

Mrs. Young gasped, and Ambrose fought to keep himself from laughing at the level of horror she conveyed with that sound. Miss Pert appeared neither diverted nor appreciative.

"You may find this difficult to believe, but not every lady is taken in by a few false words and a sickly sweet smile," she replied, her scowl coming out in full force.

"Well, you do speak your mind," said Ambrose, "and I am uncertain as to whether I find it endearing or offensive."

"As my mind is my only asset, I find it best to use it on a regular basis," she said, crossing her arms. "You certainly flaunt your only asset."

Ambrose huffed, leaning away from the sour Miss Pert, though with Mr. Bennett next to him there was nowhere for Ambrose to go. The lady made no sense. One moment she was as bright and sweet as a daisy, and the next, a stinging nettle. Though as Ambrose thought about it, there was little of her behavior towards him that had been the former, with one exception. Dottie was the only recipient of Miss Pert's sweetness, and Ambrose didn't know if he should be grateful for her benevolence to the poor child or irritated that she was incapable of bestowing it on him.

Looking down at Dottie, who was blinking with heavy eyelids, he knew the next stop could not come soon enough.

Chapter 8

N
ever had time moved so slowly. Each minute stretched into ten until Ambrose worried they would never reach their destination. Struggling beneath the weight of the oppressive silence and hateful glares of the other passengers, he wished the coach would roll faster down the country lane, but there was no hurrying the journey along.

They crested a hill, and Ambrose spied a village just ahead. Nestled among the buildings was the distinctive arch that served as the opening to the inn's courtyard. Though the clouds remained firmly closed above them, he swore a column of light shone from the heavens, encircling the blessed building as a choir of angels sang its praises. Rumbling down the road, the coach pulled into the courtyard. The Youngs and Mr. Bennett burst through the door the moment it stopped, their hasty movements knocking and bumping him, which woke Dottie and set her squalling.

Ambrose sighed.

They still had several hours to go, and he did not relish continuing on with such surly travel companions. To say nothing of Miss Pert. But there was nothing to do about it.

Stepping out, Ambrose held Dottie at arm's length as both

her napkins were soaked through and dripping. His overcoat was a lost cause, but he hoped to salvage some part of his clothing. Dottie calmed and stared at him, blinked, and then broke into a big grin, even laughing at him as he tromped over to the inn.

Ambrose wondered how any parent traveled with children. Journeys were difficult enough on one's own, but dealing with such an unexpected turn of events made it all the worse. He was simply glad that this debacle had occurred so close to a stop. With the time allotted for the passengers to get a meal, Ambrose would have a few minutes to clean the pair of them up. He only prayed that Dottie would have no further incidents.

By its very nature, a coaching inn is a noisy place. As both the respite for travelers and the social center for the village, they were rarely empty, and The Black Stag was no different. Even out in the courtyard, he could hear the bustle and voices from inside, but every sound stopped as Ambrose came through the door, trailing a dribbling mess behind him. Ambrose was already keenly aware of the horrid picture he made, and the gaping stares and disgusted looks only added to his discomfort.

"Oh, for goodness' sake!" came a sharp voice behind him. Miss Pert stood there, scowling at the gawkers. "This cannot be the first time any of you have seen a child with a messy napkin."

Turning to a man who had the air and bearing of the proprietor, Ambrose asked, "Do you have some place in which to clean her?" The man glanced in dismay at the mess gathering on the floor, but like any good innkeeper, he sensed Ambrose's heavily padded pocketbook; a smile stretched across the man's face as though nothing were amiss, and he quickly led Ambrose to a private parlor. Hurrying over to the compact dining table, Ambrose laid Dottie down, her legs kicking into the air as she babbled at him.

"I'll fetch some water and rags, sir," said the innkeeper, and Ambrose made note to give the man a large tip before they left.

"You forgot your bag in the coach," said Miss Pert, setting Ambrose's traveling case next to Dottie. "You will need it."

"Yes," he said with a sigh. But he had too much on his mind to show any gratitude. He and Dottie were filthy, and they did not have long before the coach would leave. Pulling up Dottie's dress, Ambrose peeled away the second napkin that Miss Pert had wrapped around her. He had not thought it possible for her to smell any worse than she already did, but each layer brought with it a stronger stench that had Ambrose gagging.

He forced himself to calm and focus on the task at hand. The napkin. It was tied around Dottie in an intricate series of folds, and he tried to recall the instructions Mrs. Follet had given, but it was pointless as he had forgotten the words mere minutes after hearing them. They were more helpful than the written ones she had given, but neither were of any assistance now.

But he had watched Mrs. Follet as she had changed Dottie. That was something. As he stared at it, Ambrose knew he just needed to think of the napkin as one of his machines. He had the finished product before him; he simply needed to disassemble and reassemble. Of course, his gears and springs did not kick at him while he worked. Or arch their backs. Or laugh when he bungled it.

Mary should have known better than to think her day could not fare any worse. Having the remnants of Dottie's dirty napkin trailing down her cloak was a fitting addition to an already abysmal day. But watching Mr. Ashbrook fumble with Dottie's napkin made Mary realize that some good had come from it, for the floundering gentleman was in dire need of assistance.

"May I help?" she asked as Dottie kicked at his face with a squeal of delight.

"I have it, but thank you for offering," he said in a distracted tone.

It was his first expression of gratitude that did not raise Mary's hackles. She had no idea why the fribble felt the need to slather every word with an amorous undertone, and she was grateful he was too distracted to do so now.

Stepping to the wash basin, she cleaned her hands, though she knew her linen gloves were ruined. Her cloak was made of sterner stuff, so there was a chance to salvage it; luckily, her frock had escaped most of the damage, which was a blessing. Mary sighed at all the laundry that needed doing, but at present, the only course of action was to change her clothes. She would not get a proper wash until she returned home, but at the very least, she could get out of these stinking, wet garments.

A shout came from outside, catching Mary's attention. Glancing out the parlor window, she saw the stable boys tightening the final straps of the horses' bridles and tack. That would not be out of the ordinary, except for the extraordinary speed with which they worked; the coach wasn't scheduled to leave for another quarter of an hour, and there was no need for such haste. And Mr. Young and Mr. Bennett stood nearby, dropping several coins into the coachman's hand.

It wasn't until Mr. Young bundled his wife into the coach with Mr. Bennett quick on their heels that Mary realized what was happening. Twisting the window handle, she shoved it open.

"Don't you dare leave us!" she shouted.

The passengers looked up, and Mrs. Young had the decency to look chagrined, though it did not stop her from slipping into the coach as the passengers up-top took their positions once again.

Spinning, Mary ran to the door but stopped at the sight of Mr. Ashbrook. "Hurry! They mean to leave us!"

Mr. Ashbrook gaped at her for a fraction of a second before hurrying through the napkin's final knot. Mary grabbed the babe's abandoned dress as he lifted Dottie from the table—but with a single kick, the fresh napkin came loose, landing on the floor.

Staring at it, Mary had the urge to abandon Mr. Ashbrook to his own devices and catch her coach before it left, but seeing the naked child squirm in his grip and the harried look in his eyes, Mary knew she could not do it. She doubted the gentleman would last long if he were stranded alone with the infant, and she would not abandon Dottie.

Mary reached for the fallen napkin and laid it out flat, ushering Mr. Ashbrook to lay Dottie down. Having spent a fair bit of time caring for Lydia as a babe, she was familiar with the task, though she was surprised at how readily the knowledge returned to her. With a final tie, the napkin was secure, but Mary cast her eyes to the window just as the stage pulled out of the courtyard.

"There is no point in hurrying now," she said.

Lifting Dottie from the table, she handed the child to the gentleman, who was frowning at the disappearing coach. Worry gnawed at Mary's stomach, and even Dottie's smiles could not calm her.

She was stranded.

Helping the child had seemed a simple thing to do—the right thing. But standing there with naught but a few coins in her reticule, Mary was overwhelmed. Mama had given her a little money for a meal, but Mary had nothing more. She was still a good forty or fifty miles from home with no way to pay for the journey. Though she could hope that the next coachman was merciful, Mary knew she would likely be required to pay the fare again, and she had not the funds for it. Sending word to her family would cost her; not to mention that it would be at least a day or two before they could rescue her, and she had no place to sleep nor food to eat.

Walk. That was the only option. But how would she manage her trunk? Mary sunk down onto a nearby armchair, her strength failing her.

And that was when the innkeeper reentered the parlor.

"Are you done here?" he asked.

Mary stood once more, though she had no plan. The only thing she did know was that sitting around would do nothing to fix her predicament.

"When is the next coach to Bristow?" she asked.

"As it happens, there's a coach that passes through here in two hours from Farrington," he said.

That was a possibility, though Mary would not be easy until she knew whether the coachman would show benevolence. In her experience, it was just as likely to go poorly and leave her at the mercy of her own two feet. Even a seat up-top would do. It was a decidedly uncomfortable spot, but she could manage it for a few hours.

"Then might I wait here until it arrives?" she asked.

"This is for paying customers. All others have to wait in the courtyard."

It was tempting to throw her meager coins at the innkeeper, but each was precious. Instead, Mary smiled, hoping that perhaps she might appeal to his better nature.

"I understand, and I would hate to be a bother, but it has been a long journey, and I would be so grateful if I might be allowed to rest here. I promise not to be in the way if paying customers arrive."

"Miss, I've already got to scrub down my floors because of the mess you and the gent brought in," he said, folding his arms and scowling at her. "Only paying customers are allowed here. Now, shift yourself or pay up."

Mr. Ashbrook stepped forward, donning that ingratiating smile of his, his honeyed words making sweet with the innkeeper. Watching it unfold was like witnessing her own worthlessness. She had smiled and been just as gracious and had received nothing but venom in return, but with nothing but an affable manner and good looks, Mr. Ashbrook had the innkeeper so sugared up that the man would have given them the keys to the inn if Mr. Ashbrook had asked it.

"Of course, sir. And I'll let you know when the coach arrives," said the innkeeper, giving him a properly deferential bow of the head, though he gave Mary hardly a passing glance as he left. She did not know why such treatment should surprise her, for she was a nothing. A plain, unappealing thing that few in the world noticed and even fewer cared for.

Mary gritted her teeth, forcing herself to be calm. Such maudlin thoughts were unhelpful, but it did not stop her mind from running away with them. It was an old wound that chose to pain her at the most inopportune moments, and Mary could not think of a worse time for such weakness to surface than in front of the perfect Mr. Ashbrook.

A bed sounded heavenly. It would be worth renting an entire bedchamber to get a few hours' rest before the next coach arrived. A few hours with an infant hadn't been a daunting prospect this morning, but Ambrose now knew that he had grossly underestimated just how tiring they were. Even when Dottie was behaving, it was exhausting to constantly entertain and care for her. However, when he looked down at the sweet child in his arms, he knew he wouldn't have chosen differently. Bristow would be better for Dottie, and a bit of discomfort on his part was worth it.

Casting his eyes to Miss Pert, Ambrose was uncertain what to do with the lady. Of course, he was uncertain why she had sacrificed her trip home to help him, but regardless of her reasons, Ambrose knew it was now his duty to deliver her to her destination.

"I apologize that you have been delayed," he said. "Though I am confident there will be no issues with finding another coach."

The lady's expression darkened, her thin lips disappearing as she glowered at him. "Of course you will have no issues with it. The great Mr. Ashbrook has charm to spare. You could get stranded in the middle of Abyssinia and end up on top with no effort on your part."

Ambrose gaped at her blatant hostility and was deeply confused as to why she consistently took umbrage with him. The last four hours had left his emotions taut, and that final swipe of hers was enough to snap them.

"What do you find so offensive about me?" he asked, his

anger stirring with each word. "What slight have I caused? Is there a reason you persist in sharpening your tongue on me? I have been nothing but kind to you, and you have repaid it with harsh words and sour looks!"

"I know it is difficult for a gentleman such as yourself to understand," she said with a flippant tone, "but not everyone falls at your feet the moment you smile."

Ambrose's pulse quickened, the sound of it pounding in his ears. "I am no imbecile," he said, his voice rising. "And it is easy enough to understand why such a shrew is left to travel alone. Anyone who chooses to spend the day trapped in a coach with you would have to be mad!"

Miss Pert stood rigidly in place, her eyes fixed on his, no doubt formulating her next attack, but then Ambrose saw a brightness in her eyes. It surprised him enough that he finally noticed the tremble in her chin, though nothing else in her face showed that his words had affected her.

"Then perhaps it is best if I leave you be, Mr. Ashbrook," she said with a stiff curtsy. She held her composure as she left, though Ambrose saw a tear trickle down her cheek as she shut the door behind her.

With his anger calming, Ambrose's wits returned to him, reminding him that the lady had sacrificed her coach for him. He turned Dottie around to rest her on his shoulder, but she lifted her head to stare at him with those rich, dark eyes of hers as she dribbled on his jacket. Yet another piece of his clothing that would need a thorough scrubbing. Just like Miss Pert's gown, cloak, and gloves.

Whatever else the lady said, she had been exceptionally kind to Dottie. More than that, she had been understanding and helpful to him, even though it was clear that she held him in contempt. Ambrose could not comprehend Miss Pert's behavior, but he certainly understood his own and had much to be ashamed of.

Chapter 9

Gathering her cloak about her, Mary marched through the inn, her eyes averted. Her breathing hitched, and she gathered her last bit of fortitude to keep herself from bursting into tears. Once outside in the courtyard, she sucked in a deep breath of the damp air and tried to calm herself. Swiping at her cheeks, she strode to where her trunk had been dumped.

The silly thing. Mary cursed the wide-eyed excitement that had pushed her to pack it full. Having never traveled such a distance before, she had brought everything she could possibly need—none of which had been necessary during her short trip to London.

Reaching for the handle, Mary tugged. But it hardly budged. Teeth gritted, she heaved again as hot tears spilled from her eyes, blurring the world around her as she shoved and pulled, fighting the wretched thing. Finally, she surrendered and sat on it.

Turning her face away from the inn and gawkers, Mary let the tears come.

Her heart withered in her chest, and she felt like a rag doll struggling to stay upright. Unwanted and alone. A castaway.

Her breaths came in jagged puffs as she realized that if she were to vanish, hardly anyone would notice. Her family would mourn her, of course, but Mary did not think that it would be overly upsetting for them. Lydia would be hurt, perhaps, but they were so wrapped up in their own lives that Mary doubted it would mean much to any of them.

The closest thing to a friend Mary had ever had was Henry. And then Bess. Dropping her head, Mary wiped at her face with a derisive snort. Those two were the only people who had ever cared for her, and it had been nothing but a farce. Henry wanted a friend who would stroke his ego, and Bess wanted to position herself to catch his eye.

Of course, who could blame them? Mary bit down on her trembling lip. She was plain, awkward, outspoken, and rude. Mr. Ashbrook was entirely correct in his assessment of her character. She had berated and mocked him at every turn. Thinking back on her words, Mary could not believe she had said such things. It was as though some malicious spirit had taken control of her mouth, unleashing every bitter feeling on poor, unsuspecting Mr. Ashbrook.

Sitting there alone with the sounds of the inn and stables around her, Mary felt heartily ashamed of herself and the woman she had become. Harsh. Unyielding. Critical. A shrew. It was true.

Thunder rang in the distance. Mary glanced up into the gray skies and was greeted by a raindrop on her cheek. How fitting. Pulling her cloak tighter, Mary burrowed into it; the thing still smelled awful, but at least it provided some cover from the growing rain.

"Miss?" someone called, but Mary ignored her. She was in no state to speak to anyone.

"Please, miss." A young maid came to stand before Mary and gave her a curtsy. "The weather is turning frightfully fast. You'd best come inside."

Averting her face to wipe away the remnant tears, Mary spoke, fighting to keep her words from catching. "I am not a paying customer and have been told to wait here."

The maid shook her head. "Mr. Fields was having a bit of a rough day, miss. He asked me to fetch you and told me you were to wait in the parlor until the coach arrives."

Another thunderclap rumbled in the clouds above, and though Mary had no wish to return to the inn, her pride had done enough damage today. A touch of humility was needed.

"Yes. Thank you." Mary stood, and a groom appeared, lifting her trunk with ease as the maid led them inside. Knowing what (or rather, who) awaited her in the parlor made it difficult to cross the threshold, but gathering her courage, Mary straightened and stepped into the room. However, she could not raise her eyes from the floor.

Mr. Ashbrook said nothing, but she knew he was standing there with Dottie in his arms. Except for the babe's gurgles, it was silent in the room. Mary was at a loss for words, though she knew he deserved an apology after her atrocious behavior.

"Oh, for goodness' sake," he grumbled.

Mary's gaze snapped to Mr. Ashbrook, and the gentleman was frowning at Dottie.

"We just put you in a clean napkin. How is it that you need yet another?" he groused, holding Dottie up to inspect it. Mary could see wetness spreading across the linen.

But the only response Dottie gave him was a string of gibberish.

"Allow me," said Mary, nodding at the child. Focusing on that task was infinitely easier than dealing with the larger, far more daunting issue.

Mr. Ashbrook looked taken aback but nodded. "That would be wonderful. I thought I understood what I was doing, but it is clear that I am in need of assistance."

"The knot wasn't tight enough, but it was otherwise perfect," said Mary as she ushered him to lay Dottie on the table. "Do you have a clean napkin?"

Reaching into his bag, Ambrose retrieved a fresh one and handed it to the lady. He knew he needed to say something, but prostrating himself had never been a talent of his. He preferred a compliment and one of his smiles, but those clearly did not work with this lady. She took the napkin while avoiding his eyes, and Ambrose felt the cut. He had just insulted her, and yet here she stood ready with a helping hand.

"I feel I should apologize, Miss..." he began, only to realize that he still did not know her name.

Her gray eyes finally rose to his, though they fell away just as quickly. "Miss Mary Hayward," she supplied, sliding the napkin under Dottie. "And there is no need to apologize for telling the truth. I have been beastly to you."

"That does not excuse my behavior," he said, watching her hands as she wrapped the napkin and tied it off. "You have been very kind to Dottie, and I repaid you with harsh words."

"But I have been terribly unkind to you, Mr. Ashbrook."

Before they could start arguing about who deserved to apologize most, two serving girls entered, hauling trays of food with them. Miss Hayward took Dottie into her arms, and the babe smiled, kicking and waving as she dribbled on the lady. Ambrose reached to clean it up, but Miss Hayward stopped him.

"There is no harm done," she said, bouncing Dottie. "If you like, I can hold her while you dine."

Ambrose looked at the heaping portions of food and wondered if she truly thought he was going to eat it all himself. "Dottie can play on the rug for a few minutes while *we* eat."

Miss Hayward looked at the steaming bread, soup, and slices of meat pie. "I cannot."

Ambrose ignored her protests at the sound of her rumbling stomach and took Dottie to lay her down. She kicked and squealed, and Ambrose gave her a smile before straightening. Miss Hayward positively jumped when he placed a hand on her back to lead her to the table.

"You shall need something before the next leg of the journey," he said.

She shook her head, but Ambrose led her to the chair. She came to a halt and turned to face him, though she did not meet his eye. "I cannot afford such a spread," she said, her voice a low murmur.

Ambrose turned her around and sat her on the chair. "Consider it an apology and peace offering," he said, coming around to sit opposite.

He expected her to argue, but a long moment later, she nodded and took up her spoon. Ambrose kept an eye on Dottie as he ate, but she seemed happy to lie where she was and coo at the ceiling. The lady before him was a different matter altogether for she seemed quite out of sorts and disinclined to speak; Ambrose was at a loss of how to engage her in conversation.

"Might I ask you a question?" he asked.

Miss Hayward nodded without looking up.

"What is it that you find so distasteful about me?"

Her eyes shot to his, and Ambrose nearly laughed at the surprise in her face. Though he had no interest in having his faults enumerated, it was a topic that was certain to prompt an answer.

Blushing, she glanced over to Dottie. "It is not so much that I find you distasteful, Mr. Ashbrook. But I do not care for empty flattery."

"I may have an abundance of compliments," he admitted, "but they are not empty."

Miss Hayward leveled a look at him that was incredulous, challenging, and humorous at the same time, and Ambrose smiled at it, which brought the barest hint of a smile to her lips.

"Perhaps I am a tad free with my flattery," he admitted with a chuckle, watching closely as Miss Hayward warmed incrementally.

"You are a constant stream of flimflam, sir," she said, her face the picture of stern disapproval. "The sheer volume of it is quite impressive."

Ambrose regretted opening the conversation. The lady was

hopeless, and there was no reason to waste any further words on her. But then he saw a glimmer of something in her eyes that made him reassess her words.

Leaning forward, Ambrose met her gaze. "Are you teasing me, Miss Hayward?"

And then he saw that which he had never thought to see from the frigid lady. A smile. At him. Not at Dottie or anyone else, but for the first time, she truly looked pleased with him.

"Perhaps," she said, hiding her grin behind a drink.

Ambrose chuckled, tucking into his food. He had never thought that speaking with Miss Hayward would elicit a laugh from him, but apparently, she could be quite diverting when she chose to be. Her jest was delivered with such a serious tone that he had nearly overlooked it, which only made it all the more humorous. Perhaps there was more hidden beneath that prickly exterior.

"May I ask why you find flimflam so distasteful?" he asked.

Miss Hayward stilled, the lightness disappearing as she stared down at her plate. "It's dishonest."

"Not all compliments are false."

"In my experience, they are," she said, pushing her soup about with her spoon. Her posture straightened, and she stared at her food, though Ambrose saw a hint of a blush in her cheeks. "It is heartbreaking to discover that flattery you thought was spoken in earnest meant nothing."

There was so much more Ambrose wished to ask her about that statement, but Miss Hayward looked so vulnerable that he could not bring himself to force any more confessions from her.

"And to where are you traveling, Miss Hayward?" he asked, hoping a change of topic might relax her once again. But the innocuous question seemed to do the opposite.

"Home," she said, picking at her meal. "Bristow."

"What took you to London?"

"My family is spending the Season there," she said.

"The Season?" Ambrose cast his gaze to Dottie to cover the shock he knew would read in his eyes if Miss Hayward bothered to look up from her meal. From the state of her gown and the fact that she was traveling alone, he had not thought her to be as genteel as that. If her family participated in the London Season, they must be of some means, yet Miss Hayward showed none of the trappings of it.

Miss Hayward nodded but offered up no further explanation. There was nothing overt that indicated she was distressed, but Ambrose sensed something lurking beneath her previous statement. Perhaps she did not care for London.

"And you forgot something direly important at home and are fetching it?" he asked. It sounded strange to him, but perhaps it made perfect sense to the Haywards—like having their unwed daughter travel alone on a stage with little blunt on hand.

"No. I am returning home."

There was something odd going on, but for the life of him, Ambrose could not piece it together. "You have had your fill of London, then? No husband hunting for you?"

He had said it in jest, but the emotions on Miss Hayward's face made it clear that she had not taken it as such. She met his eye once more, and in her gaze he saw a myriad of emotions, though he was unsure how to decipher them. It was clear there was much happening within her head, but no explanation was forthcoming. A single "no" was the only answer she gave.

As she was getting more succinct with each question, Ambrose decided it was best to leave things be. Miss Hayward obviously did not care to share her story nor did she ask any questions of him, so he allowed the conversation to lapse into silence as they ate, though his mind never strayed far from his mysterious companion.

Chapter 10

Clutching her book, Mary tried to ignore the strange sight before her and the even stranger gentleman in the midst of it. She had never seen a father dote on a child as Mr. Ashbrook did with Dottie. He paced the parlor with her, bouncing her in his arms, making faces and cooing at her. Watching the pair of them together, she wondered over the details of their story, but she did not have the courage to ask.

It was as though Mr. Ashbrook had a knack for finding her at her worst. Whether it was her temper getting the better of her or the shame of being sent home like an unwanted piece of baggage, Mr. Ashbrook witnessed it all. Perhaps it was best to let things lie. The next coach should arrive shortly, and then they would go on their way, never to see each other again.

Mary opened her book, but her eyes did not follow the words. She enjoyed a good, sturdy tome, but her thoughts were hopelessly tangled, and she found herself thinking about the other volume stowed in her reticule. The one she desperately wished to read.

Glancing at Mr. Ashbrook, Mary saw that his attention was on Dottie, so she slipped the other book from her bag, sliding the first into its place. She wished she had a soft quilt to wrap herself in, a good cup of tea, and the room to herself so that she might curl up before the fire. But as that was not possible, Mary contented herself with getting lost in her favorite novel.

But even those moving words could not distract her from Mr. Ashbrook. Her eyes followed him over the top of the page, tracking him and little Dottie. Mary wished she could blame it on the infant and some maternal instinct calling out to her, but it had more to do with the gentleman holding her.

"That does not speak highly of your novel," he said, glancing at her.

Mary jumped and shot her eyes away from him and back to the page. "Pardon?"

"You are staring at me more than the page, and that does not speak well of the story," he said. Mary expected some outrageous comment or suggestive smirk, but he simply looked at her with eyes that laughed more than smoldered.

"Nonsense," she said, smoothing the page.

"Admit it," he said, and then the flirt returned in full force as he smiled at her.

"Oh, must you do that?" she said, burying her nose in the book.

"Do what?" He stopped pacing and turned to face her.

"Constantly give me such looks. It is as though you cannot help yourself."

His brows shot upwards. "Apparently not, for I have no idea what you mean. I was only teasing."

Mary shut her book, affecting the same sultry expression he had employed. "'Admit it,'" she parroted.

Mr. Ashbrook laughed, which set Dottie giggling. "I suppose it is true, but why should it bother you?" he asked. Drawing closer, he looked at Mary in a manner that made her heart do very uncomfortable things. Even though she knew it was nothing more than the spell he cast over every lady, Mary could not rein in her feelings.

"Are you afraid you might lose your heart to me?" he asked. The look in his eye set Mary's stomach in knots, making her dream of things best not dreamt. But it wasn't real. She knew it wasn't. It was silly to think such things, and Mary stiffened. And then the air was gone, and Mr. Ashbrook waggled his eyebrows at her with a teasing smile.

"I am sorry to be the bearer of bad news, Mr. Ashbrook," she said, smoothing her skirts. "But not every woman succumbs to your charms. You are not the first handsome man I have seen, and I have never swooned."

That set his brows waggling even more as he beamed. "You think me handsome?"

Mary snorted. "Don't act as though that is a revelation, sir. A blind woman can see that you are quite handsome."

"On the contrary," he said. "Charming, yes. Flirtatious, certainly. But more often I am dubbed attractive. Few call me handsome, and none do so with that tone."

Mary gaped at him, but for all her control, she could not keep her cheeks from flaring bright pink.

"She thinks me handsome," he said to Dottie, bouncing her in his arms as he returned to pacing.

Mary's temper flared at the mockery. She was not a plaything. Just as she opened her mouth to give him a proper set-down, he glanced at her, and she saw the good-natured twinkle in his gaze. So few people teased her that Mary had not seen it for what it was. Rather than acknowledge his jest, Mary pulled up her book and hid behind it. She got no more than two words into it before she glanced at him again, and he gave another waggle of his brows.

And Mary chuckled. She could not help herself.

"What are you reading?" he asked.

Mary turned her burning face away from Mr. Ashbrook. "*Roman History* by Barthold G. Niebuhr." That wasn't a lie precisely. She was reading it—if not at this precise moment.

Mr. Ashbrook huffed. "That sounds shockingly serious, Miss Hayward."

"It's quite fascinating. I heard someone say that it was one of the premier books on the history of Rome, and I was curious to see for myself."

"Fascinating, eh?" he said, making a face at Dottie. "Perhaps you should read it aloud and let us judge if it's as fascinating as you claim."

Mary looked down at the book on her lap that was most decidedly not about Roman history. She reached for her reticule to see if she could switch them out, but Mr. Ashbrook was no fool.

"That is not the book you were reading in the coach. Just how many books do you carry around with you?"

"Just the two," she said, abandoning her plans. There was no point in hiding it now. "I was reading *Roman History*." Mary sighed, wishing she could hide her ridiculousness away. "But this is *Sense and Sensibility*."

"Is it about philosophy?"

At that question, Mary laughed. "No, it is a romance."

"One of those Minerva Press books?"

Mary gaped at Mr. Ashbrook. "No, indeed! It is a true romance and not one of those soppy tales."

Of course, she wouldn't admit that she had a secret weakness for those silly books, too. It was bad enough for the lonely spinster to be caught clutching novels about love; she did not need to implicate herself further by admitting a fondness for such lurid tales.

"I have read many of the author's works," she said, "but *Sense and Sensibility* is my favorite. I have been dying to read her last novel, *Persuasion*, which I hear is wonderful, too, but I cannot get my hands on the volumes."

"With such a ringing endorsement, you must read me some," he said, and Mary couldn't tell if the smile on his face was in earnest or jest.

"I doubt this would be to your liking."

"And why is that?" he asked, pausing in his pacing to look at her.

"In my experience, most think these types of books are only for brainless, lovesick girls."

"It sounds as though your experiences have been with the wrong people," he replied, and Mary was surprised to see quite a serious look in his eyes. She squirmed under his consideration and answered with only a shrug.

Mr. Ashbrook grunted and continued to pace. "Well, I am willing to give something new a try if you are."

Mary hid her smile behind the book as she opened up to the first page. "'The family of Dashwood had long been settled in Sussex...'"

...

Ambrose's feet ached. He wanted to sit down, but every time he did, Dottie fussed. It appeared that the child only wanted to be walked from place to place, bouncing along as they went. If it weren't for Miss Hayward, he would be running half-mad by now. Her voice hummed in the background, weaving the story for him in a manner that was far more engaging than Ambrose had ever thought possible for a novel. Though it was clear that she had read the story many times before, she still smiled at the good bits and mourned over the bad, sweeping herself into the plot until he wondered if she even remembered he was in the room with her.

And Ambrose was becoming quite as engrossed in the novel as she.

"'Elinor's compassion for him increased, as she had reason to suspect that the misery of disappointed love—'" But Miss Hayward was cut short when the innkeeper stepped into the parlor.

"Coach has arrived, sir," he said, "but I'm afraid that it's full up, and there isn't another until tomorrow morning."

Ambrose sagged. So much for getting to Bristow tonight. His supplies for Dottie were running low, and he was more exhausted than he'd ever been—even with his long history of haunting the gaming clubs through all hours of the night. He was uncertain if he could manage another day of this, but there was nothing to be done about the matter.

Straightening, Ambrose was about to give orders to the innkeeper when he saw Miss Hayward pale. That was when he realized he had a greater issue at hand than his own well-being.

If Miss Hayward had not the funds to pay for a meal, it was unlikely she could pay for a room and the additional costs that would come with being stranded for the night. On top of it all, some might overlook her traveling alone during the daytime, but staying at the inn would eviscerate her reputation.

Ambrose would not allow her to suffer for her kindness.

"May we have two rooms, Mr. Fields?" he asked, shifting Dottie in his arms. "And is there a woman I might hire to act as Miss Hayward's companion for the night?"

"My wife is busy, but my ma would be willing to sit with your lady." Ambrose gave the man a hard look, and Mr. Fields amended his comment. "I mean Miss Hayward, of course."

"Mr. Ashbrook," said Miss Hayward, getting to her feet, "I am grateful for your generosity, but I cannot allow you to—"

But Ambrose waved Mr. Fields away and cut Miss Hayward off before she grew more agitated. "You would be in Bristow tonight if it weren't for Dottie and me, so I will brook no refusal. I must be allowed to make up for the difficulties you face because of us."

"But a companion?"

"I may play with the bounds of propriety at times," he said, "but I am not such a bounder that I am ignorant of your precarious situation. There will be rumors enough if anyone discovers I paid for your room. The only way to stem them is if you are properly protected. A servant may not be much of a chaperone, but it will do some good."

Miss Hayward crossed her arms. "There is no need for it. No one would believe that you would compromise me."

Ambrose straightened, staring at her. "What do you mean by that?"

She scowled. "There is no need for modesty, sir. There isn't a person in the county who would believe that a gentleman like you would have designs on me."

Gaping, Ambrose felt a flare of temper threaten to loosen his tongue, but sense got the better of him, and he thought before speaking, making the fog of his own defensiveness lift enough for him to see the hint of vulnerability beneath her hardened exterior.

It reminded him of when Mina had called his flippant attitude his armor, and Ambrose wondered if this prickly demeanor were Miss Hayward's. Where he complimented and cajoled, this lady sniped and scowled. The more he thought on it, the more he saw it lurking in her eyes. Fear. Pain. For one who acted so aloof and disdaining, Miss Hayward cared deeply, and Ambrose wondered what pushed her to keep others at such a distance.

His own instincts told him to wheedle a smile from her with an outrageous comment or two, but he had learned the hard way that she would not appreciate it. If Miss Hayward disliked the dishonesty of such things, perhaps honesty was the better course.

Stepping closer, Ambrose held her gaze and gave her a respectful bow. "Miss Hayward, though you had no reason to show me kindness, you helped me through a difficult situation and are now suffering because of it, and I will not risk adding to it. You may believe yourself beyond reproach, but I will not rest easy if there is any possibility that you are wrong. Please allow me to do my duty and repay your kindness."

The edges of her armor crumbled as he spoke, and Ambrose saw the warmth in her eyes that came from his humble plea. There was no need to embellish, as the pure and simple truth worked wonders with her.

"Thank you, Mr. Ashbrook." And then she gave him another of her rare smiles, and Ambrose knew that whatever else may come, he was pleased to have brought a bit of joy to such a heartbroken creature.

...

It took several moments before Ambrose was coherent enough to realize that Dottie was fussing. Blinking away the remnants of sleep, he lit a candle and stumbled over to the armoire drawer that served as a makeshift bassinet.

"Good evening, little miss," he said, scooping her into his arms and resting her against his shoulder. Patting her back, he walked the floor with her. It was surprising how quickly it was becoming a familiar movement. Dottie's arms and legs kicked and squirmed in his hold, but he kept up the steady movement.

Ambrose checked her napkin, but it was clean. Then, he checked her bed, but it seemed suitably comfortable. She was plenty warm, but no matter how he tried to calm her, she would not settle. The answer came to him eventually, though his exhausted mind struggled to find it. Food.

Rubbing his forehead, Ambrose mulled that problem over. Mr. Fields and the rest of the inn's staff would be abed. He wished there was another option, but he saw no other recourse than to wake one of them to fetch him some milk. If he didn't, Dottie's cries would rouse the entire building soon enough.

Just as he was about to step through the door, Ambrose stopped at the sight of a small pitcher of milk sitting on his doorstep. Beside it was a note, and Ambrose snatched them both up. Tossing the paper on the table, he focused on calming Dottie first. Propping her in his arms, he placed the lip of the pitcher to her lips and slowly poured, allowing her to lap at the milk; it went far better than it had the first few times he had done this; dribbles of milk wetted their nightclothes, but it wasn't a messy disaster.

Twenty-four hours. That was all it had been. He did not have a clock handy, but it had to be around the time when he had sauntered home the night before. Only one day, yet Ambrose hardly recognized himself. Dottie blinked heavily as she finished, and minutes later, she was fast asleep in his arms. Her little foot stuck out from the edge of her nightdress, and Ambrose ran his fingers over it. She stirred, her dark eyes opening again. She met his gaze, smiled, and then promptly fell asleep once more.

Ambrose held her close. She was fed and ready to be put to bed, but he couldn't let go of her. Not yet.

"You are such a sweet little thing," he whispered. She stirred and turned her head towards him, her little lips sucking at air, and he ran a finger along her soft cheek.

Ambrose hardly recognized his own heart, for it felt like an alien thing beating in his chest. But as he reflected on his life, he was overcome with the realization that tomorrow he would hand this babe off to his sister and return to his previous existence.

There was something so special about holding her in his arms and knowing that she depended on him. Needed him. Ambrose couldn't remember the last time anyone had needed him. In truth, he wasn't certain anyone ever had. His family loved him, but if he were gone, it would not greatly impact their lives.

Standing, he walked her over to her drawer, tucking the borrowed blanket around her. Running his hand over the fine curls along her temple, Ambrose knew that whatever else was in store for their future, he would make certain Dottie found a good home. He could do that much for her.

Ambrose yawned and moved to his bed but stopped when he saw the note he'd abandoned on the side table. Bringing it closer to the candle, he hunched over the scrap of paper. There weren't many words on it, but without any context, it took an infuriating amount of time for him to decipher them. If it weren't for the fact that one of the first things he recognized was the sender's name, he would've tossed it into the fire, but his curiosity kept him fighting through it.

The minutes ticked away as he pieced each word together. For brief moments, letters coalesced into sensible English, only to scatter again, twisting into unintelligible muck. But as he soldiered on, the short missive became clear.

I thought you might need this. Consider it my apology and peace offering. — Miss Hayward

With a smile, Ambrose blew out his candle and climbed into bed, feeling lighter than he had in ages. In a little more than a day, he had taken on two rather large responsibilities. Both may be only temporary, but that did not diminish the fact that it was his duty to make sure that they were cared for and delivered to their destinations.

If he were to tell his cronies in London that he had become a nursemaid and chaperone for a pair of displaced ladies, they would laugh at him. But they would laugh even more if they knew just how much he adored it and how much he dreaded its inevitable end.

Chapter 11

Pampered was a word commonly applied to the gentry, but to Mary, it was a foreign concept. Never had she awakened to find a hot breakfast awaiting her. Nor a coach ride where she was bundled in blankets with hot bricks at her feet. Nor her expenses paid without a second thought or word of complaint. Yet all these things had happened since she had awoken that morning.

The stagecoach rolled along the road, and Mary's eyes traced the raindrops that streaked across the windows as she wondered about the gentleman beside her. Spending a few hours with Mr. Ashbrook did not make her an expert on him, but from his reputation and her own witness, Mary would say he was acting quite odd.

Not a bad sort of odd. Simply not like a gentleman of leisure.

His behavior towards Dottie was striking on its own, but today, he seemed to be taking great pains over her own well-being, too. And Mary was uncertain how to interpret it or how she would return to a life devoid of such luxury.

"Will you promise not to breathe a word of what I am about to say?" His voice came as a whisper, and Mary turned to find him bending towards her with that ever-present smile on his face.

She opened her mouth to give him the perfunctory answer, but Mary caught herself when she felt a strange urge to tease him—something that was becoming more common the longer she spent in his company.

"That depends on what you say," she said. "I reserve the right to mock you for it later."

Mr. Ashbrook's eyes widened before his grin grew and he gave a deep, rumbly chuckle. Mary fought back a smile.

"Then I have been warned," he said, shifting Dottie in his arms. "But I was hoping that you would read a bit more for us."

Mary glanced over at the other passengers, an older pair of brothers by the name of Dennehy who were fast asleep. "I would hate to bother them."

Mr. Ashbrook flashed her a simpering smile.

"You truly cannot help yourself, can you?" she asked.

"But it is so effective," he replied, adding an extra pout that was so ridiculous that Mary could not help but laugh.

The sleeping gentlemen started, their snores cutting off as they looked at Mary from under the brims of their beaver hats. She smothered another laugh as they settled and promptly fell back asleep.

"I am dying to know what happens to Elinor and Marianne," he said.

Mary rolled her eyes. "I highly doubt that."

"Is it so difficult to believe that I might enjoy it?" he asked as Dottie arched her back. Mr. Ashbrook shifted his hold on her so that she was sitting upright.

"That Mrs. Kingsley's wild brother, Mr. Ambrose Ashbrook, the scourge of gaming halls, and flirt extraordinaire cares about a silly romance story?" she asked with a raised brow. "Yes."

Though said with her usual dry manner, Ambrose sensed

the jest beneath it. However, it did not stop the words from pricking his heart. There were plenty of his set that would wear such categorization with pride, but the stark and utterly accurate assessment of his public persona was not flattering in the least.

"How did you know I am related to the Kingsleys?" he asked, latching onto something that was far more innocuous.

Dottie threw herself forward just as the carriage hit a particularly large bump, and she slipped out of Ambrose's grip. Before he could do a thing about it, Miss Hayward caught her. Dottie began tugging at the lady's cloak, but both she and Miss Hayward seemed perfectly happy with the arrangement so Ambrose let things lie.

"I am not well acquainted with your sister," she admitted, "but she is our nearest neighbor. Avebury Park sits just over the hill from Buckthorn Manor, and my parents are on good terms with the Kingsleys. We were at your brother's wedding breakfast."

Ambrose's brows ticked upwards as he scoured his memory for her. "Truly?"

Miss Hayward's eyes darted from Dottie for a quick moment. "There is no reason for you to remember me, sir. You were preoccupied with Miss Sally Hensen."

A picture of the afternoon resurfaced, though Ambrose was hard-pressed to remember Miss Hensen. There was nothing unique about her to leave an impression, and Sally Hensen's kiss in the gardens had meant as little to him as it had to her and was equally as memorable.

"Are you blushing?" asked Miss Hayward.

His eyes widened, and he tugged at his cravat.

Lifting Dottie up onto her feet, Miss Hayward cooed at her. "I do believe your Mr. Ashbrook is embarrassed." Dottie responded by clapping her hands, jerking up and down on her legs, and squealing loud enough that both Mr. Dennehys jerked awake.

"Perhaps a little," he said, once the gentlemen returned to

their naps. "It is not often that I am called to task for such things."

"But what does it matter to a gentleman about town, such as yourself?" she asked, turning her gaze from Dottie to meet his own. Gone was the lightheartedness of her earlier comments, and instead there was an earnest curiosity in her eyes.

"Perhaps I am not the gadabout I appear to be," he said.

"Then why act the part?"

Ambrose crossed his arms, turning his gaze away from Miss Hayward. The conversation had taken an unexpectedly serious turn, though it wasn't entirely unwanted. Perhaps it was the anonymity of discussing such things with a relative stranger. Or that something in Miss Hayward seemed oddly comforting at present. Or that their acquaintance had started off on such a horrible foot that there was no possible manner in which to make matters worse. Either way, some part of Ambrose welcomed the candid discussion.

"Why do you?" he countered. Turning his gaze to her, he saw her spine straighten.

"What do you mean?"

Ambrose smiled at the startled look. "No one who gets teary over a book they have read a dozen times and leaps in to help while others run the other way could ever be as cold-hearted as you pretend to be."

Miss Hayward sat there, frozen in place as she stared at Ambrose. She blinked a few times and turned away, but not before he saw the sheen in her eyes. She relaxed into the seat and turned her attention to Dottie once again.

"I did not get teary over the novel," she mumbled.

She had and was again at present, but as she wished to ignore both instances, and Ambrose had no desire to ruffle her further, he allowed the topic to drop.

Ambrose cleared his throat. "But I would have you know that I am not the bounder I appear to be. I have interests outside of cards and ladies." He had no idea what prompted him to say such a thing, but there it was. He knew it would prompt further questions, but some compulsion had pulled it from him.

"Horses?" she asked, a tickle of a smile at the corner of her lips. It was so faint, Ambrose was certain that most would not see it. To her teasing, he replied with a chuckle.

"No. They have their uses, but I do not understand the obsession with the smelly creatures," he said.

"No dandy wishes to smell of anything other than roses."

Ambrose startled the Dennehys with a bark of laughter. "No, miss," he said in low tones as the brothers went back to their slumbers. "I am certain no dandy wishes to have grease in his fingernails, yet I seem to be sorely afflicted with it." At her questioning glance, he added, "I have a growing fascination with machines."

"Machines?" she asked with raised eyebrows. "What prompted that?"

A better question would be what prompted him to reveal that to Miss Hayward. Even now, Ambrose wondered if he should shrug it off with a flippant remark and let the conversation die, but he didn't wish to. Some instinct told him that she would understand, and as he had long ago learned to trust that part of himself, Ambrose forged ahead.

"I stumbled upon a mechanical exhibition when I was wandering the city one afternoon, and it was captivating to see what they could do with a few turning gears," he said with a shrug, as though it had been a slight thing rather than the grand awakening it was.

"Truly?" she said, turning her attention from Dottie. "Like what?"

"Mostly clocks with fancy mechanisms, but they had all sorts of automata. Figures that played instruments, animals that moved about as if they were real. But my favorite was this figurine at a piano who played a whole repertoire of pieces."

Miss Hayward's eyes widened. "I read about such things in a magazine. I had hoped for the opportunity to visit one of those exhibits when I was in London. It sounds simply marvelous."

"We are living in an incredible age," he replied. "I cannot begin to describe it. I had no idea how impressive such things were until I saw them with my own eyes. I purchased a clock and promptly took the thing apart to see how it worked and found I had a knack for it. My rooms are now in a constant state of disarray as I have half-built machines scattered about."

At that, Miss Hayward questioned him about his hobby, delving deep into the topic. Never had he been free to discuss such things at such length with such an interested companion. Though she had no experience with machinery, she had a keen mind and an eagerness to learn more, and Ambrose was quite as eager to share it with her. He could hardly contain it as he rambled on. Every time he worried that he was overwhelming her with information, she countered with some question, which led into a whole new discussion. It was invigorating.

Dottie wriggled on Miss Hayward's lap, and the lady shifted the infant into a new position, her conversation never faltering. Ambrose had spent hours struggling to contain the child, yet Miss Hayward managed it with little effort, seeming undisturbed by Dottie's constant demands. Ambrose marveled at her skill with the child, for he had not a fraction of her ability.

But his mind was wrenched from that line of thought when the coach drifted to the side. Miss Hayward gasped, grabbing his forearm as they slid. The coachman righted them, but they struggled to stay aligned with the horses as they descended a hill.

The morning drizzle had shifted into a thick downpour. The clouds were heavy and gray above them, releasing a torrent onto the grasslands. Ambrose felt the wheels struggle for purchase on the muddy road, and the horses whinnied. A shout came from up-top, and the coach drifted once more. The wheels slid, bringing them perpendicular to the road, and the horses screamed as the stage came down the hill faster than the beasts pulling it. Gripping the road and then slipping again, they shook and skidded the wrong way down the slope.

The Dennehys were awake and blustering as they braced

themselves. Ambrose slid close to Miss Hayward, holding her and Dottie in place as the coach lurched, fighting gravity, the mud, and the horses all at once. The coach slammed into the bottom of the hill and heaved to the left until it stood on two wheels. The three of them tipped, and Ambrose pushed against the far wall to hold them in place.

A man up-top shouted, falling past the window.

The coach hung in the air, and Ambrose struggled to keep hold of them. Miss Hayward clutched Dottie, closing her eyes, and Ambrose held his breath. He had seen enough carriage accidents to know how much damage could be done. Clinging to them, he prayed for a safe outcome, and if not, that he would take the brunt of their fall.

And then the carriage righted itself, putting all four wheels on the ground.

"Are you all right?" he asked, holding the two of them in his arms. Miss Hayward was pale and wide-eyed but calm when she nodded.

The coachman ran past the window, coming around to the rear wheels.

"Stay here," said Ambrose. Again, Miss Hayward nodded, and he threw open the door, sending a scattering of rain across the passengers.

Within moments, any bit not covered by his greatcoat was soaked, but Ambrose ignored it and ran to the passenger who had fallen from the roof. With the water gathering at the bottom of the hill, the road had a full six inches of mud, which was a blessing for the fellow, for it had saved him from anything worse than a few bruises. Once Ambrose was certain the man was well, he came round to the coachman, who was crouching beside the rear axle. Mud buried a good chunk of the wheel, making it difficult to see any damage that might have been done.

"We'll need help if we hope to get out of this," said the coachman.

Ambrose nodded, and within minutes he had the Dennehys

and the men up-top organized. Heaving, the passengers shoved as the horses pulled. Ambrose's boots were soaked, filling with mud. Rivulets of rain crept down his arms and back as they pushed and shouldered the hulking coach clear of the mud.

But it was no use. The axle was damaged and would not make it to the next inn. No matter how Ambrose approached the issue, there was no solution that would save them from walking in this foul weather. Even sending for assistance would do little good, as the roads were worsening with each minute they stood around debating. If they wished to get warm and dry, they would have to walk. There was no other option.

It took a fair bit of money to convince the coachman to part with his oilskin jacket, but it was worth the price to see Miss Hayward somewhat protected against the elements. No matter what he did, she was bound to get soaked through during the trek, but it was better than the thin cloak she wore.

Standing in the doorway of the coach, Ambrose set his case on the floor and rearranged his clothes to make a bed for Dottie.

"What do you think you are doing?" asked Miss Hayward as he moved to place the infant inside the bag.

"She needs to stay dry, and I shan't have a free hand to hold her while carrying the bags," he replied, but Miss Hayward stopped him.

"You cannot shut her in that," she said, picking Dottie up and tucking her into her arms. "I will carry her."

"No," he said, reaching for Dottie again. "I cannot ask you to carry her such a distance."

"And I cannot allow you to stuff her in a bag."

"I will make it comfortable for her," he insisted.

Miss Hayward clutched Dottie and gave a huff of laughter. "Mr. Ashbrook, you have done a wonderful job caring for this child, but that is a terrible idea. She might suffocate in there. There is no reason I cannot carry her and keep her warm and dry."

Ambrose rubbed at the back of his neck. "Are you certain that I cannot—"

"No!" she said, though she softened the answer with a slight upward tick of her lips.

Bowing to a greater authority in such matters, Ambrose focused instead on helping the lady tie her lap blanket around her shoulders before layering the cloak over the top. Luckily, the coachman's jacket was large and the lady was thin, which allowed her to wrap it around her and Dottie. Bundled up as she was, Miss Hayward doubled in size, and Ambrose could only hope that it would keep her comfortable.

With a hand at her elbow, Ambrose helped her out of the coach and into the weather. Puffs of vapor came from her mouth as Miss Hayward gritted her teeth against the chill and drew Dottie closer. He wished he could see the child's face to make certain she was well, but she was tucked beneath the folds of fabric to keep her dry from the deluge; he had to trust that Miss Hayward would watch over her.

Shouldering Miss Hayward's trunk on one side and taking up his bag in the other hand, they began the five-mile journey to the nearest inn.

"So, how is it that your sister, who does not have a daughter, has asked you to bring Dottie from London by yourself?" asked Miss Hayward.

Ambrose faltered in his step, though he liked to think it was more due to the state of the road than the question. "Beg your pardon?"

Miss Hayward clutched her bundle closer to her chest and glanced at Ambrose as she slipped and stumbled along in a manner that made him wish he had a free hand to steady her. "You claimed that Dottie is your niece, and you are returning her to her family in Bristow. I was not about to ask in mixed company, but now, I find that I am in need of a diversion."

"And prying into my private life is the perfect remedy?" he asked with a chuckle. That secret humor of hers lurked beneath her question, removing any effrontery he might have felt from it.

"Certainly," she said, stumbling again.

Though the mud thinned the farther down the road they got, it still gripped their shoes, making it difficult to keep a sure footing. Her breath blew out in great clouds as she fought the mud, and Ambrose wished he could do something to assist her. He shifted his grip on the bags in his hands, but there was nothing to be done about it. He had no hand free to help her—not that she had one either. Besides, he was fighting the terrain as much as she.

He did not wish to dredge up Dottie's history, but as the rain was already soaking through his clothes, he knew they would need something to take their minds off the present situation and the fact that Miss Hayward's teeth were already chattering.

"I said that because it seemed the right thing to say," he admitted before launching into the story. It took a surprising amount of time to recount it all. Of course, Ambrose spent a fair bit of it entertaining Miss Hayward with his various attempts to care for Dottie, which seemed to amuse her as the passengers trudged along the sodden road like a string of sad ducklings.

Chapter 12

"**M**iss Pert?"

Mary was so lost in thought that she didn't hear Mr. Ashbrook speaking until he said that horrid name. Looking at him with a frown, she was met with a smile.

"I thought that might get your attention," he said. "Do you need a rest?"

Her arms ached from holding Dottie, her legs were nearly quivering from all the times she'd wrenched her shoes free of the mud, and she felt as though she were about to shake apart from the cold that was taking over her body. To say nothing of the agonizing crick in her back from hunching over the babe to block her from the worst of the rain. Mary wanted nothing more than a rest, but one in front of a fire, surrounded by cozy blankets. Stopping now would only make it all the more difficult to continue their journey, which she could only hope was coming to a fast conclusion.

Walking miles on end was not a difficult thing. Mary had spent many a day strolling the lush countryside, but that was when the skies were clear. Spending the afternoon among the rolling hills and verdant fields was a pleasure, but today was an entirely different venture. The world was awash in gray, looking as forlorn as Mary felt. Being far smarter than they, the wildlife had taken refuge from the torrential downpour, leaving the stranded passengers alone in the desolate landscape. It felt like hours had passed since they had started their march, but there was still no sign of an inn.

"No, Mr. Ashbrook," she said. "I don't want to rest."

"I asked if you needed one, not if you wanted one," he said with another silly grin, which made Mary chuckle—an occurrence that was becoming far more common the longer she spent in his company. It had been an age since Mary was so free with her good humor, but Mr. Ashbrook had a talent for giving her reasons to laugh.

"Whether I need one is immaterial, as sitting in the rain and cold is hardly restful," she replied—but just as she did, Mary stepped into a particularly bad patch of road that swallowed her foot in mud. With a jerking wrench, Mary tugged at it, but the sludge seeped into her boot, gripping it tightly. Before she could say a word, Mr. Ashbrook abandoned the luggage and crouched before her, digging his fingers into the mess to tug her free.

Straightening, he wiped his hands on a sodden handkerchief and looked at her, making Mary's heart stutter. Having known the gentleman for so short a time, she could not interpret all the emotions filling his gaze, but Mary saw a gleam of admiration, a shadow of worry, and even a hint of pleasure. Mr. Ashbrook was such a confusing man. He acted the part of the gadabout, yet rescued abandoned infants and stooped in the mud to help a plain nobody without a second thought. More than that, he appeared to enjoy it.

"I can leave my valise and carry Dottie if that would help," he offered.

Mary shook her head. "You will need her things, and she is lighter for me to carry than your case. But you can leave my trunk. That would free one arm to hold her, if you wish."

"You will need your things when we arrive."

"But I hate to be a burden."

The corner of his mouth turned upwards as he stared into her eyes. "You are anything but that, Miss Hayward."

Pulling free of his gaze, Mary continued down the road, refusing to look back as he gathered the baggage. She would not infer deeper meaning from his words or conduct. Mary knew her place, for Henry had taught her well; no man wanted a woman like her for a wife. Mr. Ashbrook's kindness signified nothing more than his good character. He felt a duty towards her and was executing it to the best of abilities. That was all.

She could not allow herself to run away with foolish fantasies.

Dottie's leg twitched as it often did while she slept, and Mary hugged her close, wondering what would've become of the child had she not landed on Mr. Ashbrook's doorstep; of all the gentlemen she could have been given to, he was likely the only one in the building who would expend such energy and expense on her behalf. But regardless of Mr. Ashbrook's extraordinary character, she knew it was too much to hope that such a unique gentleman would ever develop an interest in a lady such as herself.

"Miss Hayward."

She stopped and turned to see Mr. Ashbrook coming towards her. He dropped the bags once again and pulled off his greatcoat. Stripping off her oilskin jacket, he slung his coat around her shoulders before replacing her outer layer.

"Your lips are near blue," he said, straightening the collar so that it was wrapped snugly against her neck. "I fear my coat is soaking, but it is wool and will help."

"But you need it," she said.

"Not while I am hauling this load," he said, shouldering her trunk before picking up his case. "I am plenty warm."

Mary brushed her cheek against the collar, marveling at the finely-spun fabric. It was the softest she had ever felt, and though the fibers reeked of the pungent stink of wet wool, it held a hint of Mr. Ashbrook's scent. Mary could not categorize it. There was no fragrance she could think of that was similar.

It was simply his, and one that Mary was becoming all too familiar with.

The added layer did little to warm her, but it took the edge off the chill, and Mary was grateful for the raindrops on her cheek and in her eyes that hid the gathering tears. It was a simple gesture. One that many a gentleman had done before and many would do in the future, but one that Mary had never received. A little thing that made her feel cherished.

Ever since their time at the inn, Mr. Ashbrook had been unfailingly kind, and Mary was struggling to keep herself from being swept away by it. Even those closest to her did not take such pains for her comfort. If it were her family standing beside her here and not Mr. Ashbrook, Lydia and Mama would be catered to, and Mary would be expected to do the catering. And that revelation hurt as much as Mr. Ashbrook's tenderness healed.

"I believe it is not far now," he said, nodding for her to follow.

Ambrose's feet wanted to move quicker down the road, and his heart agreed, but his head refused to comply. Miss Hayward was fighting to put one foot in front of the other, and Ambrose felt desperate to run ahead and fetch help to save her from finishing this arduous journey. But he could not stomach the thought of leaving her here alone and unprotected. She was his responsibility, if only for this short time, and one did not leave a lady alone and unassisted. Besides, what help was there to find when the roads were in such a state? No carriage or cart could make it through the great ruts of mud.

With no other recourse, Ambrose kept a weather eye on the road ahead, searching for the next inn, and did what he could to keep Miss Hayward moving. Using all the powers at his disposal, Ambrose teased and coaxed a smile from the lady. And then a bit more conversation. Then a bit of flirting, which made her roll her eyes and twit him in return. Her lips regained some of their color, which made Ambrose feel a tad better, but he wouldn't be at ease until both she and Dottie were warm and dry.

And then he saw the outline of a building in the distance. It was still a good ways off, but with the end so close, it was easier to coax Miss Hayward towards it while planning what needed to be done when they arrived.

The inn was one of those lonely buildings along a long stretch of empty road, but it had rooms to let and a warm fire, which was all Ambrose needed. Once they stepped over the threshold, he set the staff into a flurry of activity. Ignoring the Dennehys, who tried to take precedence, Ambrose shouted over the brothers, barking orders at the innkeeper. The servants scattered to do his bidding, and within minutes, he had his charges bundled up by the fireplace with warm drinks.

Miss Hayward needed dry clothes, but she looked so relieved to be sitting that Ambrose couldn't bring himself to stir her. Dottie peeked out from the layer of blankets, smiling up at him, looking far more pleased with the situation than either himself or Miss Hayward—but then again, when he checked on the child, he found her warm and mostly dry. Somehow the lady had kept that sweet girl comfortable, and Ambrose suspected it had taken quite a toll on her.

The innkeeper's wife eventually took control, fussing over Miss Hayward, and that was when Ambrose noticed how her hands were shaking and the tinge of blue clinging to her fingertips. He nearly grabbed them up and rubbed at them, but propriety shoved away the urge, and he allowed Mrs. Johnson to take care of the situation. Ambrose merely watched over her as her coloring slowly warmed and her shaking subsided.

...

Jolting out of her dream, Mary blinked at the empty parlor. The light of the fire flickered, making the shadows undulate around her, and she wondered what time it was. It felt late, though she suspected that had more to do with her exhaustion.

Dottie.

Mary shot upright, knocking the blankets away as she dug through the layers of wool and cotton that surrounded her.

"She is over here."

Glancing to the side, Mary saw Mr. Ashbrook sitting in an armchair with Dottie curled up in his arms.

"How long have I been asleep?" she asked, wiping at her eyes.

"Not long," he replied. "An hour or two."

Mary was grateful for the low light, as it meant Mr. Ashbrook would not see her cheeks redden at the thought of him watching over her in such a fashion. It was a silly, fleeting fantasy that did unpleasantly pleasant things to her heart. Things that were best left alone.

Mr. Ashbrook startled her by calling to a servant standing in the corner behind her, and then a flurry of activity entered the room. Serving girls came in with trays of food, setting out a delicious array of meats and vegetables that made her stomach rumble in anticipation. They set a butler's table before her with everything close enough that she needed to do little more than lean forward to enjoy her feast.

And then Mr. Ashbrook was there, helping to prop her up with a pillow behind her back. The whole thing made her look like an invalid, but Mary did not care. Her body had not the strength to do much on its own, and her heart reveled in the gentleman's attentions. It was as if Mr. Ashbrook anticipated her every need and then exceeded it. Mary dismissed the pricks of tears in her eyes as nothing but the lingering effects of the excessive cold, though her heart burned as warm as the fire before her.

The servants bustled out the door, leaving them mostly alone with the exception of an older lady who sat silently in the corner. It took a moment before Mary realized that Mr. Ashbrook must have provided yet another chaperone; that knowledge caused the burn to consume her heart, blazing through her until she was aflame. The depth of her gratitude was overwhelming, swallowing her whole, and Mary turned her gaze to the dishes as it was far easier than facing the gentleman.

"Is everything to your liking?" he asked, and Mary let out a startled chuckle.

"It is wonderful," she said, struggling to keep her voice even. "I can honestly say that no one has ever been so generous to me. My own family cannot be bothered to go to such lengths."

The minute the words were spoken, Mary wished them unsaid. She had not intended for such a confession, but exhaustion and the sheer power of her emotions were stronger than her hold on her tongue.

Mr. Ashbrook dropped into a chair beside her, keeping Dottie cradled in his arms. Mary felt his eyes on her, and she sent out a silent plea that he would not ask the questions she sensed were hovering in his mind. She was in no fit state to talk of such things nor did she have the defenses to deflect them. Somehow she both wanted him to ask and loathed the thought of bringing her shame to light.

There was silence as the gentleman watched her, and then he said, "Mr. Johnson and his stableman assure me that the coach will take several days to repair, and there is unlikely to be any more stages to Bristow for a day or two as the roads from London are a mess."

Mary's eyes darted to him and found nothing in his expression that hinted at why he had changed tack. Mr. Ashbrook motioned for her to eat, and Mary took a bite of a warm venison pie. "Then we are stranded again?"

"Yes, but I have devised a plan that should see us home tomorrow," he said, tucking Dottie's blanket around her leg. "Bristow is only a few miles down the road, and according to reports, the storm did not travel that far. The roads between here and there are traversable—"

"Except we do not have a carriage," said Mary.

"Precisely," he replied. "The Johnsons have only one for hire at present, but the Dennehy brothers got to it first and would not give it up. However, Mr. Johnson is willing to lend me a mount."

"Oh," said Mary, putting down her fork as the food soured in her mouth. "I understand. It is no bother, Mr. Ashbrook. Of course, you are anxious to get Dottie home."

She was not his responsibility. Mary knew that. Yet it still hurt to know that he was abandoning her. Perhaps the Johnsons would allow her to stay the night. If Bristow was only a few miles down the road, she could walk it and retrieve her trunk later. All in all, it was far less disheartening than the thought that Mr. Ashbrook would go on his merry way, unlikely to cross her path again. It was a silly thought, but she had come to enjoy his company and was loath to give it up.

"Wonderful," he said, giving her one of his most brilliant smiles that made her heart flip and twist. "I spoke with the Johnsons at length, and I feel confident that I can entrust the two of you to their care. They have a room for you when you are ready to retire, and Mrs. Johnson offered to clean up the messy napkins and provide us with fresh ones."

Mr. Ashbrook continued on in that vein, explaining the situation at length, but Mary's mind was still stuck on one particular item he had mentioned so casually.

"The two of us?" she asked.

His brows drew together. "Are you uncomfortable with that? I had hoped you would not mind caring for Dottie while I am gone."

Mary shook her head. "Of course I do not mind. I am simply surprised that you wish to leave her behind."

"It does not make sense to take her there and back—" But he halted mid-sentence, his gaze darkening as he stared at her. "Did you think I was going to leave you?"

Looking down at her plate, Mary picked at the food, but she glanced at him when he leaned in closer.

"Miss Hayward," he said, his eyes grabbing hers, "I said I would get you home, and I give you my word of honor that I will do so."

Mr. Ashbrook looked quite stern as he spoke those words, and Mary dropped her gaze. "I didn't mean to give offense."

"Then why do you doubt me?" he asked, his voice low and warm.

"It is not you I doubt," she said. "In my experience—"

He grunted and stood. "I know how you are going to end that statement, Miss Hayward. I only hope that you will come to understand that I will not behave as those others who have given you such sad experiences."

While still cradling Dottie, Mr. Ashbrook gave her a low bow, and in a quiet voice he said, "I will set out at first light, I will fetch a carriage from Avebury Park, and then I will escort you to your home, Miss Hayward. I give you my word."

Unable to speak, Mary nodded, and Mr. Ashbrook strode from the room, leaving her alone with an absolute mess of thoughts in her head and feelings in her heart.

Chapter 13

Staring out the coach window, Ambrose studied the passing landscape, watching for any signs that the weather and roads had worsened since setting off that morning, but it looked much the same. Not prime driving conditions but nothing the coachman couldn't handle. With the Kingsleys' man at the helm, they would arrive home in short order—something that both relieved and disappointed Ambrose.

The past two days had been a disaster on many fronts. Having spent much of it exhausted, embarrassed, dirty, wet, and cold, Ambrose was happy to be done with it, and yet he was quite content despite the whole mess. That was the only word he could think to describe his feelings at present. Content. Pleased, even. It made no logical sense. Even now, he felt worn to the bone, but he was more at ease with his circumstances than he had been in years.

Catching sight of the inn, Ambrose let out a silent sigh of relief. He had paid the Johnsons handsomely to ensure that Miss Hayward and Dottie would receive the best care, but his heart would not rest easy until he had them in his charge once more.

Leaving the landau and the Kingsleys' servants out front,

he alighted and hurried to his rooms, taking the steps two at a time. But when he reached the threshold, he paused at the sight before him. Miss Hayward stood before the fire with Dottie resting on her shoulder. A low tune filled the room as the lady swayed, resting her cheek against the babe's forehead. Dottie gave a plaintive whimper, and Miss Hayward patted her back while rocking the child. The lady's song was naught but a simple country tune and was sung with far less skill than most ladies possessed, but its sweetness struck him.

The scene was far from unique. Ambrose had seen mothers comfort their children thusly on many occasions, but it had never held such power over him. In the abstract, domesticity was not enticing. Ambrose had no contempt for the lifestyle, but the emotional cost of securing a wife had seemed too steep with too poor a return on investment. However, seeing it standing before him brought a deep-seated longing to his heart, like that of a starving man standing before a sumptuous feast. It was no abstract thing, but a tangible desire for a family of his own.

"You miss Mr. Ashbrook, don't you?" said Miss Hayward, giving Dottie a kiss on the forehead.

Miss him? That brought a hitch to Ambrose's breath, stoking a gentle burning in his chest that warmed him through. He could not think of another person who might feel that way about him. Ambrose could not say for certain that his brothers ever did. There was no question that Mina cared enough to long for his company, but her life was so full with her own family and responsibilities that there was little time and energy for her to sit around pining for her wayward brother.

"He shall return soon, my sweet girl," said Miss Hayward.

At that, he stepped forward loudly enough to get the lady's attention, and Miss Hayward turned. Both the infant and the lady holding her broke into smiles, grinning as though there was nothing finer in the world than his presence. Ambrose's heart thumped in his chest as it swelled from the joy of their reception, and he held his breath as the strength of his own feelings grew.

Dottie reached for him, leaning forward so quickly that Miss Hayward struggled to keep hold of her, and Ambrose strode forward, scooping her into his arms. Wrapping one arm around his neck, Dottie laid her head against his shoulder, and Ambrose swore he heard a tiny sigh as she snuggled close. It nearly brought him to tears.

"It appears I have made quite the conquest," he said, struggling to get the words out in an even tone.

"That should be of no surprise, sir, as ladies throw themselves into your arms quite regularly," said Miss Hayward with that subtle twinkle in her eye.

"Certainly," he said. "But none so readily. They tend to require a few more compliments and my famous smiles first."

Miss Hayward's lips twitched, though she tried to school her expression. But then the humor faded as she looked at Dottie with a furrowed brow.

"She has already had a difficult life, Mr. Ashbrook," she said, her eyes showing a shimmer of tears that disappeared with a few blinks. "Imagine being dropped on a doorstep. Abandoned..."

Reaching over, Miss Hayward straightened the edge of the babe's dress and ran a hand through Dottie's wispy curls. Her fingers brushed Ambrose's, and the touch brought her eyes to his. They were light—a mixture of gray and blue that shifted and altered between the two—and in them he saw that vulnerability she fought hard to hide. They were so expressive. Though Miss Hayward was adept at concealing her heart, it was those eyes that gave her away to anyone willing to look.

Ambrose had wooed many a woman before, but he found himself adrift as he gazed into them. An urge pushed him forward, begging him to kiss her, which was surprising enough. He'd not thought of Miss Hayward in such terms before, but he felt that pull as clear and fervent as any he had felt before. His heart was all but jumping out of his chest, but Ambrose had no idea what to do with the sentiment.

Things had been easy in the past. The ladies were brazen

enough to make clear what they desired and inconsequential enough that their opinions meant nothing to him. But this was Miss Hayward, and she was not one of the meaningless hoard nor seeking a bit of meaningless pleasure.

And that made up his mind.

Though deflated to allow such an opportunity to pass, Ambrose sensed such affection would mean great things to her, and he would not raise her hopes without knowing whether or not this was a passing fancy. Never had Ambrose stolen a kiss nor given one to a lady who expected more, and he would not risk hurting Miss Hayward until he knew where his heart truly lay—even though it begged him to kiss her soundly.

Bringing his arm forward, Ambrose offered it up with all the courtliness she deserved. "Might I escort you home, Miss Hayward?"

...

With each passing mile, they drew closer to Bristow, and Mary struggled between relief and disappointment. For her heart's sake, she needed to escape Mr. Ashbrook. Her carefully crafted protections were quickly eroding around the gentleman. Perhaps some might call her a coward, but Mary knew better than to believe their friendship meant anything of significance to him. People like Mr. Ashbrook collected chums like spinsters collected cats. It was not his fault that Mary's heart kept inferring something more.

So, it was best that she be removed from Mr. Ashbrook and his darling Dottie and deposited back at home to be quickly forgotten by both; but looking at the child and the gentleman who held her, Mary knew it would not be so easy for her to forget them.

Mr. Ashbrook looked up from Dottie to meet Mary's gaze. "You seem awfully pensive, Miss Hayward. Might I ask what has got you so quiet?"

Mary fought back a blush at being caught in the midst of such thoughts and turned her eyes away from the beguiling sight as she gathered her thoughts. She glanced at the maid-turned-chaperone sitting beside her before fixing her attention on the world outside the window.

"I was thinking that it is good we are close to our destination."

His brows rose. "Is that so?"

"With all the trouble that has befallen us, I was certain we would be attacked by roving highwaymen," she replied and was rewarded with a rumbling chuckle from her companion opposite.

"As I have traveled this stretch of road many a time and never had such horrid luck on a journey, I lay all the blame for our misfortunes on you," he said with a smile.

"That is very unkind, sir," said Mary as she fought her own grin. She had no idea what it was about the gentleman that begged her to tease him so, but she enjoyed it far more than she should.

"It is the truth. It has taken us two and a half days to travel all of fifty miles. That is shameful, indeed!"

And that was when Mary saw her home approaching, signaling the end of this adventure. There was no denying the sadness she felt, but once again, she told herself it was for the best. Mr. Ashbrook was too charming for her good, and it was time to return to her plain, normal life. The gentleman continued to tease her, and she found herself returning it with gusto as the landau pulled to a stop in front of her home.

Looking up at the worn building, Mary felt even more keenly the difference between herself and Mr. Ashbrook. Her family's home had never been as grand as Avebury Park. Even at its best, it was dwarfed by that grand estate. It was naught but a stone square with a few additions to keep it from being wholly unremarkable, but with the paint on the shutters cracking and the bricks crumbling, it was a sad and pathetic thing.

Once the carriage door was open, Mary alighted, calling out

a farewell that was far calmer than she felt, but before she got more than two steps towards the front door, Mr. Ashbrook was there, cradling Dottie in one arm while offering up his other to Mary.

"It is for holding," he said when she stared at it. "You simply slip your arm through mine."

Mary gave him a glare, which only made his grin widen. "I know what it is for. I am simply surprised is all. There is no need for you to—"

"I said I would escort you home," he said, stepping closer. "And that includes making certain that you are inside it, safe and sound. You do have a history of meeting misfortune on even the easiest of journeys."

Mary snorted. It was far from genteel, but at such a Banbury tale, he deserved it. She took his arm but held on to her mock indignation to keep herself from feeling anything more about his gesture. It was only a gentlemanly kindness, after all.

Gibbs was there to usher them in, and Mary knew the butler was teeming with questions at her surprising return, though he knew better than to show it. With a questioning glance at Mary, Gibbs went back outside to direct the groom with Mary's trunk.

"And now I can rest easy knowing you are safe," said Mr. Ashbrook, though he did not drop his arm nor step away. The warm look in his eye made Mary's imagination run away with her, and she forced herself to rein in those wandering thoughts.

"Are you certain you wouldn't rather come and stay at the Park with my sister?" he asked. "It feels wrong to leave you here alone."

Mary pulled away, forcing some distance between them. "I appreciate your generosity, but I prefer to be at home. There is plenty of work that needs doing, and I have the servants to keep me company."

Mr. Ashbrook nodded, and they exchanged the usual parting pleasantries. Mary steeled her heart but could not stop from giving Dottie one final kiss. This was the end.

"May I call on you?" he asked.

Mary blinked at the gentleman. It was a simple question with a world of meanings—from that of a neighborly overture to something far more intimate. Shoving aside such romantic drivel, Mary nodded. "Of course, Mr. Ashbrook. I would be delighted."

The brightness in his eyes and wideness of his grin was due to his pleasure at having a friend. That was all. Mary repeated that in her mind as he gave her a final bow and departed. They were friends—something that Mary cherished, but nothing more. Friends. It had been years since she'd had one, and she wasn't about to ruin it with fanciful thoughts. Remaining firm, Mary kept from running to the front window to watch them drive away. Of course, her feet still took her there, but it was a ladylike walk and not a hurried sprint.

Hiding behind the curtains, Mary peeked out as he climbed into the carriage. Silly girl that she was, she stood there, watching him, and then he looked at the house, his grin broadening when he caught sight of her. He gave a parting wink, and Mary's cheeks blazed.

Then he was gone, and Mary felt the loss of him. He may have asked to call on her, but Mary knew the truth. A gentleman like Mr. Ashbrook had plenty to occupy his time and thoughts. Once Dottie was settled, he would return to London, and they would never meet again.

Dottie tugged at Ambrose's greatcoat buttons, pulling his eyes away from Miss Hayward's house as the landau trundled down the road and onto the next drive over. In all the times he had stayed at Avebury Park he'd never visited the Haywards. He'd met plenty of Bristow's society on numerous occasions, but he could not dredge up a single memory of Miss Hayward. He supposed it made sense as she was not one to catch his eye, but that sat uneasy with him.

Leaning forward, Dottie brought her face to his greatcoat,

but he stopped her before she stuck the filthy thing in her mouth. He handed her his clean handkerchief, and she waved it with a laugh as Ambrose readied himself to see his family again. He hoped Nicholas wouldn't be around when he arrived with an infant. That was likely to set even sensible Mina aflutter; he could only imagine how awful Nicholas's reaction would be.

Alighting from the carriage, Ambrose climbed the front steps. Jennings had the door open with a timing that bordered on the preternatural. But before Ambrose was relieved of his hat, gloves, and coat, Mina and Simon appeared on the staircase.

"Ambrose, what have you been up to?" Mina asked. "Simon and I arrived home from our morning ride to discover that you had absconded with our landau and three of our servants."

At the time, Ambrose had thought nothing of borrowing it, but hearing it described in such a manner made it sound rather questionable.

"I needed the carriage because I left Miss Hayward and Dottie at the inn—the Golden Rooster or Golden Crown or Golden something or other," said Ambrose with a vague wave.

Mina froze on the stairs. "What?"

"We were stranded there, and the only chance of getting out was to borrow your carriage," he said.

"For your lady friends?" asked Simon.

"What?" Ambrose stared at Mina and quickly realized that it sounded far worse than it was, and the pair were likely misunderstanding it all.

"Who is that?" asked Simon, gaping at Dottie.

"May we talk in private?" Ambrose asked, suddenly all too aware of the eavesdropping servants.

The couple nodded and led him into an empty parlor.

"Now, what is happening? And who is this lovely little lady?" Mina's voice and smile softened as she looked at Dottie, who grinned in return, clapping her hands. With that one look, Ambrose knew Dottie had made another conquest as Mina reached for her and took the child into her arms.

As succinctly as possible Ambrose unraveled the whole convoluted tale, though it was far less succinct than he wished as Mina and Simon insisted on interrupting at frequent intervals.

"As in Mary Hayward?" asked Mina as she alternated between listening to Ambrose and cooing at Dottie.

"Who?" asked Simon.

"Your neighbor," replied Ambrose.

"Of course, I know the Haywards, but who is *Mary* Hayward?" asked Simon.

Mina shook her head at her husband. "The eldest of their daughters."

"They have just the one."

"No, dearest, there are two, and you have met her many times before," said Mina while Simon simply tugged at his cravat as he stared at the rug.

"Are you certain?" he asked.

Mina patted her husband on the arm and continued with the conversation. "I wish I could say I'm shocked that her family would put her in a public coach alone, but I have long since learned not to be surprised at the things Mr. and Mrs. Hayward do to better their position. Thank goodness you were there to watch over her."

In truth, Ambrose was grateful Miss Hayward was there to watch over him, but he was more interested in the first part of Mina's statement. However, when he questioned her about it, she waved it away.

"The Haywards are determined to improve their social standing at any cost," said Mina. "They've hung all their hopes on their youngest, Miss Lydia, making a prime match during the Season, and they will go to any lengths to secure it. Unfortunately, sending their eldest home unaccompanied is not the first time they've put Miss Lydia's prospects ahead of Miss Hayward's well-being."

Ambrose scowled at that thought, though he was not wholly

surprised by it, either. Miss Hayward had not said much on the matter, but he had suspected her family's social machinations had everything to do with her present situation—though Ambrose could not understand why sending away Miss Hayward helped her sister's marriage prospects.

"But back to the task at hand," said Mina, lifting Dottie so that she could kick her little legs in the air. "I think you did right by bringing Dottie here. Foundlings do far better in the country than in the city. There is no reason we cannot find this dear little girl a home."

"Good," said Ambrose, though he felt decidedly ill-humored over the prospect; he already missed her.

Standing, Mina called for the servants to fetch one of the nursery staff. At his questioning look, Mina said, "With Nicholas and his family here, it may take a bit of time before I find a suitable prospect, but in the meantime, she would be more comfortable in the nursery with the other children. Between the two families, there are nursemaids enough that adding one more child should not be a burden."

Ambrose could think of nothing to say as the strangers took Dottie away. It made no sense for him to continue caring for her while there were others far more competent to do the job, but he searched for some valid reason to keep Dottie at his side. But he was pulled from his musings when Mina asked him about his own plans for the future.

"Did you wish to stay for tea or set out immediately?" she asked.

As most of Ambrose's visits ended as soon as his purpose was fulfilled, Mina's question was perfectly logical, but for the first time, he felt no inclination to hurry back to London.

"I thought I might stay until Dottie is settled," he replied.

Both his sister and her husband straightened, staring at Ambrose.

"You wish to stay?" asked Mina. "But you tore out of Bristow the moment the wedding was over. I thought I wouldn't be able to tempt you to return until after the end of the Season."

Ambrose shrugged. "I would feel better knowing for myself that Dottie is settled."

Simon's eyebrow quirked up, but Ambrose chose to ignore it. Just as Mina was about to speak, Jennings interrupted.

"Mr. Thorne is in your study, sir," he said, bowing to Simon before turning to Mina, "and Mrs. Whitmore is asking after the menu for tonight."

Mina popped off the sofa. "Goodness, where is my head? I had intended to speak to her about that hours ago. My mind has been so muddled as of late, I cannot seem to keep anything straight."

Simon stood, too, and gave his apologies before striding out to deal with his business, but Mina hung back.

"I do apologize for abandoning you like this, Ambrose, but I fear I have been run ragged with this wedding business and Nicholas's visit. I had hoped that things would calm down after Graham and Tabby left on their wedding trip, but it is still quite hectic," she said. "I shall have your usual room prepared, but feel free to use the Garden Room to freshen up in the meantime."

Ambrose followed Mina towards the door. "Might I be of assistance?"

Mina waved his offer away and smiled. "That is kind, but I have everything in hand. Go, get cleaned up and rest a bit."

And with that, she hurried from the room, leaving Ambrose alone. He sighed, dropping onto the sofa, his head resting against the back. With Dottie ensconced in the nursery and Miss Hayward safely home, there was nothing more for Ambrose to do. Once more he was unwanted and unnecessary.

Chapter 14

Reaching to the far side of the garden bed, Mary tugged at a weed. Dirt covered her cheeks and hands, though she did her best to protect both. In the short time she had been in London, the kitchen garden had become littered with noxious sprouts. Mrs. Gibbs was a fine housekeeper, but she did not have the time for such a task, and the maid, Sally, was plenty busy with the cleaning and laundry. And though Mama insisted that the cook must handle such things, Mrs. Webb was no longer of an age to be doing such labor.

Grabbing a handful of leaves, she pulled out an invader only to realize that it was, in fact, a carrot. With a sigh, she ate the meager thing, enjoying the sweet crunch even as she cursed her own distracted mind for yet another ruined vegetable. Today her work was riddled with such mistakes, each one a testament to Mary's distracted thoughts.

For goodness' sake, it had been a day since Mr. Ashbrook had escorted her home, and they had only been acquainted for two, yet she missed him. It had been an age since she'd had a friend. Though she shared close relationships with the servants, it was not the same. And Mary loved her family, but none of them truly filled the role of confidant and companion. Not that it would do much good if they were, as they were miles away in London, and Mary was here in Bristow. Alone.

Sitting on her heels, Mary stared at the mess she was making. There was little point in continuing with this butchery if they wished to have any vegetables for their meals. Wiping her hands on her apron, Mary pulled it off and abandoned it beside the rest of her gardening implements. She would have time to return to her work later, but for now, Mary was in desperate need of a diversion.

Stepping around the neat rows, Mary slipped through the kitchen door, sneaking past Mrs. Webb, who was busy preparing luncheon. Weaving her way through the house, she headed to her sanctuary. The library was an inconsequential room compared to the rest of the house. Not that the others were particularly grand or richly decorated, but funds were never used to enhance the forlorn space.

Though shelves lined the walls, they held more heirlooms than books as Hayward ancestors had sold off much of the collection that had once been housed here; Mary's own parents had certainly done their part. If it weren't for the fact that a library was positively *de rigueur* for any proper household, the room would have been stripped long ago.

A single armchair sat before the fire, but its mate was in front of the large window. To the ignorant, it would look haphazardly placed in the room, but it was the spot that allowed for the greatest light by which to read. Running a hand along the supple leather, Mary brushed away a bit of dust that had collected since she had last used it. Though it was the perfect place to curl up with a good novel, Mary could not stand the thought of being cooped up on such a glorious day. Sorting through the stack of books that sat beside her armchair, she quickly passed over *Sense and Sensibility* and settled on one that had no connection to a certain gentleman.

Clouds hung lazily in the sky like great puffs of cotton meandering through the heavens, and sunlight beamed down on her. It was the type of day that glowed with a golden, warm light that positively begged to be enjoyed, so Mary took her book out into the garden. Picking her way around the rows of vegetables, she took the path through the ornamental flower beds, taking note of the sections that needed cleaning. A clearing to one side of the path led her to a bench, encircled by great bunches of flowers, some of which stood nearly as tall as her. The scent of their blossoms filled Mary's lungs, and she stretched a hand out to brush her fingers through the taller stalks, their buttery petals brushing her skin; then she plopped down on the bench and opened her book.

Some stories were easy to begin. With no more than a few lines, she could immerse herself in that world. But this was no novel, and such a book always took a bit of work at the offset. At times, those serious tomes felt as though they were written in a foreign tongue, one that took several chapters of slogging through before she acclimated to the author's stodgy language. This book was even worse than usual. It referenced so many unfamiliar events and people that Mary struggled to understand the context itself, but she kept pushing forward. Enlightenment was worth the effort.

As her eyes ran across the page, a violet fell into view. Picking it up, Mary stared at the purple and yellow petals and then turned her eyes upwards to find Mr. Ashbrook standing over her with his most charming grin. Mary shot to her feet, her head coming scant inches from connecting with his chin.

"My apologies!" she said, stepping to a safe distance. And then remembering her manners, she gave him a curtsy. "Good afternoon, Mr. Ashbrook. What brings you to Buckthorn Manor?"

"I asked if I could call on you, and now, I have," he replied.

"Oh, of course," Mary said, tucking the book behind her and casting her eyes around the garden. "Might I offer you some refreshment?"

"No, thank you," he said, motioning for her to sit again. "I found myself exceptionally bored and thought I would come by to bother you a bit."

Mary nodded, not trusting herself to respond. She was a passing diversion to him. Nothing more.

They took their seats on the bench, though it was hardly wide enough for the pair of them. They had more space than in that first coach, but it was still too close for Mary's peace of mind.

"Is Dottie settled?"

Mr. Ashbrook nodded. "She is safely ensconced in the Park's nursery until my sister can find her a home."

"I wish you had brought her. I miss her dearly."

"I wanted to, but I doubt the nursemaids would have allowed it."

Mary started, her eyes widening. "Whyever not?"

But she was met with that rascally smile of his that set Mary grinning. Mr. Ashbrook shook his head sorrowfully, and said, "I am afraid that they are quite put out with me, for I go visit her in the nursery almost hourly, and I fear they do not appreciate my opinions on how best to care for her. If I am not careful, they will ban me from the nursery altogether."

After witnessing how avidly Mr. Ashbrook watched over the child, Mary could imagine just such a scene, and she laughed at the picture it made.

"And what is it that has you occupied this afternoon?" he asked, pointing to the book. "Finishing our novel without me, are you?"

Shaking her head, she laid the volume on her lap. "Nothing so entertaining, unfortunately. It is *History of the Rebellion of 1745* by John Home."

At that Mr. Ashbrook guffawed, and she blushed. "You have the most extraordinary taste in books, Miss Hayward. Quite unusual."

Mary shifted in her seat, tapping her fingers against the cover, uncertain how to respond. "I had an unusual education, so it is quite fitting."

Mr. Ashbrook leaned over, nudging her with his shoulder. "I meant no offense. It is quite refreshing to meet someone with such varying tastes."

Placing the book on the ground beside her, she replied, "In all honesty, I cannot claim to have diverse tastes. I simply do not wish to be a dunce." Having not intended to say so much, the confession startled her, and though Mary tried to shift to a safer topic, Mr. Ashbrook would not be swayed.

"You are no dunce, Miss Hayward. What makes you think you are?"

"It is nothing," she said, casting her eyes away from Mr. Ashbrook to stare out at the garden. "It looks to be a beautiful summer."

He huffed and turned towards her, forcing Mary to meet his gaze. "No prevaricating, Miss Pert. What makes you think you are a dunce?"

Miss Pert tried so hard to hide the conflict churning in her head, but Ambrose saw the struggle written in her eyes. So much of her expression remained stoic that Ambrose couldn't blame others for not seeing it, but it was clear that she was embarrassed to admit whatever truth lurked in her heart. Instinct told him that she wanted to reveal it to him, but Ambrose understood the power of shame, and he would make no move to force a confession. For several silent seconds, he waited, hoping she trusted him enough to share it.

"I did not receive much of an education," she finally said. "In order to economize, Mama undertook my schooling, and she was never much of an academic."

Again, that pinched expression took hold of her, hardening her features and making it appear as though she did not welcome further discussion. But Ambrose saw the sadness hidden beneath. Even while the rest of her body gave every impression that she desired nothing more than a bit of distance and solitude, her eyes gave away her heart. It was an internal struggle with which Ambrose was well-acquainted. Fear warring with loneliness, mingled with hope and despair.

And there was something more to what she had said. Many a young lady was educated by her mother and not a governess, so that was no shameful thing. Mulling it over, Ambrose fairly tripped over the truth when he came upon it.

"They would not spend the funds on you, but what of your sister?"

Again, her feigned frigidity reared its head, her spine straightening until it might snap. But her eyes revealed a world of emotion that Ambrose was certain Miss Hayward did not wish to be seen. All that coldness she conveyed to others hid a warm heart that he sensed was as fragile as glass. One does not become so frightened and build such fortifications without cause, and that made Ambrose ache for her.

"Lydia's education was more important. But it is of no consequence. Mama did not care for teaching, but I learned to read and study on my own and supplemented our sparse lessons." Reaching up, Mary tucked a stray lock of hair behind her ear. "When I hear people speaking of a subject I don't understand, I read a book on it. That way I will not be so ignorant in the future. That might sound silly—"

But Ambrose cut in. "No, it doesn't. No one enjoys feeling ignorant and out of their depth." The conversation had steered suddenly into uncomfortable territory for him, but just as he had not allowed her to divert attention away, Miss Hayward was intent on keeping him from altering course.

"You speak as though you know from personal experience," she said.

Ambrose swallowed, wishing he could tug off his cravat; until Turner arrived, one of Mina's footmen was acting as his valet, and the lad had a tendency to tie them too tightly. He turned his eyes away from Miss Hayward, though he could not keep silent. Not with her. "I was often called a halfwit in school, and it is not pleasant."

Miss Hayward reached over, placing her hand on his forearm, and though she said nothing at first, the small gesture carried great relief with it. For the first time in his life, Ambrose felt like someone truly understood, even without a word spoken.

"I find it hard to believe that they would say such things about you, for you are nothing of the sort."

Ambrose's eyes moved from where her hand rested and up to her eyes.

"A rogue, yes. But certainly no halfwit." She spoke with such seriousness that it gave the teasing a deeper level of wit that set Ambrose laughing. A good, long laugh that started as a low chuckle and built until he struggled to control it.

"You, my dear Miss Pert, are a gem," he said, taking her hand in his. It was an easy movement. Comfortable. As though they had sat thusly many a time before.

"And you may be the only one who thinks that," she said with a self-deprecating shake of her head. It was clearly meant to be a jest, but a flash of hurt tinged her lighthearted affectations.

"You are," he said with complete sincerity. "Though it pains me to know that your family left you to travel alone, I am extremely grateful that it put you in my path."

Plucking a few sprigs of flowers from the bushes behind them, Ambrose offered them to Miss Hayward, who stared at them as though they were an alien thing. She made no move to take them, but he took the liberty of tucking them behind her ear. The purple blossoms looked lovely against her dark hair, and Ambrose was rather stunned to realize just how pretty she was. Not in an obvious manner, but she had a stateliness to her that was quite appealing.

His hand fell to her shoulder, and Ambrose found himself gazing at her lips. Her eyelids lowered, and Ambrose felt the invitation emanating from her. Inching towards her, he leaned in to close the distance. The dreamy expression in Miss Hayward's face shifted into shock as she shot to her feet, forcing Ambrose to rear away.

"I must go," she said, hurrying to the house, and Ambrose scrambled to catch her.

Fool! An unmitigated fool. Mary held back the tears, refusing them permission to fall. How could she have let this happen again? To think that she had actually wanted him to kiss her! Fawning over Mr. Ashbrook like a simpleton. A bit of flattery and a few flowers, and she was ready to throw herself into his arms. Tricking herself into believing that his kindness meant something. In her daze, she had almost missed the truth; she was simply re-enacting the self-same scene Henry had used to steal those kisses all those years ago. The flower in her hair. The sweet words. The fervent look.

Mary heard Mr. Ashbrook calling after her, and she moved faster towards the house. She needed distance or she would never clear her head.

A bit of fun. That was all Mr. Ashbrook wanted. It was all any gentleman wanted. A diversion. Something to clear away the boredom. It meant nothing, and Mary hated herself for believing that this moment was any different.

"Miss Hayward, please," he said, catching her by the arm. "What is the matter? Have I offended you?"

"I am not a plaything!" she said, pulling free and continuing on her way.

"Of course you are not," he said, stopping her again. "Why would you say that?"

"I may be uneducated, but I am not brainless," she said, allowing the anger to flow into her words. Standing before her was not Mr. Ambrose Ashbrook, but her family who had abandoned her, Henry and Bess who had betrayed her, and her own foolish self for allowing this to happen again.

Mr. Ashbrook opened his mouth, but Mary spoke over him.

"Gentlemen like you do not flirt with ladies like me," she said with hitched breaths. "They do not give us flowers. They do not tell us sweet things!" Even though her anger was blazing, tears pushed through, and Mary swiped at them. "And I refuse to be your plaything!"

Mr. Ashbrook gaped and said, "You are not that to me.

Please, let me explain. I promise that I—"

But Mary shook her head, pulling away from him. Whatever Mr. Ashbrook wanted from her, it had nothing to do with love.

"No, Mr. Ashbrook. It was made clear to me long ago that I have nothing to recommend myself to a gentleman, so do not ply me with any more false compliments."

With that, she ran into the house, barring the door behind her.

Chapter 15

S tanding in front of his bedchamber mirror, Ambrose tugged at his coat sleeves and fiddled with his cravat. Neither required any more attention, but he fidgeted nonetheless. Turner's careful work was slowly being undermined as Ambrose picked at it, but he needed the distraction. Of course, it was not overly effective as his thoughts continually turned to Miss Hayward.

She believed him shallow and insincere. Ambrose straightened his waistcoat for the tenth time. He had not intended to throw himself at the lady, but it had felt right. Natural. And the antithesis of shallow and insincere.

"Mr. Knight invites you to attend a horse race in Dixon in two days," said Turner, picking his way through a stack of correspondence.

Ambrose gave the same reply he had to the rest. "Send my apologies."

Turner merely looked at him with a questioning raise of his brow and continued on. "Mr. and Mrs. Pike have invited you to attend a house party in July."

"Charles invited me to a house party?" Ambrose turned away from the mirror to look directly at his valet. "Whatever for?"

Turner chuckled. "My guess would be that the invitation comes from Mrs. Pike, who is looking to arrange an eligible match with one of her unmarried friends." But when Ambrose did not shudder or laugh at the absurdity, Turner stared at him. "You wish to attend?"

"Of course not," said Ambrose, turning away from his valet and the mirror. What he wished to do was go straight to Buckthorn Manor and see if Miss Hayward would speak to him. She had been repeatedly "occupied" the times he had called on her, but Ambrose was not ready to cry defeat.

"Mrs. Kingsley will find the babe a good home," said Turner.

Ambrose returned his gaze to the fellow. With his mind so full of one particular lady, it took a moment before he understood what Turner was alluding to. And that was another topic which Ambrose had no interest in pursuing. The nursemaids had not made good on their threats to bar him from their domain, but prudence told him he needed to limit his visits to once a day. That was better than none. Being denied Miss Hayward's company was difficult enough, he would not risk losing Dottie's as well, and the nursery staff did not find Ambrose's newfound preoccupation with the nursery as diverting as the rest of the residents of Avebury Park did.

"I am certain Mina will," said Ambrose, the words souring his stomach.

Turner grunted, his eyes narrowing as he examined his master. "Then what has got you so flustered that you've undone my work?" he asked as he set about fixing Ambrose's clothes.

"Merely a lady," he said with that same roguish tone he had used many a time to insinuate far more than the truth.

He reached to touch the cravat, but Turner slapped his hand away. Ambrose scowled at the man, but the servant replied with a challenging raise of his eyebrows. Any other gentleman would sack a servant for such belligerence, but Ambrose was not a usual gentleman, and Turner was much more than a mere valet. The man was a combination of housekeeper, butler, valet, personal secretary, and jack-of-all-trades, and Ambrose could not survive without him. And in truth, he enjoyed Turner's familiarity. In most instances.

"You mean Miss Hayward?" asked Turner with a look that dared Ambrose to deny it. "Don't look so surprised. It wasn't a difficult guess. You mention either her or Miss Dottie every few minutes."

Ambrose harrumphed, but he unraveled the entire tale to Turner as the man finished his work.

"I have never met a lady so disinclined to be wooed. She shouted at me and stormed off when I gave her a flower," he said, reaching to tug at his waistcoat, but Turner slapped his hands away again.

The valet chuckled. "Then I like her already, sir, for you have met your match. Most ladies throw themselves into your arms at the slightest invitation, and you have had it too easy."

"You sound like Miss Hayward," Ambrose grumbled.

"Even better. For the first time in your life, you may have to exert yourself to win a lady's affections, and that's good for you." But then the humor in Turner's expression faded. "Assuming you are serious about courting the lady and not toying with her."

"Courting?" The word was both thrilling and terrifying.

Ambrose did not doubt that he cared deeply for Miss Hayward. In their short acquaintance, she had inserted herself into his life so thoroughly that he found himself constantly wishing to talk to her. Throughout the day, he wondered what Miss Hayward would think about this or say about that. And if the number of times he daydreamed about kissing her were any indication, he was certainly attracted to the lady.

Yes, he desired a relationship with Miss Hayward, but there were lingering questions that kept him from leaping headlong into courtship. Was this matrimonial desire in earnest or a by-product of their unusual adventure together? Did he truly wish to open his heart to a wife? For a man who had never thought much about marriage and children, simply considering the possibility was a rather large step. To openly declare that he was pursuing a courtship was one step too far.

Turner sighed, rolling his eyes. "And you wonder why the lady is skittish? If you cannot decide where your heart lies, you cannot blame Miss Hayward for protecting hers. Especially considering your history with women."

His advice was sound, but that did not stop Ambrose from snipping at him. "Most valets keep their opinions private."

Turner shrugged. "Most masters do not need it."

Ambrose scoffed at the jest and shook his head before leaving his bedchamber in search of breakfast. When he arrived in the dining room, he found both his sister and brother seated with their respective spouses. He was in no mood to engage them, but it was too late to disappear. However, they were caught up in their own conversation about people and things in which he had no interest, leaving Ambrose to silently eat his breakfast and contemplate Miss Hayward.

There was no denying that he liked her. Was fond of her, even. The lady may have prickles that would rival those of an ornery porcupine, but she was warmth and softness beneath it. She sacrificed for others. Helped, even when she disliked the person. She was more entertaining and engaging than any lady of his acquaintance. Or any gentleman, for that matter.

If any other person had rebuffed him as Miss Hayward had, Ambrose would have walked away without a backward glance, but instead, he spent countless minutes wondering when he might see her again. And Ambrose always thought of it as a "when," not an "if." He may be denied entrance to Buckthorn Manor at present, but he would not allow things to stand as they were. For once he would knowingly put himself in a situation that might prove quite embarrassing because the thought of losing Miss Hayward was far more painful.

With a secret smile, Ambrose knew he just needed a plan. Perhaps a peace offering. And with that thought, he knew exactly what Miss Hayward would like.

"Why would you purchase a threshing machine?" asked Nicholas, smearing a bit of butter on a piece of toast with a distinctly imperious manner.

Simon sighed, scrubbing a hand through his hair. "It seemed a good idea at the time, but the machine is causing more problems than it solves."

Mina murmured something to her husband, patting Simon's hand before taking a sip from her teacup.

Nicholas shook his head and tossed his napkin onto the table. "Mechanizing farm work is absurd. It might help in small ways. Perhaps. But why change things when the system we have works beautifully?"

Ambrose rarely paid any attention when they discussed their estates, but for once, they had touched on a topic that was not mind-numbingly dull. "What is the matter with the thresher?"

Simon huffed, tapping the table beside his plate. "I haven't the foggiest. My man says it has something to do with a cylinder or some such part that doesn't rotate properly, but that means nothing to me other than that an expensive piece of equipment is going to sit idle during harvest."

"That is unfortunate," said Ambrose, "but that doesn't mean mechanizing is worthless. Machines can be temperamental, but the amount of labor and time they save overall makes it well worth the investment."

At that simple statement, Mina, Simon, and Nicholas paused to stare at him; Louisa-Margaretta continued to munch on her toast and stare out the window at the front lawn.

Mina recovered first, dabbing at her lips with her napkin and saying, "I do hope you are right as that is precisely why we invested in it."

"And what of those farmers' livelihoods?" asked Nicholas, shaking his head. "With machines doing their work, what would my tenants do? I could never take away their income like that."

Simon did not reply, but the muscles in his jaw tightened,

and for the first time, Ambrose wondered if the pair's camaraderie wasn't as perfect as it appeared on the surface. Not that they were coming to blows on the matter, but it was clearly an old subject—one that Simon did not care to discuss again and one that Nicholas would not abandon.

"We would never do that to our tenants, either," said Mina, reaching over to touch her husband's knee. "There is always more work to be done, even if we mechanize parts of it."

"Not that it matters, as we cannot get the silly thing to work," grumbled Simon.

"Precisely," said Nicholas, leaning forward. "What good does it do if it is constantly breaking?"

There were a few annoyed utterances from both gentlemen before Ambrose interjected, "Such things often have flaws in the beginning. No new innovation works perfectly in the early stages. I have heard that threshers need adjustments, but as a whole, they are quite a useful tool to have."

Again, the others stared at him as though he were speaking ancient Greek.

This time, it was Louisa-Margaretta who spoke, tittering in that manner of hers that was growing more irritating over the years. "And what would you know of such things, Ambrose?"

"Louisa-Margaretta!" said Mina with a disapproving frown.

"I happen to know a fair bit," said Ambrose, his face heating.

Nicholas snorted.

"That is enough from you both," said Mina, scowling at their brother and his wife.

"You have to admit it is a tad ridiculous that he would weigh in on such matters," said Nicholas between bites of his breakfast. "He has no aptitude for such work."

Ambrose's gaze dropped to his plate, and he clenched his jaw to keep from saying another word. It was futile to defend himself against Nicholas for there was no changing his mind.

Mina threw her napkin on the table and glared at Nicholas. "I am fully sick of hearing you speak of him in that manner!

Ambrose is not a half-wit, and I will not allow you to treat him so."

"I meant no harm," said Nicholas, lifting his hands in surrender. "I was simply pointing out the humor in the situation. Talking about farming and mechanization is not his forte."

Ambrose stood. He may not have eaten more than a few bites, but he no longer had an appetite. The smile he always used in such situations came without bidding.

"Nicholas is right. I'm afraid I have no aptitude for such things." With just the right tone, the words came out as good-humored, and Ambrose gave them a polite farewell and a parting bow before striding out the dining room door.

Once out of sight, his pace quickened. Ambrose wanted nothing more than to see Miss Hayward. She may be brusque at times, but she never laughed at him. Never mocked him.

Ambrose paused mid-step and chuckled at just how wrong those thoughts were. Shaking his head, he continued down the hall. Miss Hayward certainly did both, but it was not cruel. And even as she poked fun at his solicitous behavior, she did not think poorly of him. Perhaps at first, but not anymore. A lady who had known him for such a short time showed him more consideration and kindness than his own brother.

At that thought, Ambrose was determined to see her again. Turning his feet towards the library, he went in search of something to tempt Miss Hayward. Just as he reached the threshold, he heard Mina calling after him. Hurrying down the hall, she sped towards him until she was nearly breathless.

Puffing, she pressed a hand to her stomach. "I don't know what is wrong with me. It is only a few hours into the day, and I am already spent."

Ambrose took her by the elbow and led her to a sofa. "Should I fetch something for you? Or call for Simon?"

"Goodness, no. It is nothing," she said with a smile before pulling him down to sit beside her. "I came to speak with you."

"Not again, Mina," said Ambrose with a sigh. "Every time this happens, you come to me and defend his behavior, and I am sick of it. Tell Nicholas to stop being such a pompous wind-bag."

Mina's eyes narrowed. "He has already gotten an earful from me, and I am tired of you two sniping at each other. You are brothers, but that doesn't guarantee an easy relationship. Do you think that I enjoy Louisa-Margaretta's immaturity? Or Nicholas's heavy-handedness? Or Graham's grumpiness? Or your defensiveness? For goodness' sake, we all have flaws, but we are good people at heart."

She paused. "Save Tabby. I have to admit, I adore her without caveat, but the rest of us can be very trying. Even Simon is so obtuse at times that I want to shake him."

Ambrose chuckled at that image, fairly certain that Mina had done so with her husband on many an occasion.

"We all have our shortcomings," said Mina, reaching over to rest her hand on Ambrose's forearm. "But we love each other, and that means forgiving our pigheaded siblings when they do not behave the way we wish them to. It means supporting them when they are trying their best and giving them kind nudges to help them overcome those flaws. We each need help if we are to improve and should not hold on to past grudges that poison the relationship."

Ambrose stiffened, but Mina continued. "Do not pretend that you have not held on to every wrong Nicholas has ever committed. I know you both too well to believe that you are the sole victim in this scenario. Nicholas may instigate things frequently, but he rarely means to. You, on the other hand, enjoy provoking him."

And Ambrose knew he had no defense against that. Certainly, he could claim that it was only when Nicholas provoked him first, but that was untrue. However, he was not ready to admit it aloud.

"But that is not the reason I came to find you," said Mina, turning the conversation away once she'd spoken her piece. "I was hoping that you might go with Simon to inspect the thresher. He and our steward, Mr. Thorne, are going out to see if they can salvage it, and since you seem to know a bit about such things, I was hoping that you could help Mr. Thorne convince Simon that it is not a waste."

"I don't know much about threshers."

"But having another voice of reason might help."

"And Simon would listen to me?" Ambrose asked with a scoff.

"It couldn't hurt. Unless you have something else planned this morning—other than hiding in the library, of course."

"I was not hiding," he grumbled.

Mina gave him an arched brow. "So, you were looking for something to read?"

"Is that so shocking?" Ambrose tried to hide the bitterness in that statement, but at Mina's startled expression, he knew he had failed.

"I meant no offense," said Mina. "But I have never seen you open a book."

"As it so happens, I was looking for one," he replied.

Mina's eyes widened. "Is that so? What are you looking for?"

"*Persuasion*," said Ambrose.

"Is it a philosophy book?" asked Mina with a puzzled look.

"From the title, one would think so, but no. I am told it is a romance."

At that, Mina's puzzlement grew, adding in a dash of surprise. "You are looking for a romance?"

"I was reading one of the author's earlier works and quite enjoyed it," he said, carefully skirting the fact that he had not, in fact, read it himself.

Mina shook her head and sighed. "You are a puzzle at times, Ambrose."

"But an entertaining one," he added with a waggle of his brows.

Mina grinned. "Most assuredly. But I'm afraid I don't have that novel. I can have Mrs. Whitmore check with the lending library. Mr. Sims keeps a wide selection, but if he does not have it, perhaps the bookstore in Manning might, though I am afraid it is far enough away that we don't go there often."

"My thanks, but I would prefer to get it myself," said Ambrose.

Mina's eyes narrowed, and her grin grew curious. "And why is that?"

Ambrose cleared his throat, and Mina beamed.

"This isn't for yourself! Though I can guess the intended recipient."

Retreat was the only viable option, so Ambrose got to his feet. "If I am to join Simon, I'd best change into my riding clothes."

"It's Miss Hayward, isn't it?" asked Mina, jumping to her feet to follow him into the hall. But he was much faster than she, and Ambrose was able to escape her prodding, though he heard her laughter long after she had lost sight of him.

Chapter 16

B ristow was truly a beautiful corner of the world. Though Ambrose had visited many times, the landscape around his sister's home still awed him. The rolling hills dappled with trees, the long stretches of grass dotted with wildflowers. Sitting atop his borrowed mount, Ambrose breathed in the scent of fresh earth and clear air. In this place and at this moment, Ambrose was hard pressed to understand why he spent so much of his time in dirty, crowded London.

Just over the hill to his right was Buckthorn Manor. He would much rather ride there, but Mina had asked for his help, and he was not about to throw her over. This may be the only time his family had ever or would ever ask him for anything, and Ambrose was determined to do it justice. He nudged Sheba into a trot, and the mare launched after Simon and Mr. Thorne, who had gotten far ahead as he had been daydreaming. She was a rather good mount, and Ambrose loved the feel of the wind pulling at his hair and coat as he pulled up beside them at the new barn.

Workers grabbed the reins when the gentlemen dismounted. Stepping through the doors, Ambrose halted at the sight of the massive machine. It was not the most intricate he had seen, but it was one of the largest. The size of it was quite extraordinary considering its simple purpose, but threshing grain took significant effort, and Ambrose knew this would be a boon to Simon's workers.

To one side there were horses lashed to a wheel, which provided the propulsion for the gears. The sounds of the other gentlemen faded from Ambrose's mind as he stepped closer to the behemoth, his eyes following the line of the machine, picking apart the various pieces and seeing exactly how they worked together. Arriving at the heart, he threw off his jacket to squeeze through a tight space to examine the gears. The machine was dormant, but his mind saw the parts working together to create the desired outcome.

And there it was. Two misaligned wheels. He had seen similar situations in his clocks and automata. Ambrose rolled up his sleeves and reached inside.

"What are you doing?" asked one of the workers, drawing the attention of the others.

Ambrose did not bother to explain and simply tugged at the smaller wheel.

"Leave it be, Ambrose," came Simon's voice. "It is broken enough without us mucking about in it."

Popping back out, Ambrose motioned for his brother-in-law. "I can see the problem. Two gears are misaligned."

Simon crouched beside him but said, "I see nothing wrong."

Guiding Simon's gaze, Ambrose pointed it out. "Just there."

"It looks right to me."

When Mr. Thorne joined them, neither gentleman could see what Ambrose was referring to.

"You're right," said the foreman. "It's ever so slight, but I see it."

Simon and Mr. Thorne stood back as Ambrose and the other man wrenched at the gear until it shifted into its proper place. Moments later, the foreman had the horses moving, which set the gears turning, and everything was running exactly as it should.

"Well done!" said Simon, clapping Ambrose on the shoulder as they stood, watching the thresher.

"It's a wonderful sight," said Mr. Thorne.

"How did you see the problem?" asked Simon, turning to look at Ambrose.

He shrugged, straightening his shirtsleeves. Simon handed him his jacket, but it was clear his nonverbal answer was insufficient.

"I find machines interesting," said Ambrose, pulling it on and straightening his waistcoat. "I've been to a few exhibitions in London that display these sorts of things."

"More than a few, if I had to hazard a guess," said Simon.

The three men left the foreman to his work and strode out of the barn; with the threshing machine back in operation, there was nothing more to be done there.

"I tinker with them from time to time," said Ambrose, but that was as much as he was going to admit.

Simon pulled Ambrose to a stop, though Mr. Thorne continued to his horse, giving the two of them some distance. "You were brilliant in there, Ambrose. Even the foreman did not see the problem until you pointed it out. Have you thought about investing in factories? There is money to be made in such things, especially under the guidance of those who understand them."

Ambrose snorted. "I have no head for figures, Simon. Investing would be a disaster."

Grabbing Sheba's reins, he moved to mount but stopped when Simon spoke again. "I would be willing to assist you."

Turning, Ambrose looked at his brother-in-law, seeing actual interest in the gentleman's eyes. In the years they had known each other, he could not think of a time that Simon had been anything other than annoyed with him.

"Why?" asked Ambrose. "I'm surprised you even allowed me to come along to see the thresher."

Simon's gaze fell away, and he shifted from foot to foot. "I know I've not always been welcoming." Simon paused and tugged at his cravat and then continued. "Mina is forever fretting about you, and causing her such distress does not endear a person to me, as your brother, Graham, can attest," he said with a hint of a smile.

"There is nothing to fret about," said Ambrose.

"Isn't there?" Simon held his gaze, firm and unwavering, and it was Ambrose's turn to look away. "I would love nothing more than to assist you in such a venture. I don't know enough about machinery to know what the possibilities are, but there is an exhibition at the fair in Abbott I've been eager to visit. Perhaps we can go together and do a little investigating. We could bring everyone and make an outing of it. Mina has been looking for something to do together before Nicholas and his family leave."

The thought of Nicholas being there was enough to make Ambrose pause before agreeing, but the lure Simon had set was too enticing to pass up. With a few words, they set their plan and mounted their horses.

The ride to Avebury Park was thrilling. Less because of the world around him and more because of the possibilities Simon had presented. Perhaps there was a way for him to do something more than lurk about London. Cards had been the only thing he had ever excelled at, but Ambrose wondered if perhaps—just perhaps—there might be more opportunities for him. A way to use the few talents he had.

At that thought, they crested the hill, and Ambrose's eyes turned towards Buckthorn Manor. And just maybe, he might be able to talk a certain someone into attending the exhibition with him.

Chapter 17

C urled up in her favorite armchair, Mary stared out at the
overcast day. It was positively miserable. Even rain
would be preferable to the grim clouds hanging in the
air, casting everything in muted grays. Mary turned her eyes to
the book propped on her thighs, but she could not focus on the
words. She leaned her head against her knees, the edges of the
book poking her arms and legs.

Knowing she had been right about Mr. Ashbrook did not
lighten her spirits. Days had passed, and he was nowhere to be
seen. The cad must have been toying with her, or he would have
visited again.

Of course, another unpleasant possibility pricked Mary's
conscience. Shoving the book aside, she leaned her head against
the armchair, and her eyes tracked the swirling clouds outside.

The whole interlude in the garden had been intoxicating,
and Mary was no longer certain if those feelings had been Mr.
Ashbrook's doing or a silly fantasy of her own making. Perhaps
she had simply misinterpreted what was intended to be an overture of friendship, and she had repaid his kindness by behaving
like a Bedlamite. No gentleman in their right mind would wish
to visit again after being mistreated in such a fashion.

Either Mary had allowed another scoundrel into her life or she had misread the situation and run off the only true friend she'd had in years. Neither possibility brought her any peace, making her feel as dreary as the weather.

Turning, Mary set her feet on the floor and abandoned her book. There was no point in sitting there, languishing away over what had or had not happened. There must be something she could find to pass the time other than wondering if Mr. Ashbrook was thinking of her.

Stepping out of the library, she wandered to the kitchen. With the family gone, Mrs. Webb had far less work, but perhaps there was something for Mary to do. Passing a cupboard, she caught sight of Gibbs seated on a chair amidst the shelves of linens, fast asleep. Mary looked at the man who had been a fixture at Buckthorn Manor longer than she. His hair had turned white and was growing more sparse and wispy with each year, his face more lined and cragged. Mrs. Gibbs was still spry for her age, but her husband was not so blessed. Sneaking a blanket from one of the stacks, Mary tucked it around him and let the old fellow sleep. There was no master or mistress at home to be bothered by it, and he had earned a bit of a rest.

Mary continued on to the kitchen to find Mrs. Webb and Mrs. Gibbs seated at the table with cups of tea.

"Come sit with us, dear," said Mrs. Gibbs, patting the bench next to her. "You've been keeping yourself so busy since you arrived home."

Mrs. Webb looked at Mary with raised eyebrows that were one part humorous and one part accusatory. However, the woman remained silent as she raised the teacup to her lips.

Mary took the drink Mrs. Gibbs offered her. "There's much work to be done."

Mrs. Webb smiled and murmured, "Not that much."

"With the family gone, it is an opportune time to get the deep cleaning done," said Mary, tapping her fingers along the edge of the saucer.

Mrs. Gibbs nodded, but Mrs. Webb said, "Aye, but not in a

matter of days."

"Moira," said Mrs. Gibbs with a hard look.

Mrs. Webb feigned an innocent expression and sipped her tea.

"I do apologize if I've been running you ragged," said Mary, abandoning her spoon on the saucer with a clink.

Mrs. Gibbs leaned forward, patting Mary on the hand. "Don't you listen to that crone, sweetheart."

"Hag," replied Mrs. Webb in a prim tone, placing her cup down with the elegance of a fine lady.

The other woman shook her head at the cook, her lips twitching with a smile as both their eyes twinkled.

"Keeping yourself busy won't fix the situation," said Mrs. Webb.

"Moira!" hissed Mrs. Gibbs, sending the other a hard look.

"If I had a good looking fellow like that sniffing around, I wouldn't send him packing," said Mrs. Webb, which made Mary blush as she had never blushed before. Which, in turn, made both of the women chortle, though Mrs. Gibbs had the decency to stifle hers.

"He's not sniffing around," said Mary, but before she could say another word, Sally entered with a bob to ask about some detail concerning her work, and Mary was grateful for an excuse to escape those well-meaning and meddlesome women.

"I'm so sorry to bother you, miss," said the young maid. "I just couldn't remember—"

"It's no bother, Sally," said Mary, putting an arm around the girl as a show of support while they left the kitchen. She may be inexperienced and in need of a lot of assistance, but Sally was a good girl who was eager to learn.

And then a knock sounded at the front door.

Mary's heart thumped at the possibilities of who stood on her doorstep. A tradesman would go to the kitchen entrance, and there was only one person in Bristow that would wish to call on Mary Hayward. Sally stepped to the door, and Mary held her breath as it opened.

Bess Cavendish.

Mary's first thought was to order Sally to slam the door in Bess's face, but no matter how much Mary fantasized about such behavior, she did not have the gumption to do so. Apparently, she could only act blatantly rude to strangers in coaches.

"Mary, it is so good to see you," said Bess.

Sally stood there, wide-eyed, her eyes flicking from Bess to Mary and back again. The girl clearly sensed the chill wind blowing from Mary, though she was ignorant as to its source. With the exception of Mrs. Gibbs and Mrs. Webb, who were too wise for Mary's good, no one else knew.

Mary kept a civil tongue in her head but could do no more than that.

"I brought some blackberry preserves," said Bess, lifting a basket. "The last I saw your mother, she mentioned how much she enjoyed them, and I thought I should bring some by. They are the last jars until the fall harvest."

Mary took the proffered basket with a curtsy. "I am certain she will appreciate your generosity. She is not home at present, but I shall write and tell her."

Sally moved to shut the door, but Bess stepped forward. "I was hoping that we might visit for a few minutes."

Through significant effort on Mary's part, she had avoided being alone with Bess since the lady's engagement had been announced. With an audience, there was no need to worry, for the Cavendishes were intent on keeping their past a private affair. However, Bess had just caught Mary during one of the few times in her life when there was no family member around to serve as a social buffer. Nor could she slip away without Bess noticing.

Mary calculated her options and decided an awkward visit was preferable to a scene on their doorstep. Best get it over with and hope it would be their last private encounter.

With a nod, she stepped out of the way to allow Bess entrance, hoping she had the fortitude to keep her composure for the next few minutes. It was hard enough to know that Henry thought her a fool for how she had behaved all those years ago;

she did not want another embarrassing interlude for the Cavendishes to privately mock in the years to come.

Ordering Sally to bring tea and cakes, Mary led her guest to the parlor, in which they awkwardly stared at each other for a solid minute before Bess deigned to speak.

"I understand you were in Town."

Mary nodded.

"That must have been delightful. I have always longed to see London."

"It was impressive," said Mary. In truth, she had not seen any of it except for the view from the coach, but she was not about to admit it.

The conversation continued in a stilted manner. Mary did offer up the occasional polite question, though it was a struggle to know what to say to Mrs. Henry Cavendish. But then Bess shifted the conversation towards an unwelcome, uncomfortable, and far too intimate topic.

"I miss our friendship," she said, her eyes dropping to her lap.

"Our friendship?" Mary parroted, for it was all she could think to say.

Bess nodded and met Mary's eyes once more. "You were the best friend I ever had, and this distance between us pains me."

"Distance?"

Another nod, but this time, Mary saw actual tears in the lady's eyes, which left her fully shocked and speechless.

Bess reached forward, gripping Mary's hand, and said, "I feel terrible about how things fell out between us, and I've wanted to mend it, but this is the first time I have gotten you alone since that awful fight."

Mary opened her mouth, though she had no thought as to what she should say. The parlor door opened, and Sally entered with a tea tray, giving Mary a brief respite as they silently waited for the maid to lay out the spread and disappear once more.

That silence continued for several moments before Bess hazarded to speak. "I know that you are upset with Henry, and

I cannot blame you for it, but does that need to force a wedge between us?"

At that, Mary's breath seized. A low, simmering anger bubbled inside her as Bess sat there, looking so sweet and innocent.

Once she found her voice, Mary spoke with soft but pointed words. "I will admit that I have been angry with Henry—he led me to believe that he loved me while courting another. Clearly, he did not care about me in any fashion, for even a friend or brother would not be so cruel. And it has been painful to accept that I meant nothing to him."

Mary took a breath. Admitting that much was difficult enough, but there was more to say. "However, I have long since abandoned any disappointment I felt at his rejection. I do not love your husband and feel quite relieved that I did not marry such a man. Though the boy was my dearest friend, the man Henry grew into is not someone with whom I would wish an acquaintance."

Bess opened her mouth to respond, but Mary held up a silencing hand.

"But my feelings towards Henry do not nor have they ever factored into the death of our friendship," said Mary, leveling a cold stare at Bess. "*You* betrayed me. *You* hurt me. The distance between us is not about Henry. It is about you."

"I know I was wrong to treat you so, but can you not forgive me?" asked Bess, clenching her hands in her lap. She was contrite enough that Mary's heart nearly softened towards her, and part of her wished to say yes. She had long hoped for such an acknowledgment, but it did not give even a drop of satisfaction, for it did not address the full scope of Bess's sins.

Mary swallowed, sucking in a quiet breath before speaking. "Answer me one question."

Bess nodded, but Mary suspected she would not be so enthusiastic once she heard it.

"I have thought about what happened," said Mary. Far too many times, if she were honest, but she would not give that to Bess. "It was some time before I realized there was something strange about it all."

Pausing, Mary gathered her thoughts, feeling calmer than she would have expected. But that was likely because she was certain that her suspicions were true.

"When you moved to Bristow, there were many girls vying to be your friend. You could have ingratiated yourself among any of the finest girls in society, yet you chose to befriend the lonely daughter of a minor family." Mary paused. She knew what the forthcoming answer would be, but asking the question and removing all doubt pricked her heart.

Steeling herself, Mary pressed forward. "Did you do so to get at Henry?"

Bess paled, and that was all the answer Mary needed. "The past is the past, and I cannot change it, but I did care for you. I still do."

"You cared for me?" Mary gave a jerking laugh. "You used me. You lied to me. Whether or not I can forgive you for what you have done, do you think that there is any way I could ever trust you?"

"Oh, my dear friend," she said, leaning forward to clasp Mary's hands, but Mary pulled away. "You know how my family was struggling. We had lost everything, and I was desperate. I needed a good match, but without a dowry, I had few prospects. I could see that Henry was never going to marry you, so I did what was necessary to catch his eye. But though my motives were mercenary at first, you became so dear to me. It broke my heart to see you hurt."

Closing her eyes, Mary took a calming breath. Though she understood the difficulties Bess had been facing, and perhaps even sympathized with her plight, the betrayal ran far deeper than that, and the duplicity disgusted her.

Mary waited until she had enough control to speak. Opening her eyes, she glared at Bess. "You say you knew that Henry would never marry me, yet you encouraged my feelings for him. Under the guise of friendship, you eagerly offered up advice on how to win his heart, all while ensnaring him for yourself. Even if I could accept your greedy motives for befriending me, I cannot comprehend why you bolstered my hopeless dreams!"

Bess opened her mouth to defend herself, but at that moment, Gibbs opened the door and announced another visitor. Flustered by her current conversation, Mary could hardly focus on the words the butler spoke or the fact that Mr. Ashbrook strode in after him.

"Good afternoon," Ambrose said with a deep bow, hardly containing the great grin on his face. He had finally gained access to Buckthorn Manor, and that victory filled him with joy. But it fled when he straightened and saw Miss Hayward's distress. Her posture and expression were as rigid and stoic as usual, but there was a tightness around her lips and a faint hint of tears gathering in her eyes.

His gaze shot to her companion, who was covertly brushing aside her own tears. He opened his mouth to ask what was the matter, but Miss Hayward's gaze begged him to leave it be.

"I am sorry if I have interrupted your visit," said Ambrose, though he felt quite the opposite.

Miss Hayward shot to her feet. "Mrs. Cavendish was just leaving," she said, though Mrs. Cavendish's expression did not agree. However, she rose to her feet.

"Might I be allowed to call on you tomorrow?" asked Mrs. Cavendish.

"I am afraid that I shall be quite busy," replied Miss Hayward with a tone that no one could mistake for anything other than a firm dismissal.

Mrs. Cavendish nodded, curtsied, and followed the butler to the front door. Miss Hayward watched the lady go, her hands held stiffly in front of her, and Ambrose had no idea what to say, though he felt a desperate need to speak. She motioned for him to sit in Mrs. Cavendish's vacated seat, while Miss Hayward took hers once again.

Ambrose sorted through his thoughts, wondering what he

could say, but it all felt uncomfortable with the maid standing in the corner, watching over them. He wasn't even sure when she had appeared, but their silent chaperone watched them with far more interest than most servants did in such situations.

"Are you well?" he asked. That was decently innocuous.

Miss Hayward nodded, though it was not convincing. "Well enough."

"Might I do something for you?"

"Not unless you can undo the past," she said, gazing down at the floor. "Or shut off my heart." At that, her eyes snapped to his, widening at the slip of her tongue. She fidgeted, and Ambrose wished he might take her hands in his and calm her agitation, but he knew that would not help the situation.

"Regret is an unpleasant thing," he said. "I am sorry you are burdened with it."

"Who isn't?" she said, giving him a sad smile. "But I do apologize for my behavior. You stumbled upon an unpleasant scene, and I had not expected callers today, though I am grateful for an excuse to cut the previous visit short."

"In that case, I am surprised that you did not let your feelings fly," said Ambrose, the edge of his mouth quirking upwards. "You don't strike me as someone who allows civility to keep you from airing your true thoughts."

Miss Hayward averted her face, but not before he saw the crimson flush in her cheeks. "I was terribly rude to you when we first met, so I cannot fault you for thinking that. The only excuse I can offer is that I was especially cross that day. Much had happened to put me in a foul mood before we ever met, and you were the unfortunate recipient of all my frustrations. I do apologize."

Ambrose was losing control of things, and it brought a slight shock of panic. The last thing he wanted was to hurt her, and Miss Hayward was clearly distraught. Ambrose could feel the maid's eyes burning into him as he scrambled to salvage things.

"It was only a jest, Miss Hayward. A sorry attempt to

lighten your mood. I'm simply grateful to be allowed entrance into your home. I feared you would close your door to me again."

Miss Hayward stared at him. "Again? I was not aware that you had called."

Ambrose cocked his head and turned his eyes to the small maid in the corner. "I was told you were occupied every time I visited."

Miss Hayward followed his gaze to the girl in the corner. "Sally?"

"You have been very busy as of late," she insisted.

"But you never mentioned Mr. Ashbrook stopped by."

The girl scowled, glaring at Ambrose with a fierceness that rivaled any he had ever seen. "He upset you," she hissed.

"Sally," said Miss Hayward with a sigh and a shake of her head. "We shall talk about this later."

And with that, the girl returned to her silent, watching state, though her gaze grew no warmer.

"I cannot blame her for being so protective," said Ambrose, giving Sally a genuine smile to match his genuine words. "I did upset you, and I wished to apologize for that."

Reaching into his pocket, he pulled out the parcel and handed it to the lady.

"A peace offering," he said in response to her puzzled gaze.

With a tug, Miss Hayward pulled the twine off the package and unwrapped a copy of his brother's book. "*My Life at Sea*," she said, brushing her fingers over the cover. "I have wanted to read this."

Ambrose smiled at the eager tone in her voice. It wasn't what he had wanted to give her, but after scouring much of Essex for *Persuasion*, he had settled for second-best. And at that thought, he sent a silent apology to his brother for calling his book second-best.

"I thought we might read it together," said Ambrose. "You have such a fine reading voice. After we finish *Sense and Sensibility*, of course."

She looked up from the book to give him a disbelieving stare, though there was a hint of humor to it. "You cannot help spouting tripe, can you?"

"You know what I am," he teased with a shrug. If Miss Hayward chose to disbelieve his words, there was nothing he could do about it at present. Perhaps with enough time, she might come to accept the truth.

Miss Hayward shook her head with a wry chuckle and turned her gaze down to the book, her fingers brushing the leather and paper.

"And I was hoping that I might beg you to join me and my family," he said, shifting in his seat. "We have plans to attend the fair in Abbott next week to view the machinery display."

There, he'd got it out. It was a simple enough request, and his casual tone and wording hid how much he hoped she would agree. This trip was just another excursion for his family, but for Ambrose, it was revealing things he had not thought to share with anyone. He loved his gears and springs and had no interest in opening that passion up to ridicule. Fear kept his nerves in a constant state of agitation over the forthcoming outing—except when he pictured Miss Hayward among the party. She brought him peace, as though her presence alone gave him an extra dose of strength.

But Ambrose knew it would not do to let this skittish lady know how much her answer mattered to him.

Staring at the book in her hands, Mary nearly missed the invitation. Her eyes flew to Mr. Ashbrook, and she fought to keep her composure after such a shock. He wanted her to attend a fair with his family. Mary had met the Kingsleys on many occasions, but she could not claim a close acquaintance. Certainly not the type to include her on a family outing.

Mr. Ashbrook continued to speak, listing the various reasons why she should come, but Mary heard not a single word of it. She simply watched the draw of his brow and the pinching at the edge of his eyes. And then there was a fidgety quality to his gestures. Beneath that debonair facade, Mary swore he was nervous.

"Why?" she blurted, unable to keep her astonishment in check. "Why would you want me there?"

Mr. Ashbrook stilled, looking into her eyes with the same intensity she knew was in hers. He opened his mouth but closed it again. And opened it once more. He cleared his throat and finally said, "Because it is important to me, and you shan't laugh."

The gentleman hid it well. He truly did. Though his words were intimate, he spoke them in a blasé manner, as if he were describing the weather. But Mary knew it was no little thing to him. It mattered a great deal, and he was nervous. Very nervous. She was uncertain how she knew it, but she did not doubt it.

"Who would mock you?" she asked.

Mr. Ashbrook gave a careless shrug, his eyes drifting away from her. He did not need to give more of an answer than that, for Mary understood him clearly. Mr. Ashbrook had been hurt before, and those hidden wounds still pained him. Her own throbbed sympathetically, and there was no way she could deny his request.

"I would love to," she said, and Mr. Ashbrook broke into a smile that did terrible things to her heart.

Chapter 18

W hat had she been thinking? That question haunted Mary's thoughts after she accepted Mr. Ashbrook's invitation, yet she couldn't regret it—even if she re-peated that question time and time again as she set out for Ave-bury Park, and when she was bundled into a coach with Mr. Ashbrook and several of his kin, and throughout the day as they explored the fair.

Mary had attended festivals many times in her life, but Bristow's offerings were meager compared to Abbott's. Stalls of every kind filled the enormous patch of grass adjacent to the town. There were food and treats, performers and games, sights to see and a myriad of things to buy. And to the west sat dozens of machines and exhibits showing the latest innovations available for farming.

It was invigorating and overwhelming, made all the more enjoyable by Mr. Ashbrook escorting her from stall to stall.

"Uncle Ambrose!" shouted one of the many Ashbrook children, running over to tug on Mr. Ashbrook's coat as he pointed to a group of jugglers. "Look at that!"

Mary smiled at the lad's enthusiasm as he tore off after one of his brothers. With five boys, all under the age of six, their party was quite raucous as they ran from one sight to another. Mary could not imagine how much worse the chaos would be if they had brought the youngest along as she had originally hoped. As much as Mary missed the opportunity to see Dottie, she was grateful they did not have an infant to add to the confusion.

Mr. Kingsley called after Mr. Ashbrook, beckoning him to some metal giant that was making an awful racket. Leading Mary to his brother-in-law, Mr. Ashbrook launched into a discussion with Mr. Kingsley about its merits. Catching sight of a seed planter, Mary stepped away to see the fascinating machine at work. It was not the most intricate apparatus on display, but there was something mesmerizing about the ease with which it cut through the earth.

The children ran back and forth, bumping into the adults as they played whatever games they had created to entertain themselves as a pair of nursemaids and their mamas tried to keep them out of trouble. One of the younger Ashbrooks, Noah, came up beside Mary, one hand wrapping around hers as he stared at the movement of the drills that dug into the soil. He watched it and then reached a hand towards the mechanisms, but Mary scooped the lad into her arms. Holding him tight, she stepped closer to give him a better view while keeping him firmly in hand.

"Look at that," she said, bending so that they might see the interior mechanisms, and the boy gave her a grin.

"Closer," he said, leaning forward, but Mary kept him at a safe distance and babbled to the child, pointing out the interesting bits.

"What do you think?"

The voice startled her, and Mary jumped, bumping straight into Mr. Ashbrook. With a hand, he steadied her and smiled.

"It's quite fascinating," she said. "Noah and I were just admiring this seed planter."

Mr. Ashbrook smiled at his nephew and ruffled the boy's hair. Noah squirmed, shoving the hand away with a wrinkled nose.

"You should visit the displays in London," said Mr. Ashbrook. "It is amazing to see what they can make these bits of metal do, and what the future will bring."

He watched the machine with a look of awe, excitement, and a dash of boyishness that had Mary grinning. Noah wriggled in her arms, and she put him down but kept his hand in hers.

"And how are things with your family?" she asked in a whisper so that those little ears would not overhear.

Mr. Ashbrook turned his gaze to her and gave her a brilliant smile that made her breath catch. "Better than I could have imagined. For some reason, Simon has listened to his half-wit brother-in-law and is investing in a number of pieces today."

Though thrilled at what that meant to Mr. Ashbrook, Mary scowled at the way he phrased it. "Do not speak of yourself in that manner. You are no half-wit, and you are far more capable than you give yourself credit for."

Mr. Ashbrook held her gaze, his sketch of a smile warming as he looked at her. They stood silently for a moment before he said in a quiet voice, barely loud enough for her to hear, "When you say it, I can almost believe it. Thank you for coming with me."

He offered up his arm, and Mary took it and whispered, "Thank you for inviting me."

Holding onto Noah's little hand, the three of them walked along, and Mr. Ashbrook pointed out various sights, all of which she found terribly interesting. He spoke with such authority and understanding that Mary was awed by his knowledge of it all.

"Why are *you* not investing?" she asked.

There was a scant second where Mary swore she saw redness flashing through Mr. Ashbrook's cheeks. "It's hardly in keeping with my carefully crafted persona of the mindless lech."

Mary pulled him to a stop and forced him to meet her eyes. "We both know that is not you."

But the look in his eyes broke her heart. His expression showed nothing but disinterest, though she saw the truth hidden beneath his gaze. Uncertainty. Fear. Sadness.

"You have a brilliant mind for this sort of thing," said Mary. "It's clear to anyone who talks to you on the subject. You should pursue it."

Mr. Ashbrook began to reply, but Mr. Kingsley called to him. Glancing between his brother-in-law and Mary, he sighed.

"Go," she said, giving him a smile of encouragement.

With a nod, Mr. Ashbrook strode away, leaving Mary to watch him as he crossed the fairgrounds. Standing there with Noah tugging on her arm, her heart burned in her chest at that flicker of warmth she had seen in his gaze. It filled her, making her feel flushed though the sky was cloudy, and Mary bit on her lip to keep herself from smiling. It was just a bit of silliness.

Wasn't it?

Since their reconciliation a week ago, they had spent many an hour in each other's company. Whether reading aloud together or simply walking the garden, Mary had spent a significant portion of every day with Mr. Ashbrook. Yet there was nothing overtly romantic to it. But from time to time, there were these fleeting moments. A look in his eye. A touch of his hand. Minute details that hinted at something deeper. A thought that was not particularly comforting, for it left Mary confused as to the gentleman's motives.

Standing together, Mr. Ashbrook and Mr. Kingsley fell into a deep discussion, one that was clearly enjoyable to them both. As the two gentlemen made their way through the crowd, Mr. Ashbrook nodded and smiled at everyone they passed. The sight of it wrenched Mary straight out of her ridiculous dreaming. She was—once again—inferring more than was meant. Mr. Ashbrook had an effervescent personality and a gift with people that allowed him to buoy a person's spirits. It was what made him charismatic and her a fool.

Hands tugged at her skirt, and Mary picked Noah up again. He was too big for her to hold for very long, but she appreciated the distraction.

"Noah!" called Mrs. Kingsley, coming up beside Mary. "There you are. You had us very worried when you disappeared. Thank you, Miss Hayward, for watching over him."

Mary nodded and mumbled a few cursory things, but she had nothing more to say as she knew little about the lady.

"I hear you had an eventful trip from London," said Mrs. Kingsley.

Mary nodded once more.

Mrs. Kingsley's hands clenched before her, and the conversation lagged until she asked, "And your parents are still there?"

Another nod. "With my sister, Miss Lydia."

More silence and another question. "And are they enjoying their time in Town?"

Mary had no inclination to speak about that subject, but as it appeared to be the only ready topic of conversation, she forged ahead. "Lydia's letters say they are. It sounds as though she is having great success in London society."

"That is no surprise," said Mrs. Kingsley, reaching over to tweak Noah's cheek. "She is a sweet girl."

Noah wriggled out of Mary's arms again and went in search of the other children, leaving the two ladies alone. Mary glanced to the seed planter and then over to Mrs. Kingsley. Then her eyes traveled to Mr. Ashbrook.

"It is good to see him so happy," said Mrs. Kingsley, her eyes following Mary's gaze. Mr. Kingsley laughed at something Mr. Ashbrook said, making Mrs. Kingsley beam. "It is rare to find my brother so at ease."

Mary's brows shot upward. "That is surprising as he seems to have an overabundance of ease. I would say he is one of the most agreeable people I have ever met."

Mrs. Kingsley's smile shifted, curling her lips thoughtfully as she studied Mary. "I am afraid that not all our family understands him, and he often is seen in a disagreeable light, which sets him on edge."

Mary looked over at the gentleman with a furrowed brow,

trying to see if there was any hint of that, but the scene before her was all that was amiable. "I suppose I can understand their frustration. I was not particularly kind to him when we first met because he seemed so frivolous, but that is not who he truly is."

Reaching over, Mrs. Kingsley entwined their arms, which made Mary start. "I have decided we are going to be great friends, Miss Hayward, for anyone who can see my Ambrose for his true self is well worth befriending."

"Fixing a loose gear is one thing, but this is quite another," said Simon, clapping Ambrose on the shoulder. "Where did you learn such things?"

Ambrose paused mid-shrug, the old tendency coming out before he'd thought better of it. Simon had treated him and his opinions with respect and cordiality, but old habits were hard to shirk.

"This has been a passion of mine for a few years. I have spent hours combing mechanics exhibits and even a few factories and mills." Just saying it aloud was freeing, lifting a weight from his soul that he had not known was there.

Ambrose's eyes flicked over to Miss Hayward, who was walking along arm-in-arm with Mina. The sight of it brought a warmth to his heart, and Miss Hayward gave him a nearly imperceptible smile.

"Have you traveled up to Lancashire?" asked Simon. "I hear they are doing revolutionary things with manufacturing."

"Not yet, though I would like to," he replied, turning his attention back to his brother-in-law.

"Perhaps we can plan a trip together. There is money to be made in such things, and I've been anxious to invest in it."

Ambrose nearly gaped at the invitation. In the years he had known Simon, the gentleman had not been openly hostile (unless provoked) but neither had he been affable. This shift in his personality was still a bit unsettling though welcome, all the same. The gentlemen stood together, watching the moving arms and wheels of the machinery around them, and for the first time in a very long time, Ambrose felt at peace with his family.

Investing. The thought of it had always terrified him, but perhaps with Simon so willing to assist, it was possible. Ambrose wondered what Miss Hayward would think about the venture; the lady had a keen intellect, and he had no doubt she would have much to say on the matter.

"If you gentlemen are interested in investing," said one of the purveyors, offering up a pamphlet, "here is some information about our operations."

Ambrose held the bit of paper in his hand, staring at the words he had no hope of interpreting. There were too many letters, and they scrambled themselves so thoroughly that Ambrose knew it was pointless to try. The purveyor continued to prattle away while the reality of his situation settled into his heart, weighing it down until it felt like it had fallen to his feet.

How could he ever hope to invest when the written word eluded him? Numbers and letters were the very foundation of business, and Ambrose had no control over either. A few words here and there he might manage, but tackling the scores of documents and ledgers were beyond him.

Shoving the pamphlet into his pocket, he mumbled some semblance of a farewell before stalking away.

Something was wrong with Mr. Ashbrook. Mary saw the shift in his posture, the tensing of his mouth as the tradesman spoke. Mr. Ashbrook stared at the pamphlet in his hands, his lips moving in the barest manner that could not be spoken words, and Mary wondered what was distressing him so. The urge to go to him nearly had her dragging Mrs. Kingsley to his side, but Mary kept the desire in check and watched as Mr. Ashbrook stuffed the pamphlet into his pocket.

"Do you think so?" asked Mrs. Kingsley.

The lady nudged her, but Mary kept her gaze on Mr. Ashbrook as she replied, "Pardon?"

"I was asking whether you think my brother will stay in Bristow for a bit after Dottie is settled in her new home," said Mrs. Kingsley.

Mary straightened, swinging her eyes to stare at her companion. Of course, he would return to London, and she had known it all along, but in the passing days, she had forgotten that this was not his home. When his business was concluded, he would return to Town. Mary didn't know why it surprised her, but the revelation left her stomach twisted into knots.

Her chest tightened, but Mary managed to say, "I suppose so. London is his home."

"Whose home?" asked the gentleman in question.

Mary swallowed again, hoping to loosen her dry throat, but it was no use. Luckily, Mrs. Kingsley replied, "Yours, of course. Though I hope you will stay for a good long visit, I have no doubt that you will skulk back to that dirty city as soon as you can."

"I do not skulk," said Mr. Ashbrook. "And I shan't be leaving Bristow for a good long while."

His words made Mary's stomach flip and flop, leaving her entirely confused about whether she was glad or terrified at the prospect. Likely a bit of both.

Chapter 19

Having never expended much effort to conform to the rules of society, Ambrose had never given those dictates much thought, but now, he was thoroughly vexed with them. How he wished Miss Hayward were beside him. She saw things so clearly, and he was in desperate need of clarity, for the choice before him was no simple thing.

The Princes' cottage was small but sturdy. Clean. Simple but well appointed. Clearly, Mrs. Prince took great pains with her work, and Mr. Prince was a capable provider. The home was not as fine as Ambrose wished for Dottie, but she would be comfortable. Yet there was more to happiness than one's physical needs.

A table took up most of the main room, and Mina and Mrs. Prince sat at one side, chatting over a pot of tea while he and Mr. Prince silently stared at their cups. Mrs. Prince's words coming in a rapid string as she described how they would care for Dottie, but Mr. Prince remained mute. Perhaps it was only his imagination, but the fellow seemed indifferent, which left a sour taste in Ambrose's mouth. Dottie deserved to be cherished.

His Dottie. Arriving in his life only a few weeks ago, she had shone a great light on the pointlessness of his existence. She showed him what life could be. The joy of being needed. The satisfaction of fulfilling one's duty. Of having purpose. With her sweet disposition, Dottie had forever altered him, and Ambrose's heart wrenched at the thought of losing her.

Propriety. The word irritated him. Ambrose needed Miss Hayward's opinion; his instincts were too conflicted, and this decision was too important. But he would not credit the lady's cynical belief in her reputation's infallibility. Gossip had already claimed him as Dottie's father, and Miss Hayward's presence at the Princes' cottage would have set the rumor mill churning. No matter how illogical or impossible, she would have been tied to Dottie in some scandalous manner. So, Ambrose would content himself with her opinion based on his account of the afternoon.

The visit came to a close, and Ambrose followed his sister to the door as she made their farewells.

"They are perfect!" said Mina with a grin as their coach rolled away. Taking his arm, she sidled closer to him on the seat. "Mrs. Prince longs for children, and I know she is going to be an excellent mother. What do you think?"

"What makes you think your bachelor brother is a sound judge of such things?" he replied with a chuckle.

Mina stiffened and looked at him. "What is the matter?"

Ambrose gave her his patented smile. "What makes you think anything is the matter?"

Mina's face fell, her brow furrowing. "You are acting as you always do when avoiding uncomfortable topics, Ambrose. Are you unhappy with the Princes? I promise they are good people."

"They seem nice enough."

"But?"

Ambrose sighed. "Mrs. Prince seems a lovely lady who would treat Dottie as a daughter and not a servant. However, I do not feel the same could be said of Mr. Prince. He is not the right man to be her father."

Mina gave a slow nod. "I do admit that he seems a tad stoic because he prefers a child of his own flesh and blood, but they have a comfortable home and a good living."

"But will he love her?" Just the thought of his sweet Dottie being raised by an indifferent father had him gritting his teeth.

Instead, he pictured Dottie resting on Miss Hayward's hip, her little hands clapping. Her dimpled smile shining at him. Miss Hayward's gorgeous eyes glittering as he took them into his arms. It was a golden image shining through his dark thoughts. It had long hovered in the recesses of his mind, but it no longer startled him. It called to him. His family. His future.

Mina continued to prattle on about the merits of the Princes, but Ambrose's mind lingered on that daydream, and he wondered if it could become reality.

They arrived at Avebury Park in due course, and Ambrose made his way directly to the nursery. With Nicholas's brood now gone, it was far quieter in that section of the house. From a far ways off, he heard Dottie fussing, and Ambrose quickened his pace.

"Stop that right now," a woman hissed, but Dottie continued to cry. "If you don't quiet down, I'll toss you back in your corner, you brat!"

Ambrose stepped into the room and found the culprit standing by the window while Oliver was building block towers in the center with his nursemaid. Dottie's eyes were closed, but she was screaming with all her might, fighting against the nursemaid's hold. Her cheeks were drenched, and she arched her back, fairly bending herself in two, but it was no use. Through her tears, she caught sight of Ambrose, and Dottie shrieked louder. Her arms reached for him, her fingers opening and closing, begging him to save her.

Taking the babe into his arms, Ambrose glowered at the woman, who scowled right back at him. Dottie snuggled into him, wrapping her arms around his neck, and gave a few halting sniffles.

"What is going on?" he demanded.

"Children cry," said the woman, putting her hands on her hips. "There is nothing to get worked up about."

"Master Oliver was showing her some of his blocks," said

the other nursemaid. "But Mrs. Smith wouldn't allow it."

"Speak when spoken to, Nurse Mullens," said Mrs. Smith with a scowl. Nurse Mullens ducked her head with a blush, pulling Oliver onto her lap.

"You wouldn't allow Dottie to play?" asked Ambrose as he rocked the child.

"She's a filthy by-blow." Mrs. Smith's tone and expression made it clear she thought he should understand the situation without needing clarification. "Her very existence is an affront to morality, and she should not be allowed anywhere near Master Oliver or any other decent children. She is lucky to have a roof over her head and needs to learn her place."

With each word, Ambrose's anger grew until he felt liable to burst into flames. The fury pushed him to speak—begged him to put that self-righteous crone in her place—but Ambrose kept his composure. Calling on every ounce of self-control, he took a breath, calming the rage.

"I understand," he said in a tone that was surprisingly calm. "I shall remedy the situation immediately." And with that, Ambrose carried Dottie straight out of the nursery. Mrs. Smith called after him, and he paused. As the woman seemed so bent on putting others in their place, Ambrose gave her a look that allowed for no confusion as to what hers was, and she snapped her mouth shut.

Though the whole scene had run its course in a matter of moments, it shook Ambrose. Coming on the tail of his visit to the Princes, Ambrose's heart was in upheaval, and there was only one way for him to find some peace.

...

Blinking at the periodical, Mary tried to focus on the article. Having never studied mechanics and other such scientific achievements, she found it a difficult subject to tackle. Luckily, the whole thing was fascinating enough that she enjoyed the struggle.

Drawing up her knees, she leaned against the great oak and stared out at the vibrant green surrounding her. She ought to be doing chores inside, but the weather was so magnificent that she could not allow herself to be cooped up, away from the sunshine. The smell of blossoms and ripening fruit and vegetables filled the air, mixing with the sounds of insects and birdsong.

And then there was the view. She swore she could see the entire county from her spot on the hill, though her eyes fell most often to the building not more than a fifteen-minute walk away. Avebury Park. It was a handsome enough home to be sure, but not enough to warrant Mary's current preoccupation with it.

She huffed at her sappy heart and put the periodical aside, for there was no use forcing herself to focus on it. Instead, Mary picked up the book that had been her near constant companion ever since she had been gifted it nearly a month ago.

The passage of time astonished her. Their trip from London to Bristow had seemed a long thing, but the time since had sped by, each day quickly ticking closer to when Mr. Ashbrook would return to London. And that day was far closer than she feared. There was no reason for him to deny the Princes; they were good people who would care for Dottie like their own. And then Mr. Ashbrook would return home.

Flipping through the book he had given her, Mary stopped at the page that held a sprig of dried violets. Brushing the delicate petals and leaves, she thought herself a very silly woman indeed for saving such a trifle, but she could not bring herself to throw them away. The memory and keepsake were such a bittersweet thing to her. Mary could no more stop her feelings for Mr. Ashbrook than she could hold back the march of time that was destined to steal him away from her, but the sentiment was fruitless. Some masochistic part of herself hoped for a future with him, but Mary knew too well that it would come to naught. She was not the type of lady to inspire romantic feelings. If Henry's words on the matter weren't proof enough, her history with gentlemen confirmed it.

"Miss Hayward!"

Mary looked up to find the gentleman who occupied her heart strolling up the hill towards her with a footman in tow, both men weighed down with bundles. She stood, brushing the dirt from her skirts, and abandoned her book and periodical on the ground beside her. As he drew closer, she saw Dottie smiling at her from his arms, and Mary scooped up the child and kissed her sweet, chubby cheek.

"I was hoping you might join us for a picnic this afternoon," he said, beaming at her as brightly as the afternoon sun.

"That sounds lovely," said Mary, and Mr. Ashbrook motioned to the footman, retrieving a blanket from the fellow's load. Within moments, it was laid on the grass, the feast spread out around them, and the pair and child were seated comfortably in the perfect summer afternoon.

"How good of you to bring Dottie," said Mary, sitting the babe on the blanket so that she might wiggle to her heart's content. "I find myself missing her at the oddest times."

Retrieving a pasty from the basket, Mr. Ashbrook offered it to Mary with another smile, though it was tinged with sadness. "I know exactly what you mean."

"How was your meeting with the Princes?" she asked without preamble. It was no good pretending it was not foremost on her mind.

His smile disappeared, and Mr. Ashbrook shook his head. "It has been a trying day. The Princes seem like good enough people, but it does not feel right to give Dottie to them."

With a few prompts, Mr. Ashbrook unraveled the day, telling Mary about all that had passed. But then he revealed what had motivated his visit.

"She called Dottie filthy?" Mary's voice grew shrill as it rose. Dottie flinched and looked at her. In an instant, Mary had the infant in her arms again, holding her tight as though the child had understood Mrs. Smith's vitriol.

"What a horrid woman," she mumbled, burying her kisses into Dottie's neck until the child chuckled. Leaning back, Mary looked at Dottie and whispered, "You are precious, sweetheart."

Watching Miss Hayward show such unrestrained affection to Dottie warmed Ambrose far more than the sun beating down on him. If he'd had any doubts, seeing that precious interaction confirmed the feelings in his heart. As much as he feared baring his whole self to another person, Ambrose knew that if it made Miss Hayward and Dottie permanent fixtures in his life, it was worth the risk.

"I suppose I shouldn't be surprised," she said, laying Dottie on the ground once more; her little legs kicked, and her arms waved, a great, big smile filling the child's face. "Her parentage may be beyond her control, but that won't stop others from judging her for it."

Sorrow shone in her eyes, though Miss Hayward continued to smile at Dottie and pulled a silly expression, which brought out another giggle from the lass.

"It is not your fault, dearest," she said, grabbing one of Dottie's flailing hands and kissing it.

Seeing the pair of them together drew Ambrose in until his arm brushed hers. Miss Hayward started, turning to look at him.

"You are so kind-hearted," he said.

Miss Hayward harrumphed, shifting into the aloof person she pretended to be. "You are the only person who thinks so."

Ambrose ignored that and took her hand in his. "You feign indifference, but I am awed by how deeply you care for others."

Reaching with his other hand, he brushed back a lock of her hair. Miss Hayward stiffened, tracking his movements as he tucked it behind her ear. It brought him closer, and her eyes widened as he paused there, mere inches from her face.

"I know that you might not feel for me as I do for you," he whispered, "but I cannot go another minute without telling you how deeply I admire you."

At that, Miss Hayward gaped. It was not the reaction Ambrose had hoped for, but she hadn't run away screaming. Yet.

"I love you, my dear Miss Hayward," he said in hushed tones, leaning forward to close the distance.

"What are you doing?" she asked, leaning back.

Mr. Ashbrook's brows shot upward. "Declaring my love, though I'm obviously making a muck of it. And then I was hoping to kiss you. Thoroughly." That suave facade stared at her as he leaned in again, but Mary jerked away.

"No. No. No," she said, repeating the word as she shook her head and stood.

"Miss Hayward?" he asked.

"Love?"

"Yes," he said as he rose to his feet and took her hands in his.

Mary pulled free, shaking her head some more. Love? The gentleman spoke of love? Mary covered her face and turned away, but the feel of his hand on her shoulder had her heart melting.

"What is wrong?" he asked.

She spun to face him, her hands trembling as though they were one of Mr. Ashbrook's machines shaking itself apart. "You cannot love me!"

But then Dottie chortled, and the reality of the situation snapped into place. Mr. Ashbrook did not love her. He loved Dottie. She was the reason behind his mad declaration.

Mr. Ashbrook stepped forward, taking her hand once more. "I do—"

"No," she said, brushing away a tear that had slipped past her defenses. "You wish to keep Dottie. You met with the Princes today, and the thought of giving her to them is breaking your heart, so you are piecing together a makeshift family in order to keep her."

Dropping her hand, he stared at her. "That has nothing to

do with it."

"You want a wife so that you may keep Dottie," she said, putting distance between them. "And I am just the easy choice."

"No," he said with an equally fervent shake of his head. "That is not true. I love you!"

Mary gave a great burble of hysterical laughter at those ridiculous and utterly ludicrous words. The handsome and incredible Ambrose Ashbrook was declaring his love for the plain nobody, Mary Hayward. One might even say he was begging her, but it couldn't be real. It was impossible to believe that the only gentleman to ever show an inkling of interest in her was someone like him. He was everything Mary could hope for, and fate was never so kind to her. She was born to be the overlooked Hayward spinster—not Mrs. Ashbrook.

He drew closer, and a calm settled over Mary. It was a numbing peace that allowed her the clarity she needed to see the truth. She loved Mr. Ashbrook. Loved him so dearly that she would protect him from his own blindness. Whether or not he knew it, his feelings weren't real. They couldn't be, and Mary would not allow him to make such an irrevocable decision in his desperation to be Dottie's father.

"You may think you love me," she said, drawing a protest from him, but she continued. "You may think you do, but I know you do not."

Again, he tried to speak, but Mary squeezed his arm, drawing him into silence.

"You cannot love me," she said.

Ambrose could not believe what he was hearing. The way she spoke, it was so definitive and unwavering. And absolute tripe.

"Why not?" He stepped forward, drawing her into his arms, but she would not have it, pulling clear again. "You say it with such authority, but you cannot know what lies in my heart."

"I can," said Miss Hayward, her voice quiet and weak, her

eyes dropping away from him. She tried to hide it, but Ambrose could see pain plaguing her, and he wanted to take her into his embrace and show her how wrong she was. But every time he drew near, she moved away.

"I am a terrible dancer. Just awful," she said. The sudden shift in conversation startled him, but Miss Hayward continued before he could question it. "My parents never saw a point in wasting funds to teach me something for which I have no aptitude."

Ambrose struggled to understand how this tied into their mess of a conversation, but the obvious hurt it was causing her forced him to be patient.

"But I was still so excited for my first assembly," she said, a hint of light glimmering in her eyes. "To see the ladies in their fine dresses and the dancers moving about the floor. I may be hopeless at it, but I do love watching them. The grace in their movements. It is beautiful." Her words trailed off, and Ambrose wished to take her to a ball. Anyone who spoke so lovingly could not possibly be content with merely watching.

Miss Hayward swallowed and continued on, the light in her eyes fading as her shoulders sagged. "Imagine my surprise when I arrived and had a queue of lads asking to stand up with me. It was like a dream. I never once thought it strange that they should wish to escort a partner who trod on their toes and tripped over her steps. Not until Jeremy Wilson explained it."

There was silence for several good moments, and Ambrose waited for Miss Hayward to continue.

"He thanked me for assisting him," she said, her face that hard mask she wore to hide her feelings. "He was able to do his duty without raising speculation. Any other dance partner might set tongues wagging, but no one would suspect him of having designs on Miss Hayward."

"That imbecile." That was the only thing Ambrose could think to say that would be appropriate for a lady to hear. Miss Hayward kept feigning indifference, but he sensed her heartbreak.

"He was not the only one," she said. "Apparently, all the lads in town had the same idea. Duty forced them to dance, and I was harmless to their reputation for I incited no speculation. Even their sweethearts felt no jealousy if I was their partner. And I came with the added benefit of being 'too sensible' a girl to get swept away into thinking a simple dance meant anything."

With that, Miss Hayward straightened her spine, meeting his gaze with conviction. "I know you cannot love me because I am so ugly and undesirable that not one of them thought I dreamed of finding love. Of being courted. They all assumed that I knew better than to hope for such things. Never has a gentleman shown the slightest interest in pursuing me, and I cannot accept that the world has suddenly shifted and someone like you would fall in love with me."

Ambrose gaped at that assessment. To hear such horrid words about her was painful enough, but to hear them from her own lips tore at his heart. "Someone like me? You think me that shallow? That outward appearance is what matters?"

Miss Hayward's eyes shone with tears, though her expression remained stony. "Then you do not find me attractive?"

Ambrose had an urge to strike his head. Perhaps that might bring the world to rights again, for it was all out of sorts at present. "You are putting words in my mouth."

"They are the words you are speaking, sir!"

"They are not!" Ambrose fought to keep control of things, but this conversation was twisting itself into a knotted mess.

"You want a mother for Dottie," she said, jutting her chin out. "And I am a convenient lady to fill the position. Convenient is all I have ever been, and all I will ever be!"

"You think I cannot..." But his words faded at the flash of fear in her eyes. Beneath all the posturing and surface emotions, she was terrified. His sweetheart was a prickly lady with a soft heart beating inside her, and he suspected there was more to her story than what she had shared—experiences that had taught her to protect herself from ever hoping for happiness.

Staring into her frightened eyes, Ambrose wanted nothing more than to spend his life ensuring that her tender soul was never bruised again.

"Who made you so afraid?" he whispered, holding her gaze as he drew closer. Her eyes widened, but she remained in place. "Who made you believe that I could never see your beauty? Your goodness? For I would count myself lucky to spend the rest of my life with you."

Miss Hayward remained there, still as a statue. Only her eyes showed the emotions buffeting her. Disbelief and anxiety were prominent, but hidden among them was a hint of longing, though he suspected she was more frightened of that than she was of him breaking her heart. Ambrose knew too well the terror that accompanies hope when one has had it dashed too many times.

They stood toe-to-toe, her skirt tangling with his legs, and Ambrose breathed in her scent. She was not some fancy lady who doused herself in perfumes to mask her true essence. She was a mix of fresh soil, soap, and some indefinable aroma that was uniquely hers. A hint of flowers, but not ones that came from a bottle, for it was more intoxicating than any aroma Paris could manufacture.

With careful movements, he brushed her cheek. Her eyelids lowered, and despite her earlier denials, she leaned into his touch.

"Mary," he whispered. Though many called him a libertine, Ambrose had never taken such a liberty before, for he had never felt such a fervent desire to address a lady so intimately. But this was not harmless flirtation. This was his love. His Mary.

But at the sound of her given name, Miss Hayward jerked away from him with wide eyes. Shaking her head, she hitched up her skirts and sprinted away. Ambrose shouted after her and took a few running leaps before remembering that Dottie was alone on the blanket. Scrambling to her, he scooped her up and gave chase.

Chapter 20

Though tears blinded her, Mary knew the way to her house. She could hear Mr. Ashbrook calling, but she would not stop. She could not. Mary would feel embarrassed for this display later, but for now, she needed distance. Desperately.

Mary's lungs burned as she sucked in great heaving breaths and forced her feet to move faster. Cutting across the grounds, she took the shortest route home and finally saw Buckthorn Manor drawing closer. But Mary did not stop until she was safely inside with the door bolted behind her.

Leaning against the wood, she slid to the floor, curling up and covering her face as she allowed the tears to overtake her.

Love.

Mr. Ashbrook said he loved her. But it wasn't possible.

Handsome. Charming. Of good family and good fortunes. A gentleman like that did not want for female attention. Someone with so much could never love someone with so little. It was ridiculous. Even more ridiculous than her casting aside her better judgment and allowing her heart to fall so completely for him.

There was a knock, and Mary heard Mr. Ashbrook pleading

with her to open the door. Holding her breath, she quieted, hoping he might not hear her making a cake of herself. But it only made his voice clearer, and Mary knew she would hear those desperate, pleading words for the rest of her life.

But she could not open the door. To do so would be her ruin. Regardless of his motives, Mr. Ashbrook would regret his declaration. Even if he truly meant it here and now, there was no future Mary could foresee in which a lady like her could keep the attention of a gentleman like him. He would lose interest but still be bound to her. Mary could not face the thought of seeing resentment grow as they trudged along in life together. Stuck.

For both their sakes, Mary would remain strong.

Eventually, the sounds faded, and she was left alone with her thoughts and heartbreak. Mary had not the strength to move and allowed the tears to flow until she had no more to give. Until she was nothing but a dry husk beneath the blazing summer sun.

Mrs. Gibbs bustled past the entrance but stopped when she saw Mary. "Good heavens! Are you all right, dear?"

The intrusion gave Mary a resurgence, allowing her enough will to get to her feet. Luckily, her tears had already dried on her cheeks, so only the redness in her eyes showed her distress. Closing down her heart in a manner that was all too familiar, Mary nodded at Mrs. Gibbs. "Quite all right."

"Well then, thank goodness you are home," she said, handing over a letter. "We received word from your family not an hour ago, and we are all in an uproar!"

Mrs. Gibbs was not one for hyperbole, but the woman was working herself into quite a state; her mobcap was askew, and there was a blaze of wild panic in her eyes. Mary scanned the letter, quickly realizing that uproar was quite a tame word for their situation.

"Lydia is engaged?" Mary gaped at the letter. Though she had known that was the intended outcome, it was shocking to know that her sister had done so in less than two months.

"Yes, yes," said Mrs. Gibbs with a vague wave, "but that is not the issue at hand."

Mary read on and gasped. "They are returning tomorrow? With guests?"

"A baronet and his mother!" said Mrs. Gibbs. "How can we ever make things ready in time?"

Folding up the letter, Mary knew she would have time to think over Lydia's news at some later time, but for now, there were more important things to be done. Though Mary despaired that they could make the house presentable by the time their guests arrived, she was grateful for the distraction.

...

"Where have you been?"

Mina accosted Ambrose before he had taken more than two steps into the entryway. The last thing he wanted or needed was to be greeted thusly while he was in such a state, but his plan to disappear into his bedchamber evaporated when his sister appeared at the top of the stairs.

"The nursery is in chaos," she said. "Mrs. Smith fairly accused you of berating her and stealing little Dottie."

"She should never have been entrusted with Dottie in the first place, so do not scold me for protecting her!" he said, his voice rising.

Mina's eyes widened, and she blinked at him. Motioning for him to follow, she led him to the parlor. Once the door was shut, she crossed her arms and faced him. "I was not accusing you of anything, Ambrose. Now, what is the matter?"

He shifted Dottie in his arms. "Nothing."

That was the wrong thing to say. If he had given any excuse, Mina might have accepted it and moved on, but his blanket denial only roused her suspicions.

Mina gave him a hard look. "Nurse Mullen told me what happened, and I am very upset that Dottie was treated so poorly. I know you must be, too, but I can only think of one or two times you have ever raised your voice to me. There must be more to the story."

The fight seeped out of Ambrose, and he slumped onto a sofa. Dottie reached for his cravat, but he pulled away. With a dimpled grin, she tugged at it again, and he let her; there was no point in fighting either her or his sister. Mina sat opposite him, watching him with that all-knowing motherly gaze of hers.

"It's Miss Hayward, isn't it?" she asked.

Ambrose nodded. "I told her that I care for her, and she does not believe me."

"You care for her?" Mina said the word with awed reverence. She tried to keep the smile hidden, but Ambrose saw it quivering at the edge of her lips.

With a sigh, he admitted the whole truth. "I love her. I want to marry her."

Mina's hands flew to her mouth, and she came over to his sofa, forcing him into a hug.

"You are squashing Dottie," he grumbled.

"She is fine," said Mina, but she sat back and took the babe from him and cooed at her. "And you are to be my niece."

"Mina," Ambrose growled. It was true that such bouts of temper at Mina were rare for him, but between the stresses of the day and her current obtuseness, he was at the limit of his patience. "She rejected me."

Turning her gaze to her brother, Mina gave him a look that was sad and understanding with just a hint of irritation, though Ambrose could not fathom why.

"What did you say to her?" she asked.

"It is of no significance. She ran away and barred me from her home. Again."

"Nonsense," said Mina, resting Dottie against her shoulder. "Tell me what happened."

Ambrose had no desire to recount that dreadful scene, but fighting Mina was futile. So he began to speak. And speak. It was good that his sister had taken charge of Dottie, for Ambrose got to his feet and paced the room as he told her every detail. In all, it took far longer than the original scene had taken, but at length, every word that needed saying was said.

Standing at the window, Ambrose stared out at the garden. The sun still shone, casting the room in a warm afternoon glow, but a coldness gripped his heart.

"Dearest, come here," said Mina, and Ambrose had no strength to withstand the summons. When he got close enough, she took his hand and tugged him onto the sofa. "I know this may be difficult for you to understand, but Miss Hayward was not rejecting you."

Ambrose opened his mouth to speak, but Mina silenced him.

"She said that she did not believe you—not that she did not want you." Mina paused, gathering her thoughts as Dottie squirmed on her lap. "Miss Hayward's life is filled with people who tell her she is ugly."

That harsh word struck Ambrose, and Miss Hayward's voice echoed in his thoughts as he recalled the trembling way she spoke it. He had never given that small word much thought, but said thusly, it held a world of pain. He heard it in Mina's voice, too. Reaching for her hand, he squeezed it, and she smiled, blinking away a shine of tears in her eyes.

"Even her own family treats her so," said Mina. "Her parents dote on her sister, Miss Lydia. They've spent every penny they can on buoying her prospects to gain themselves a wealthy son-in-law, yet they can't be bothered to buy Miss Hayward a decent dress. I've heard her own mother praise the fact that the girl has no marriage prospects because she is so good at caring for them and running the household. What do you think that would do to Miss Hayward?"

Ambrose had known enough of the situation to surmise that her family neglected her, but Mina's words gave him a clearer picture of the mountain he was attempting to summit.

"In my experience..." She loved using that phrase, and it was always followed by some harsh lesson she'd had to learn.

No wonder she struggled to believe him.

"For right or wrong, such things shape one's self-respect," Mina said with a sigh. "And it is not easily overturned—even with someone you love telling you otherwise. Ambrose, you are fighting against a wealth of experience that tells her she is unwanted, and you are not going to change her mind by simply telling her once. Or twice. It will take time and effort for her to trust it."

Leaning forward, Ambrose rested his elbows on his knees. "What can I do?"

"Don't give up!" said Mina, poking his shoulder with her free hand. "Keep telling her. Keep showing her. When she pushes you away, try again."

Ambrose took a deep breath, thinking through various courses of action, but then Mina poked him again.

"Get going," she said.

"Now?"

"Of course," she said, standing. "With our guests gone, we can manage Dottie without Mrs. Smith, and you need to get started if you wish to convince Miss Hayward that you are in earnest. Now, go secure me another sister-in-law!"

...

Anxiety is such a useless sentiment. It does not divert impending disasters nor does it help in preparing for them. And it is by no means an accurate portent of doom, for more often than not, it signifies nothing. Anxiety simply stretches out the torment so that one feels it long before the pain strikes and ensures that if those fears prove unfounded, the afflicted person suffers nonetheless. And Ambrose was terribly anxious.

Standing at Buckthorn Manor's door, he waited for someone to answer. If they answered. He straightened his waistcoat and picked a bit of lint from his jacket. Then tugged at his sleeves and checked his cravat. By all accounts, he would think himself well turned out, but then he worried that perhaps he was too turned out. As he had never formally courted a lady before, he had no experience in the matter. Not that it would be particularly helpful, as Miss Hayward eschewed convention.

Shifting the bouquet of peonies to his other hand, Ambrose worried whether he should have left them at Avebury. So far, his overt displays had not worked, but they reminded him so much of her. The blossoms were a large explosion of petals. At first glance, they were white, but there was the barest hint of pink to them that made them quite lovely. But most of all, it was their scent that called to him like Miss Hayward's did.

Ambrose groaned at his own soppiness.

The door opened, and old Gibbs appeared.

"Is Miss Hayward at home?" asked Ambrose, glancing at the bouquet in his hand and wondering what to do with it. Present it right off? Or make it a surprise?

But his musings were cut short when he heard a feminine grunt. Ambrose leaned around Gibbs to see Miss Hayward dragging a rug. Shoving the flowers at the elderly butler, Ambrose stepped past the man and took the burden from her.

"Excuse me?" She stuttered a few words before she noticed who had taken her burden. "Mr. Ashbrook?"

"Where do you need this?" he asked. Though he had strength enough to hold it, the thing was difficult to grip, and he was ready to put it down.

"Allow me," said Miss Hayward, but he gave her a look that silenced the protests.

"Where should I place it?" he asked with enough authority for her to know that he was not going to be thrown over so easily. Even still, he expected more of a battle, but Miss Hayward nodded and led him into the drawing room.

Having never been in this part of Buckthorn Manor, Ambrose did not know what the room should look like, but at present, it was in disarray. A pile of sheets sat in one corner, and young Sally was brushing down the furniture, which pushed out of the way to make room for the rug. He dropped it down where Miss Hayward ordered, and the two of them un-rolled it.

"Sally," said Miss Hayward, "there is no need to brush down the furniture. The sheets should have protected them from dust. Please take that pile of linens to Mrs. Webb."

The girl scooped up the dirty sheets and hurried to do Miss Hayward's bidding.

"What is going on?" he asked, and Miss Hayward started, turning to look at him as though she had forgotten he was there. Her mouth was pinched and strands of hair fell loose from her bandeau, but it was the strain in her eyes that had Ambrose on edge.

"I do apologize, but I have not the time to entertain visitors," she said, straightening the armchair beside her.

"What has you in a dither? Might I be of assistance?" Miss Hayward looked at him, wringing her hands, and Ambrose wanted to grab them up in his. She opened her mouth, and he knew she meant to send him away. Before she could do so, he said, "Please."

Silently, she stood there for several long moments before giving him a tentative nod. "I know I should not accept, but I am in desperate need of help. My family is returning with my sister's well-to-do fiancé and his mother. They shall be here to-morrow morning, and there is so much to be done to make things ready that I am afraid I shall never do it all in time!"

With each word, she grew more agitated, casting her gaze at the room about her, but Ambrose stepped closer to draw her attention away from all that needed to be done and smiled. "I have two hands and a sturdy back. I may not be well versed in housekeeping, but with your guidance, I'm certain I can be a decent footman. Put me to work, Miss Hayward."

The lady blinked at him, her eyelashes fluttering in a way that might look coquettish on any other lady, but in her eyes, Ambrose saw only bewilderment. "You would do that?"

"Of course," he said, reaching over to give her hand a reassuring squeeze. "What needs to be done first?"

Chapter 21

During the course of her life, Mary had made many beds. Thousands, perhaps. It was a task that required little thought. The flip of the sheets. The tucking and straightening. It was a familiar chore that she was bungling quite thoroughly today. Having another set of hands should help to speed the work along, but not when they belonged to Mr. Ashbrook. Mary was so addled by his presence that simple tasks were becoming far more difficult than they should be. With a sigh, she refolded the bedsheet. Again.

"Is this right?" asked Mr. Ashbrook. His voice drew Mary's eyes to him, but she glanced away when her gaze met his. Her cheeks pinked, which made her even more embarrassed, further deepening her blush. For all her ability to remain composed, Mr. Ashbrook was equally able to discompose her. Especially after he stripped off his suit jacket.

He'd shed the restricting article, rolled up his sleeves and procured an apron from Mr. Gibbs. Mr. Ashbrook was now attired like any number of male servants Mary had seen in her life, but none had ever made her so decidedly uncomfortable while in such a disrobed fashion. The fact that the gentleman was fully aware of her flustered state made the whole situation all the more difficult.

"Is this right?" he asked.

Coming round to his side of the bed, Mary found a near perfect replica of hers. "Very good."

"But?" he prompted, and when she did not answer, he said, "I can hear it in your voice."

With a quick movement, Mary shifted one of the tucks, and Mr. Ashbrook leaned close to watch what she was doing. Very close. Too close. Mary looked at him from the corner of her eye and saw a little smirk on his face. With the lateness of the hour, the only light in the room was that of a few flickering candles, and she had hoped that the darkness would mask her agitation, but the scamp knew the effect he was having on her.

"Must you stand so close?" Mary had meant the words to have a bite—something to put him at a distance—but they came out in a hoarse whisper.

"I need to see your handiwork in order to do better next time, Miss Pert," he said, straightening.

The gentleman remained in place, blocking her escape. Mary glanced at Sally, but there would be no help from those quarters. The girl scrubbed the floors, ignoring what was happening on the other side of the room. For all her former dislike, Sally was now a thorough admirer of Mr. Ashbrook.

Inching around the gentleman, Mary reminded herself of all the reasons to keep her heart in check. He wanted a mother for Dottie. That was it. A convenient wife. But those rationalizations were weakening with each passing hour he worked beside her.

Mr. Ashbrook reached for the pillows and plumped them before handing them over for Mary to arrange on the bed. When she looked up, she saw that his smile had shifted to something more introspective.

"What is going through your head?" she asked, unable to stop herself from speaking.

As he straightened the edge of the blankets, his grin grew. "Only a few weeks ago, I was sitting in one of the finest clubs in

London wrapped around a glass of brandy and a deck of cards. My life has taken a strange turn."

Mary met his gaze. It was full of mirth and warmth, and she found herself quite trapped in it.

"But a happy one," he added.

"The bed is finished," she said, scanning the bedchamber for what else needed doing, but only Sally's chore remained. Retrieving another scrub brush, Mary knelt down and joined her. She did not bother arguing with Mr. Ashbrook when he did the same; his trousers were already stained, and Mary had accepted that he was determined to help in every aspect.

"Do you miss your friends?" she asked. She'd thought it an innocuous question, but Mr. Ashbrook paused, sitting on his heels as his expression grew pensive.

"I don't believe I have any friends in London," he said as he returned to work.

Mary swiped at her forehead. "Nonsense. You have a knack for collecting friends wherever you go."

Mr. Ashbrook grunted. "Acquaintances, perhaps, but not friends. They are people with whom I waste time. Relationships built on pleasure and frivolous conversation. People who do not know who I am because they have no interest in digging past the surface."

It was Mary's turn to pause and sit on her heels. He said the words casually, but the fervor with which he scrubbed at the floor made it clear that it was of significance to him.

"Then they are fools," she said.

His head jerked up to stare at her, and Mary's cheeks blazed until she was certain that she was as bright as a strawberry. And then that grin of his grew, making Mary's stomach somersault.

"It looks like we are done here," she said, getting to her feet. Her muscles ached at the movement, begging her to rest, but there was still much to be done. Rubbing at her neck, she stretched, working out the tension, but there was nothing to do about it until she got a good night's rest, and there was little chance of that tonight. And with all the extra work that came with hosting guests, Mary doubted she would get any until they left.

Sally retrieved the scrub brushes and scooped up the bucket before walking through the door; she left it propped open, but in essence, Mary was alone with Mr. Ashbrook. This was not the first time, but with everything that had passed between them in the last few hours, it felt far more intimate than Mary was prepared for.

Focus on the task at hand! Mary told herself that quite frequently while she worked, and she hoped her thoughts would comply. Patting her apron pockets, she searched for her list of chores.

"Might I ask you a question, Miss Hayward?" asked Mr. Ashbrook, wiping his hands on his apron.

"Of course. You've spent hours scrubbing down my home; you have earned the right to ask a question." Where was her list? She glanced around, searching for where she had laid it.

"But only one?" he teased. The gentleman had such a way of turning a few words into a reason to smile, and though Mary was moments from collapsing into an exhausted heap, she grinned.

"Just one," she replied, and then caught sight of her paper sitting on the side table beside the bed. But thoughts of lists and chores fled from her mind when he spoke.

"Why are you working yourself to death for people who dumped you in a carriage without a thought about what might happen to you?"

It was a foolhardy thing to say. The lady was sensitive and frightened, and Ambrose had just asked something he doubted she wished to discuss, but her situation bothered him to such a degree that he could not contain the question any longer. And it hung there for several silent moments.

When she did not speak, Ambrose continued, "I apologize if that offends you, but I cannot understand why you care for people who could not be bothered to give you an escort for protection and money for emergencies. I find myself worrying at the oddest moments about what would have happened if I had not been there."

Miss Hayward raised her eyebrows and crossed her arms. "I would not have been in any trouble if not for you."

The prickles had returned in force, and Ambrose knew it was time for caution, but he would not retreat. If this time as her temporary footman had taught him anything, it was that Miss Hayward felt deeply for him. A lady did not get that flustered over a gentleman who meant nothing to her. Unfortunately, it was buried under such fear that Ambrose knew earning her trust would be difficult. If he were to gain ground in this venture, it would take persistence and care.

"Travel is always a gamble," he said. "I may have been responsible for the first delay, but there was the foul weather and a subsequent breakdown, both of which are common enough occurrences that your family should never have left you in such a precarious state."

Miss Hayward shrugged. "We don't have funds for such things."

"Then they should have kept you in London or not brought you at all."

"They needed assistance during the move to Town," she said, her pert facade failing as her voice grew quiet and weak. There was a sad, pleading look in her eyes, as though she were grasping for any justification and begging him to accept the lies she chose to tell herself. "And they could not afford to keep me in London."

That was a load of rubbish, but Ambrose knew to push no further. Miss Hayward held herself with dignity, but there was a fragility to her that he had no desire to test. She saw the truth beneath the tripe, and she was not ready to accept it.

"You are a treasure. You may not see it—and for some reason that I cannot fathom, it appears no one else does—but you deserve so much more than this," said Ambrose, meaning every word.

"You are going to return to London," she whispered, her gaze falling to the floor.

Ambrose could not tell if the words were spoken to herself or to him, but he would not let it stand either way. "I shan't," he said with a shake of his head, but then reconsidered. "Not without you, at any rate."

"I have no talent for society, and if you married me, your social calendar would disappear. Do you truly think that living as an outcast with a plain wife is what you want?" she asked, refusing to meet his eyes.

"You are not plain!" he said, growling at the word she threw around far too casually. Stepping forward, Ambrose nudged her chin up until she looked at him. "You are lovely, and I would be happy for any life that had you in it."

Miss Hayward shook her head as if she could not believe it, and Ambrose supposed she couldn't. Mina's counsel came to mind, warning him that this would not be an easy victory.

"What about in a year?" she persisted. "Ten years? Are you certain that you wish to surrender what you have for me?"

Ambrose's hand still hung on her chin, and he used the opportunity to brush his thumb just below her lips while thoughts of kissing them muddled his mind. "I am certain that I have had more fun scrubbing floors and washing windows than I've had in all my years of London society—because I was with you."

Her eyes were bright, though her body was rigid. There was so much about Miss Hayward that called to him, begging for his help. Not because she was weak, but because she was forced to shoulder a burden too great for one person. She had the strength of character to weather it alone, but Ambrose did not want that for her. He wanted to lift her. Protect her. Give her the joys she had been denied by circumstance, society, and her family.

Leaning away from his touch, Miss Hayward turned and snatched a bundle of linens and a bucket of soapy water.

Ambrose sighed to himself. That line of conversation was

over. For now. The lady needed time and space, which he could give, though she was a fool if she thought that was the final word on the subject.

Miss Hayward stopped. "My list," she said, nodding at the paper resting on the side table behind him. Ambrose retrieved it but faltered when she asked, "What is next?"

He offered it to her, but she had not a free hand.

"Can you please tell me what is next?" she repeated, moving toward the door.

With her back to him, Ambrose searched the letters, but they formed no words he could decipher. When he glanced up from the page, he saw her watching him. A voice in his mind said he should tell her the truth—explain why such a simple request was beyond him—but fear kept him silent. With things so tenuous between them, the last thing Ambrose wanted was to hand her a reason to reject him for good.

Miss Hayward would understand. Ambrose felt that. But he crumbled. Years of hiding that aspect of himself returned in force, seizing his tongue. Eventually, it would come out. He could not hide it forever, but did he have to tell her right now when she was still flinching at every compliment he gave her?

His mouth opened, but the words would not form.

"Allow me," she said, coming over to exchange her load for the list. She said nothing, though she glanced into his eyes. He smiled, hoping that it might cover the awkwardness, but Miss Pert looked more disappointed than placated. Taking the list, she led him from the room without a backward glance.

Chapter 22

Their work stretched into the wee hours of the morning, the sun readying itself to peek over the horizon when Mr. Ashbrook took his leave. Though Mary's body cried out for sleep, she watched as he walked across the lawn and wondered how she could already miss his company. If only she could shake some sense into her troubled heart, but Mary had no idea what she should feel towards that confusing gentleman.

"Miss."

Mary turned to see Sally. The poor girl looked liable to fall over; she had worked hard beside Mary and Mr. Ashbrook, even after the Gibbs and Mrs. Webb had been ordered to bed, leaving the younger crew to soldier on alone. Mary's thoughts were far from coherent at present, and it took her several moments before she recognized that Sally was offering up a bouquet of peonies.

"Mr. Ashbrook had these with him, miss, and forgot all about them in the chaos," she said. "Left them with Gibbs, he did."

Their sweet fragrance filled her nose, their soft petals brushing her cheek as she breathed them in. In the dim candlelight, she couldn't tell their color, but they looked near white and utterly perfect. Mary was too exhausted to keep her tears at bay as she thought about that lovely gentleman.

"He's very sweet on you, miss," said Sally with a smile.

But Mary retrieved her candle from the side table and said, "We'd best go get some sleep. There is no need for you to be up until the party arrives, so feel free to rest until then."

Turning away, she ignored the disappointment on Sally's face. Mary was in no fit state to discuss Mr. Ashbrook, for she had too much to say on the subject and was too exhausted to keep hold of her tongue.

Better to remain silent.

But Mary clutched the peonies to her chest as she walked to her bedchamber, her thoughts fixed on the man who had brought them. These were not wildflowers, plucked as they lazed about the fields on a spring day. These were purposeful, even tied together with a silk ribbon.

Forced to leave the flowers on her vanity as she dressed for bed, Mary's thoughts remained fixed on them. She moved like one of Mr. Ashbrook's automata, going through the motions without conscious effort. Before she crawled between the sheets, she placed the blossoms in her water pitcher beside her bed.

For being so exhausted, Mary thought she would be rewarded with a long, deep sleep, but that comfort fled her. Her body was drained, but her mind spun with all that had happened in only a few hours. Clutching her blankets to her chest, Mary stared at the canopy.

Great, fat tears rolled from her eyes, dropping onto the pillow as she thought of Mr. Ashbrook scrubbing her dirty floors. Without a thought, he had cast aside his pride and finery to lower himself to the level of a servant for her. Regardless of what the future held for them, she would never forget it.

Mary could not believe that his declaration had been earnest, yet he had done more than spout sweet words. Mr. Ashbrook had worked himself to exhaustion for no other reason than that she needed the assistance. It had been unbidden and freely offered. More than that, he had fought her any time she'd tried to dissuade him from a particularly nasty chore or send him home.

But could such a gentleman truly care for her?

Mary fought to empty her mind and slip into sleep, but memories plagued her. The fervor in his gaze as he made his tender declaration. The smile as he took the rug from her. The vulnerability as he stared at her list.

Yet another issue to steal away her sleep. Mary would never have expected someone like Mr. Ashbrook to be afflicted with self-doubt, but it had been clear that he was well-acquainted with it. She had not the mental faculties to identify what bedeviled him, but that peek past his polished facade made Mary care for him all the more.

Sleep.

Mary rolled onto her side, curling into a ball, and closed her eyes. For one blessed moment, she was at peace, but then she thought about how grateful she was that her thoughts were silent. That led to thinking about how much she needed to sleep. Which led to thoughts of why she needed it.

Lydia.

The whole purpose behind her family's London Season was to secure her sister a husband, but the speed with which it had happened startled Mary. Could two people fall in love so quickly?

And that question brought her full-circle to Mr. Ashbrook.

Hours passed as she stewed, fidgeting in her bed as she fought to quiet her mind. There were stretches when she dozed, but true sleep eluded her. Through slits in the curtains, Mary watched the growing light as the sun rose, and there was no helping it. She could only hope that she would have the strength to get through the day and be allowed to retire early tonight.

Stumbling through her morning ablutions, Mary dressed in her finest gown, which was not terribly impressive by most standards. All in all, though her eyes showed her exhausted state, she looked as fine as possible for her. Pulling her hands away from her cheeks, she forced herself not to pinch them. There was no point in rosing her complexion. Or hoping that Mr. Ashbrook would visit.

...

"Good heavens, child," said Mrs. Gibbs as Mary entered the kitchen. "What are you doing up? You should be resting after such an effort."

Mary sighed and snatched a fresh pastry from the table. "Would that I could, but sleep eludes me. There is still much to plan before they arrive."

Joining Mrs. Webb at the stove, Mary stirred the steaming pot of jam as the cook shook a pan of vegetables that were likely heading into the pie tin waiting on the table. The kitchen was stuffed with raw ingredients ready for Mrs. Webb and Mrs. Gibbs to form into tasty dishes. Seeing the food piled around, Mary was overwhelmed by the sheer volume.

"Did Mr. Brown put up a fuss about this? Our grocer bills are in the rears," she said.

"Don't fret," said Mrs. Webb. "Your father wrote the grocer directly and sent him an advance for this. It seems your sister has caught herself quite the swell."

"Where are the jars?" asked Mary, lifting a bubbling pan from the flame.

"I am not canning that quite yet," said Mrs. Gibbs, pointing to a dish beside her in which Mary could pour the freshly made jam.

The three women moved about the kitchen with the familiarity of those who worked together regularly. Pastries and bread were set out to cool, pies and vegetables prepared, and herbs cleaned for the coming dishes Mrs. Webb would cook.

"Are we going to ignore that Mr. Ashbrook was breaking his back to impress you or are we going to discuss what you are going to do about your young man?" asked Mrs. Webb.

"He is not my young man," said Mary, coring yet another apple for tonight's dessert.

Mrs. Gibbs shook her head at Mary as she scrubbed the dirty dishes. "I hate to disagree, but a man does not willingly clean chamber pots."

"I cannot think of many courting bucks who would," said Mrs. Webb. "Your Mr. Ashbrook is a special one."

"He is not my Mr. Ashbrook," Mary insisted, wiping her hands on her apron.

"And why would you say that?" asked Mrs. Webb, turning from her burbling pot to stare at Mary with her hands on her hips. "That young gentleman has been a permanent fixture in this house since you arrived home. He dotes on you. He even came by yesterday all fancied up and with a handful of flowers for you."

Mary paused in cutting her apple and gave each woman a hard look. "You know perfectly well that it is ludicrous. You have seen enough of my history with gentlemen to know that there is no possible way that I have attracted someone so handsome and charming and kind and perfect. Such a man does not lack for female attention."

Mrs. Webb snorted, returning to her pots with a disgusted shake of her head, and Mrs. Gibbs gaped at her. Mary turned her attention back to the apple, but then Mrs. Gibbs was there beside her, taking the thing out of her hand. Sitting beside her on the kitchen bench, Mrs. Gibbs held Mary's hands.

"Dear," she said, her brows pinching together, "just because those other gentlemen weren't intelligent enough to see your worth doesn't mean that Mr. Ashbrook can't. He has a good head on his shoulders. He sees you for what you are and loves you all the more for it."

"My worth as a mother perhaps," mumbled Mary, though even as she said it, the words felt false. Visions of Mr. Ashbrook working beside her hour after hour came to mind, and Mary was no longer certain what his motives were anymore.

Mrs. Gibbs stared long and hard into Mary's eyes, her expression hardening at what she saw there. "You are a good girl, and if you cannot see your own value then no one—not even your Mr. Ashbrook—can make you see it. But do not assume that everyone is as blind as—"

But whatever lecture Mrs. Gibbs had intended to give was cut short at the sounds of approaching carriages.

"They've arrived!" said Gibbs, bursting into the kitchen with unnecessary volume.

"Set the kettles on," said Mary. "Get trays ready. It is too early for luncheon yet, but they might want a bite to eat."

The two women nodded and snapped to work, bustling about the kitchen while Mary popped up from her seat, pulled off the apron, and hurried with the old butler to the front door. Sally was waiting for them there, though the poor dear was asleep on her feet. Mary wanted to send her to her room for a bit more rest, but there was nothing to be done about it. Without a footman on staff, they needed her.

Gibbs opened the front door, and Mary stepped through it, arriving at the carriage just as her father alighted and handed down her mother.

"Dearest!" Mama swept her into a hug and whispered in her ear. "A baronet, Mary! I cannot wait to tell you all. Oh, and I brought you the most lovely ribbons and lace from London."

Mama released her but gave a worried frown as she looked at Mary. "I told you to wear your finest dress. Sir Duncan must see us at our best."

"It is my finest."

"But you should have gone to Madam Notley's and purchased a new one," replied Mama as she glanced to the other carriage where an elderly woman was being assisted down by a gentleman. "The future sister-in-law of a baronet should not look so shabby. It would not do for us to appear too poor to properly clothe our daughters."

"Madam Notley will not allow us any more credit, Mama. And even if she did, there was not time for it. You did not give enough notice—" But the others in the group drew closer, and Mary was hushed by her mother.

"Lady Whiting and Sir Duncan, might I be allowed to present our eldest daughter, Miss Mary Hayward?" said Papa, taking Mary by the elbow and drawing her forward to stand before the pair.

The lady was far older than Mary would have expected. But then, so was Sir Duncan. From her family's descriptions of the gentleman, she had expected someone far more dashing and a good deal younger. Lydia stood at his side, and he looked more like her father than her intended.

Lady Whiting sniffed, her wrinkled lips pursing as she raised a lorgnette to give Mary a full perusal of her person.

"Not very pretty," she said with another sniff. "Quite plain, in fact. But I am pleased to make your acquaintance. Your sister speaks of you often, and she is such a dear girl."

From the corner of her eye, Mary saw Mrs. Gibbs emerge and give Lady Whiting a most fearsome scowl, though she hid it before anyone else witnessed it. Mary didn't know what to do with that statement, but it was fitting that someone would offer up such bold criticism on the subject that had tormented her ever since Mr. Ashbrook had appeared in all his romantic glory.

But such thoughts were diverted when Lydia gave Mary a hug. With a smile in her voice, she whispered, "I cannot wait to tell you about my dear Sir Duncan."

"Charmed," greeted Sir Duncan with a nod when Mary was finally released. The gentleman held a cane with a practiced air that said it was more accessory than necessity.

Mary heard a mighty yip as a ball of white and black fur collided with her feet and pawed at her hem before tearing after the horses. The grooms struggled to keep the beasts in hand as the little creature barked and nipped at their hooves.

"Pepper!" Lydia laughed at the pup and patted her knees as it came running for her, and she scooped him up. "Isn't he a dear? My sweet Sir Duncan gave him to me."

Lydia smiled at her fiancé, looping one of her arms through

his. To all appearances, Mary would say her sister was aglow with happiness, but there was something in Lydia's eyes that made the back of Mary's neck prickle.

"How very thoughtful," said Mary with a stilted tone; she was pleased for her sister, but she suspected Lydia would not be the one cleaning up after the pup.

"Dearest, we are so worn from our journey," said her mother. "We could all do with a bit of refreshment and a lie-down. The grooms will handle the luggage but will need you to direct them."

"I don't know if I could ever rest," said Lydia, beaming at Sir Duncan while stroking his arm. "My love and I shall be married by the end of the month!"

"So soon?" asked Mary.

"There is no need to postpone," said Sir Duncan. "It's best to get things underway now that it has been decided."

"If you care to follow Mrs. Gibbs," said Mama, "she will show you to your rooms where you can rest and freshen up."

"We have tea trays ready and will deliver them shortly," said Mary, but the group was already heading towards the front door in a flurry of words and yipping. A moment later, they abandoned her on the front steps to see to her work. As befitting their station, the Whitings had brought a small contingency of servants with them. The lady's maid and valet were hounding her for information regarding their master's and mistress' things while the postilions and grooms unloaded the trunks.

And Mary kept wishing Mr. Ashbrook were there to assist her, which was beyond silly. She had shouldered such work before he had appeared and would do so after he vanished. But having his help made it so much easier to deal with the chaos. And far more enjoyable.

With a few orders to her staff and theirs, the guests were situated, and Mary could retire to her bedchamber. There was still a mountain of things to be done throughout the day, but she gave thanks for a bit of peace. If only her thoughts would allow it.

There were Mrs. Webb's and Mrs. Gibbs' words and the mystery surrounding Lydia to consider. But more than that, Mary pondered what Mr. Ashbrook had said about her family. He had all but called her a drudge. The accusation had been too stark for her to accept it then, but the manner in which her mother had given her orders as though she were one of the Gibbs supported Mr. Ashbrook's assertion.

Walking to her bedchamber, Mary pondered it all, the thoughts swirling through her mind in a great, tangled mess.

"Mary!" Lydia shot from her door and snatched her sister, pulling her inside. "I have so much to tell you, I fear I shall burst if I wait another minute!"

Herding Mary to the bed, Lydia climbed atop and dropped a package onto Mary's lap. With a quick pull of the twine, she unwrapped the brown paper to find a book of poetry. On the whole, Mary was not a keen reader of verse, and Byron's works were among her least favorite, but she gave her sister a hug.

"Then you like it? It took me forever to decide what to get you," said Lydia, beaming.

"You are a sweetheart. I love it," said Mary, for the sentiment behind the gift made up for any deficiencies.

Lydia sighed and leaned against the headboard, wrapping her arms around a throw pillow. "Mama and Papa are so thrilled with Sir Duncan. I hoped for a good match but never believed I would find a baronet. They cannot stop talking about it. Mama is positively awed by Lady Whiting, and Papa is enamored with Sir Duncan's income. It is everything they wished for."

Mary toyed with the tassel on one of the pillows. "But is he everything *you* hoped for?"

"Of course," came the quick reply. Such an answer would have been reassuring if it had not been for the speed and tone of it. On the surface, it appeared to be everything that it should, but it sounded rehearsed.

"Then you are happy with Sir Duncan?" she pressed.

"How could I not be?" Lydia's tone was bright, but her

smile had a touch of brittleness to it. But before Mary could pursue the topic further, her sister launched into the details of her time in London, scarcely pausing to breathe. Mary listened and nodded at intervals, but the knot in her stomach warned her that all was not right with her sister.

Chapter 23

Standing outside the conservatory, Ambrose propped himself against a faux pillar and stared at the hill on the eastern boundary of the Kingsley's estate. This was not the first time he had stood thusly over the past few hours, for it was now his favorite spot in all of Avebury Park. If he squinted hard enough, Ambrose swore he could see the top of Buckthorn Manor peeking over the crest, and he didn't know whether to laugh at his love-sick fixation or simply embrace the sweet madness that consumed him.

Footsteps caught Ambrose's attention, and from the corner of his eye, he saw Simon join him on the veranda.

"There must be something exceptionally fascinating about our landscape for it to have captured your attention so," said Simon, and Ambrose sighed. He'd been avoiding Mina and her husband for precisely this reason. After all the times he had teased them about their romance, it was only fitting that they should do the same—but he need not give them an easy target. Being on the receiving end was far less enjoyable.

"No doubt Mina has told you about Miss Hayward, so I won't feign ignorance as to your meaning," said Ambrose.

"She did," said Simon, coming to lean against a pillar beside Ambrose. "Though I had guessed something was afoot before she confirmed it. Nicholas owes me a fiver."

Ambrose snorted. "My brother has a knack for misunderstanding me."

Simon nodded, crossing his arms. "Nicholas is a fine man with many excellent qualities, but he often believes himself infallible, though he does not always show sound judgment."

"You mean he is pig-headed and rarely in the right?" Ambrose asked with a chuckle.

"Stubbornness and Ashbrooks go hand-in-hand."

"I shall tell Mina that."

Simon smirked. "She would be the first to agree with me. And in her, I find it endearing. But I came out here to thank you for all your help. Mr. Thorne and I are trying our best to keep up with all this modernization, but I fear our understanding of it is limited. Without your expertise, we would be lost."

Ambrose blushed, and he cleared his throat. Then he twisted his lips into that comfortable smile of his. "My expertise lies more with cards and where to find the best brandy, but I am glad to be of service."

Silence followed that statement, and Ambrose turned his gaze to his brother-in-law, only to find the gentleman studying him. There was no hostility there. No judgment or irritation. But it was no meaningless inspection, either. Having spent so much of his life hiding in plain sight, Ambrose was unfamiliar with such scrutiny, and his cheeks burned even brighter. Simon gave a little huff and an introspective smile.

"It appears I owe Mina a fiver," he said, looking out into the distance.

Ambrose's brows drew together. "For what?"

"She has always insisted that her dear brother is not the flippant flirt he pretends to be. I thought her overly sentimental for seeing something that was not there."

Giving a lazy smile, Ambrose replied, "Well, you mustn't let the secret out, or I fear I shall lose all standing with society."

Simon pinched his nose and sighed. "You have a talent for driving sensible people quite mad with your evasions."

"Miss Hayward has told me so on many an occasion." Just the thought of her calmed his agitation, and Ambrose was able to give a genuine smile.

"Any lady who withstands your charms and takes you to task for them is well worth having around."

"I certainly believe so," said Ambrose, his mind wandering to his hopeful future with her and Dottie. "Unfortunately, she does not."

Simon nodded, his face growing grim. "That is an all-too-familiar problem, and one not easily remedied. With so many critical voices in her ears, it can be difficult for yours to be heard. And even more for her to believe it."

Pushing off the column, Ambrose turned to give his brother-in-law his full attention. "How did you manage it with Mina?"

Simon's jaw clenched, his muscles tensing. "As much as I wish I could erase it all, Mina still struggles at times. She is the most incredible lady I have ever known. Talented and generous, and just so beautiful." As he spoke, his eyes drifted into the distance, a smile on his lips.

Snapping back to the conversation, Simon continued, "My reassurances help some, but they only do so much. In the end, she must overcome it herself."

Crossing his arms, Ambrose fell against the column with a grunt. "And here I hoped you had the solution to all my problems."

With a shrug, Simon gave a non-committal grunt. "From what Mina has told me, Miss Hayward has been taught to devalue herself. You cannot expect that to change in a matter of weeks."

Ambrose thought over what Simon had said. There was quite a bit of sense in it, but it did not help his cause, for it required more patience, which was not one of his strengths.

"If I could give you one piece of advice," said Simon, "it

would be to never give her reason to doubt your feelings."

"That is all she does," said Ambrose.

Simon shook his head. "Likely, she doubts she could inspire such feelings, but that does not mean she doubts you. Do not give her reason to, for it will break both your hearts."

"I would never betray Miss Hayward's trust in me."

"I thought the same of myself," replied Simon in a low voice. "I hope you do not make the same mistake I did."

He stared at his brother-in-law, curiosity and shock begging him to ask more, but Simon's expression made him hold his tongue. Instead, Ambrose said, "I have a present for her. It took some hunting, but I—"

"Presents are fine and well, but they are not enough. Honesty is the most important thing you can give her." Simon tugged at his cravat, and his eyes drifted into the distance. He cleared his throat before he continued, "It is easy to justify secrets, especially when there is so much at risk. It's terrifying to take that leap and open yourself fully to another. To trust that they will still love you once they know all of you. But it is imperative—especially when you love someone who believes they are unlovable. You cannot hope to gain her heart if you are unwilling to give her all of yours."

A lump formed in Ambrose's throat, choking him as he pictured telling Miss Hayward all. No more prevaricating. No more procrastinating. Miss Hayward was the first lady for whom Ambrose cared enough to consider such a confession, but to do so at this crucial junction made his heart feel as though it were wedged between the gears of a threshing machine.

"It is a terrifying prospect, isn't it?" asked Simon, eyeing his brother-in-law. "So you must decide which is worse, pushing through that fear or losing her."

And that made his heart stop altogether. Lose her. Never see Miss Hayward again. No more talks. No more reading. No quips and teasing. Just the possibility made Ambrose break into a sweat.

"I think you have your answer," said Simon with a smile.

"So why are you standing here, looking forlorn, when you can simply walk over that hill and be precisely where you wish to be?"

"Her parents and some visitors arrived yesterday," said Ambrose. "With all the commotion, I thought it best to give them a day or two to settle in before bothering her."

Simon grunted with a roll of his eyes. "The baronet and his mother. The neighborhood is abuzz with news of Miss Lydia's engagement, but I would hazard a guess that things are not going to settle until after the wedding. They are bound to have a stream of callers to bow and scrape for Sir Duncan and Lady Whiting's amusement. I fear that Mina and I are bound to pay a call in the next few days."

Ambrose chuckled at Simon's sneer but shook his head. "You are right, but I'm still not keen to meet her family after how they have treated her. I fear what I might say to them."

"They are not wicked people," said Simon. "Simply selfish. And altogether unpleasant if you do not care for the company of sycophants."

Ambrose sucked in a deep breath, letting it out in a slow sigh. If Miss Hayward's heart weren't at stake, he would never bother with such an odious task. But it was, and Ambrose would endure far worse to secure her hand in marriage.

"Get a move on," said Simon, pushing off the column. "The Ambrose I have come to know over the past few weeks is a gentleman I am pleased to call my brother and my friend. And we both know that is due in large part to Miss Hayward. You have found your match, so go and get her before she talks herself into turning you away permanently."

...

The Hayward property was by no means a large one. It was pretty in its own right, but no one of their class would ever deign to call it anything more than modest. Being fond of walks, Mary had made the tour of the grounds on foot many a time and could not think of a single outing in which they'd bothered with a carriage. Yet, there they were, stuffed into the Whitings' landau.

Mary wished she could have begged off, but Lydia had been so desperate for her to join them that there was no choice but to agree, even though she was forced to take the groom's rumble seat on the back end of the carriage. Mama, Papa, and Lydia were squashed together on the backward-facing bench. Of course, Sir Duncan and Lady Whiting had claimed the premier seats, for their dignities would never allow them to be uncomfortably situated—which was their loss, for Mary thought her seat the finest in the group. It was raised, affording her a better view, and isolated, allowing her to ignore the inane conversation of her companions and ponder on her favorite subject.

Mr. Ashbrook had not called yesterday, and Mary readily admitted that his absence distressed her. The visitors' condescension and her family's obsequiousness were already wearing on her, and Mary longed for Mr. Ashbrook's company. For conversation that did not revolve around social standing and gossip. For words spoken without disdain. A sensible discussion.

At the crest of the hill dividing their property from the Kingsleys', her father called for the coachman to halt so that they might admire the view. Lady Whiting and Mama were content to remain in the coach, but Mary and the others went to explore. Lydia strolled arm-in-arm with Sir Duncan while Papa followed, droning on about the vastness of the Hayward estate. Though he was not outright deceitful, Papa took some liberties with the boundaries of the property and heavily implied that certain portions of Avebury's grounds belonged to Buckthorn.

Meanwhile, Mary was pleased to find a solitary spot beneath the great oak tree that stood on the crest. She could not understand why Lydia had insisted on her accompanying them on this outing, as all attention was on Sir Duncan and Lady Whiting, and the pair did not care whether Mary was here or in the heart of Abyssinia.

Tucking her legs beneath her, she sat at the base of the tree.

From her perch in the carriage, Mama sent a pointed look to Mary; she did not go so far as to scowl at her daughter, the look in her eyes was a clear condemnation of such boorish behavior. But since Lady Whiting's back was to Mary, she ignored Mama's proddings to stand.

Leaning her head against the trunk, Mary stared at the canopy, loving the way the branches shivered and danced in the breeze. Just the rustling sound of the foliage brought a semblance of peace to her overwrought heart. Closing her eyes, Mary shut out the world and her worries, breathing in the scent of summertime and growing things, and turned her thoughts to the happy memories of her picnic with Mr. Ashbrook beneath this very tree.

Something fell onto her lap, and Mary's eyes snapped open to find a violet resting in the folds of her skirt. And then there was Mr. Ashbrook standing over her. A slow smile spread across her face, and Mary beamed at the person she most wanted to see at that very moment.

"Good afternoon," he said in a low voice.

"Good afternoon," she thought she replied, though the words were garbled and her heart thumped at the manner in which he looked at her.

"I'm very happy to see that you are still among the living. When I left here, I was certain you were going to expire on the spot," said Mr. Ashbrook, offering her a hand. With a gentle tug, he had her on her feet; they stood so close that Mary's cheeks reddened, though she did not move away.

"I am no wilting flower," said Mary.

Mr. Ashbrook's gaze softened. "No, you are not."

"We are taking in the grounds today," said Mary, struggling through the words. To say nothing of the erratic thumping of her heart.

"It is a fine day for it," he said, looking up at the sky.

Mary looked upwards, too, and saw nothing but gray clouds. "You have odd taste in weather if you think this fine," she replied in a dry tone.

And then he turned his face down again, and somehow used the movement to maneuver closer to her. With only a slight lean, they would be in quite a compromising position. Mary's eyes widened, and just one side of Mr. Ashbrook's lips quirked upright, his eyes sparkling with that wicked humor. His move had been deliberate, and he knew full well what effect it was having on her.

"It is always a fine day with you," he said in a low voice. In any other circumstance, Mary would have laughed at that, but at present, she was struggling to keep herself from closing the distance.

"Ridiculous." Mary had meant it to sound gruff, but it came out as a breathy whisper.

"Mary?" called Lydia, breaking the spell Mr. Ashbrook had cast. Stepping away, they turned to see that the party had reconvened at the coach.

"Miss Hayward, would you do the honor of introducing me?" asked Mr. Ashbrook, offering up his arm to Mary—but with her family watching on, she couldn't bring herself to take it. Leading him to the carriage, Mary made the proper introductions.

"Ah, yes," said Mama. "Mrs. Kingsley's youngest brother, correct? I remember seeing you at your brother's wedding, though we did not have the opportunity to meet. Your sister must have invited all of Bristow to the thing."

"An absolute shame that we did not. I am very sorry to have been deprived of an earlier acquaintance," said Mr. Ashbrook with that affable air of his.

"Ambrose Ashbrook," said Sir Duncan, the upper class ennui fleeing from his eyes for a brief moment. "I have long wished to make your acquaintance, sir. One of the finest card players in London, or so I hear."

"You flatter me," said Mr. Ashbrook, though he did not deny the claim.

"We must get together for a few hands," said Sir Duncan. "I have wanted to test my skills against yours, but I cannot abide the clubs you frequent. Far too coarse for my liking. How is one to enjoy an evening when at any moment the members might fall into a round of fisticuffs?"

Mr. Ashbrook chuckled. "You make it sound as though those places are filled with savages rather than gentlemen."

"I detest such brutish behavior," said Sir Duncan with a sniff. "It's barbaric, and I refuse to be party to such things."

Mr. Ashbrook coughed to cover a laugh. "Indeed, sir. But unfortunately, the finer clubs have barred me after their members grew tired of me draining their coffers."

Sir Duncan's eyes positively lit up at that. "I hear you laid waste to Mr. Hamford."

"I shall remain mum on the subject, though I will admit we played a particularly brutal game that may have led to my being banned from Dervish's," said Mr. Ashbrook.

"Good show," said Sir Duncan with a laugh and a stomp of his cane. "That pompous imbecile deserves everything you gave him."

"We are holding a dinner party tonight," said Mama, cutting into the conversation with an eager grin. "You must join us, Mr. Ashbrook, and then stay for cards."

Mary stared at her mother, shocked at the blatant falsehood she was spinning.

"Just a few friends from the neighborhood," she continued. "But we would adore it if you would be among the guests."

"I would be honored," said Mr. Ashbrook with that charming smile that had the other ladies tittering. Even Lady Whiting thawed enough to give him a playful tap on the arm as he offered up some ridiculous compliment.

Mary's heart constricted as she watched him flatter and flirt with everyone, ingratiating himself into their good graces so thoroughly that one could be forgiven for believing that he was a dear family friend and not a relative stranger. It was sobering, though Mary was grateful for the reminder of what Mr. Ashbrook was. A good man, certainly, but it was in his nature to make everyone fall in love with him.

His infatuation—if Mary could call it that—was likely nothing more than a byproduct of her rebuffing his advances. Mr. Ashbrook was merely rising to the challenge, working harder to win her over. It was in his nature.

Yet she could not reconcile that Mr. Ashbrook with the one who had cleaned her family's home.

"Mary?" Mama spoke with a hard tone, and she snapped from her reverie to discover the rest of the party seated already inside the carriage.

"Mr. Ashbrook," said her father, "I am afraid we do not have room for you, but we look forward to you joining us tonight."

"It would be my honor," Mr. Ashbrook said with a suitably humble bow, though there was a tightness in his voice that Mary could not understand. "However, I thought I might stroll your lovely grounds. May I ask Miss Hayward to walk with me?"

"Certainly," said Papa with a dismissive wave. "She knows the grounds better than anyone."

Mary gave a bob to the party, but Mama called her over and whispered, "Do not take too long, dearest. There is much to do for tonight's dinner, and I shall need you posthaste."

The carriage rolled away, and Mr. Ashbrook said, "They are a lively bunch."

"Yes," Mary replied. "And tiring. Mama is determined to spend every waking moment entertaining Sir Duncan and Lady Whiting. She is terrified he might cry off if he grows bored for even one moment. The marriage contracts are signed, yet they are still determined to impress him." Mary tried for an air of humor, but her heart hung too heavily in her chest.

Mr. Ashbrook motioned for Mary to walk with him, but she studiously avoided the arm he offered up and the furrowed look he gave her at the rejection. She held her hands behind her (for it was the only safe thing to do with them), and they strolled towards the house.

"Were they pleased with our preparations?" he asked.

"I believe so," she replied.

"They have not said as much?"

The accusation in his tone pricked at her. "I doubt they understand how much work is put into such things, but it is of no importance."

"Yes, it is," said Mr. Ashbrook, kicking at a rock. "You spent hours in a panic to get everything ready in time, and the very least they could have done was acknowledge your efforts."

Mary snatched a tall blade of grass from the side of the path and ran it through her fingers. "Yes, but I am just a drudge, remember? Isn't that what you were implying the other day?"

Mr. Ashbrook froze mid-step, though Mary did not pause. The sooner she arrived home, the better. Distance and time were all she needed. It had worked with Henry, and it would work again with Mr. Ashbrook. Theirs was such a short acquaintance that her feelings were unlikely to linger long. Though Mary feared they would.

"I hate seeing you mistreated, and it is clear that your family takes you for granted," said Mr. Ashbrook.

Mary shredded the leaves and picked another blade. "You suppose that I have a choice in the matter, or that there is something I might do to change my circumstances, but this is the best I can hope for."

"And why is that?"

"Because I am poor and unmarried. Spinsters are of no value to a family."

Mr. Ashbrook pulled her to a stop. "You cannot believe that."

Staring at the grass in her hand, Mary would not meet his gaze. "It is fact. A woman is a wife and a mother. If not that, she is a financial burden to her parents. When they are gone, she is passed around to whatever relatives will take her in, and they resent her for it. So, I make myself valuable instead."

Mr. Ashbrook began to speak, but Mary continued. "It's not so bad. It's far better than becoming a governess. Those poor creatures are mistreated, underpaid, and overworked. They rarely have a moment to themselves, but I am allowed my freedom. As long as the work is done, my time is my own."

Continuing down the path, Mary discarded the shredded grass and replaced it with a new stalk. "I have a good life. Though it is not always obvious, my family appreciates what I do for them. And for the most part, they ask very little of me. I am much better off than most spinsters. Quite blessed, in fact."

Mr. Ashbrook matched her pace, though he remained quiet as they walked along; Mary did not mind a comfortable silence, but there was a thickness in the air that had her babbling.

"I am quite content with my place in this world," she continued. "There have been times in my life when I've envied my sister and the way my parents dote on her, but if it means marrying a man like that pompous bore, Sir Duncan, I am much happier being the spinster servant."

Mary did not look up at Mr. Ashbrook, but she felt his scowl. For the life of her, she wished to simply stop talking, but the words grew more brittle and harsh with each utterance, and she could not rein them in. "Perhaps I have discovered a blessing to being so desperately plain."

Chapter 24

The lady hardly paused for breath as she rambled, but Ambrose would not let such a statement pass unchallenged. "You are not plain!"

Halting, he grabbed Miss Hayward's arm, but she wrenched from his grip, turning to look at him with such apathy that he hardly recognized her. But then, this was not his Mary. This was the infuriating Miss Pert.

"Even if I were to ignore the many people who have called me plain, I have the evidence of my own eyes, Mr. Ashbrook," she said, casting away the remnant bits of grass. "Mirrors do not lie."

"Rubbish," said Ambrose, stepping closer, fixing her with a look that brooked no refusal. "You are lovely. Elegant. Regal—"

"Now, *that* is rubbish," she grumbled, folding her arms. "Unless, of course, you are about to spout such nonsense to my father, too, for I bear a striking resemblance to him."

"You do not!" Ambrose's voice rose, and he fought to keep his temper in check.

"Do recall, Mr. Ashbrook, that not five minutes ago you claimed my mother looked far too young to have a daughter engaged to be married. You have a silver tongue, sir, and an over-abundance of honeyed words," she said, continuing down the path.

Ambrose's heart dropped. For all his confidence, he had done precisely what Simon had warned him not to. For Ambrose, that conversation had been meaningless banter. A way to ingratiate himself with her family. Nothing but hollow words. For Miss Hayward, his false compliments bolstered every doubt and fear. Cast shadows over his earnest declarations. Painted him a fraud.

Having always thought himself a man of honor, Ambrose was disheartened to realize how much of his life was a lie. He was steeped in dishonesty and deceit, yet he expected her to believe him. If he wanted her trust and love, Ambrose had to give her his completely.

Miss Pert marched down the path with rigid composure. Head high and shoulders straight. Unmovable. Unbreakable. A woman made of stone. But the heart in her chest was no granite rock. It was warm and delicate and so easily bruised. And he would not give up on it.

Ambrose rubbed his palms against his trousers as his pulse pounded in his ears. Words had always been his friends, yet they failed him now, for he was at a loss. Taking several steadying breaths, he tried to think of what to say. How to explain it. Even as the panic took possession of him, his resolve hardened. There was one way in which to heal what he had broken, and he would do it. For her.

"I am generous in my praise," he began. Ambrose swallowed the lump in his throat and pondered what to say next. Honesty was well and good, but he needed to explain himself in the best manner. "Too generous, in fact. It has become so second nature that I do not realize when I am acting the flirt. But I do it because I am terrified of people."

Miss Hayward halted, turning to look at him with a cocked brow. "What reason could you have to be terrified of people?"

Carefully, Ambrose crept towards her as he spoke, lessening the distance between them. "Because they might discover what I truly am."

"And what is that?"

He swallowed and let out a silent breath. "A simpleton."

Miss Hayward huffed and turned away, speaking to him from over her shoulder. "You do not fool me with your false modesty, Mr. Ashbrook. I know you have a keen mind, so do not treat *me* like a simpleton."

Though her words stung, Ambrose ignored them. He had danced with Miss Pert too many times to mistake his partner, and her carefully crafted persona was working hard to keep him at a distance.

With Simon's advice ringing in his mind, demanding he take the leap, Ambrose steeled himself. "I cannot read."

He'd thought his voice too weak to carry, but Miss Hayward paused and faced him. She did not speak, but she did not run away, either, so Ambrose counted it a temporary victory. However, her expression was inscrutable, leaving his heart pounding as he forged ahead, though he could no longer meet her eyes as he spoke.

"I've tried but cannot," he said. He tugged at his jacket, his eyes tracing the ruts at his feet. "I know what letters are, but it is as if my eyes cannot see them. At times, I can grasp one or two words, but then the scribbles shift and move, tangling into an incomprehensible mess."

Miss Hayward's feet came into view, and Ambrose followed the line of her skirts, his eyes inching up to see her staring at him. He searched her gaze and found compassion.

Ambrose clenched his jaw, blinking rapidly. A moment later he continued. "At home they thought me lazy, but at school they dubbed me an imbecile. And no matter how hard I worked, I couldn't keep pace with the other boys. So I pretended that my academic failures were purposeful, and I learned to charm my way through my classes. Of course, it helped that my father gave hefty bribes to the headmaster—for no son of his was going to fail."

His gaze dropped again, and Miss Hayward took hold of his hand. Perhaps it was enough to stop there, but having opened the door to that hidden place, Ambrose found it impossible to close. Not with her standing before him.

"Idleness and apathy are acceptable in society, but idiocy is not," he said. "So I play the charming rogue to keep people from seeing that beneath it is a halfwit who cannot read the invitations he receives nor pen a simple response."

Miss Hayward squeezed his hands, drawing his eyes to hers. "You are no halfwit."

He let out a huffing chuckle, shaking his head. "And you wonder why I love you? What other lady would hear that confession and then defend my intelligence?"

"But I have seen it time and time again," she insisted, her brows drawing together as her gaze bore into his. "Your eyes may play tricks on you, but they also allow you to see the world in a manner that is unique. I am constantly amazed at the insights you have. And your memory! You need only see something demonstrated once or twice and then you can mimic it. That is incredible. I can hardly keep my chores straight without writing everything down in my diary."

Years of fearing this very moment had been for nothing, for here stood the lady he loved, clinging to his hands and insisting with all her heart that his secret was not shameful. Ambrose struggled to breathe steadily as gratitude overtook his heart. Whether chance, destiny, or divine intervention had thrown them together in that coach all those weeks ago, Miss Hayward was the greatest blessing he had ever received, and Ambrose had no idea how he would ever be worthy of it.

"I did not confess that to elicit such beautiful words, Miss Hayward, though I do treasure them," he said, lifting her fingertips to his lips. "I am too effusive in my praise and too loose with the truth, and I know that gives you cause to doubt my sincerity, so I am giving you the one thing I have never given anyone else. My true self."

Miss Hayward's eyes widened as she stared at him, a shimmer of tears forming at the corners. Staring into her face, he wondered why anyone would call such a magnificent creature plain. She was a lady of pure elegance. Her features were clear and unique, the type that grew more handsome with the years.

She was beyond anything he had ever hoped for in a wife, and Ambrose knew that whatever else he accomplished in his life, he would fight to make her a permanent part of it.

Mary had never given much thought to breathing. It was simply a given in life. But at this moment, she was finding it near impossible to do so. Mr. Ashbrook's strong hands kept her steady, but she struggled to keep her legs from trembling.

Those words. Those timid, heartfelt words. They held more power than the volumes he had previously spoken, for Mary knew they were true. And this proud and private gentleman would not open his heart in such a manner for a mere flirtation. One did not share the darkest parts of oneself on a whim.

"I nearly forgot," he said, freeing one of his hands to dig into his jacket pocket. In a flash, the vulnerability in his eyes was gone, replaced by that suave smile of his, and Mary was facing the careless fribble once more. "I brought you a present."

He placed a brown parcel in her hands, and even with it covered in paper, Mary knew it was a novel. She thought back on all the hours she'd spent reading aloud to him and saw those memories in a new light. With a tug, she pulled the string free and read the title.

"*Persuasion*? You bought me a copy?" Her breath hitched, and her tears blurred the title. Mr. Ashbrook smiled at her astonishment, and Mary could not form words. She didn't recall mentioning how much she wanted to read it, but she knew—positively knew—that it was no coincidence that he had chosen this for her.

"It was nothing," he replied with the practiced ease he gave everyone else.

Clutching the book to her chest with one hand, Mary took his in her other. "Where did you get this? I have been begging Mr. Sims to carry this for months."

Mr. Ashbrook smiled that infuriating smile, but before he could give some other nonsensical remark, Mary squeezed his hand and gave him a look as stern as steel. "Where?"

His expression shifted, peeling away to reveal that vulnerability Mary understood all too well. It was the look of a lost soul begging to be loved all while terrified to face another rejection.

"A bookstore in Ainsley."

Mary gaped at him. "That's a half day's journey from here."

Mr. Ashbrook shrugged. "It was the only place I could find it."

"Then there were others you searched?"

He nodded but offered no other explanation. Mary could only imagine how much time and effort he had spent to hunt down this little novel for her. Letting out a shaky breath, Mary could not keep the tears from trickling down her cheeks.

"Why?" she whispered, clutching the book.

Mr. Ashbrook's brows rose, and he drew close, leaning in until he was all she could see. "I have told you why, but you refuse to believe me."

Mary blinked at him, trying to swallow past the lump constricting her throat. The weakness in her legs spread through her until she felt liable to drop, but Mary held firm. She had to speak. To explain. Mr. Ashbrook deserved her secrets.

"I am not the sort of woman that inspires loves," she whispered as tears clouded her words.

"You have said that before, and I still think it absurd," he replied.

Ambrose could see her fighting her nerves, struggling to get the words out, and as much as he wished to calm her, he knew that this was necessary. He had to understand the demons she was fighting against.

"I was in love once," she said, forcing the words out.

As he had long suspected that, her revelation came as no surprise, but Ambrose remained silent, hoping his quiet strength would help her overcome her fears.

"He was my closest friend. One of my only friends, in fact. But I loved him deeply." In halting words, she continued, describing the childhood playmate that grew into the man she had hoped to marry. Each bit of the narrative pained him, for he knew there was no happy ending for the young Mary who had placed so many of her hopes on such a feckless man.

"I was so certain he was going to propose," she said, tears coursing down her cheeks. "But he announced that he was marrying someone else. A girl who pretended to be my friend in order to catch his eye. I am not someone who is at ease with people. And two of the only ones I let into my heart tossed me aside like rubbish."

Brushing away her tears, Miss Hayward stiffened, and Ambrose watched as Miss Pert tugged on her armor, protecting her heart behind that awful apathy she pretended to feel. "But I am better off without them. With time, I came to see that he was a cad and she was a poor excuse for a friend. Neither was much of a loss."

"Do not do that, Miss Pert," he said, putting a touch of humor into the nickname while reaching to rest his hands on her shoulders. "Do not pretend it doesn't hurt, and do not shut me out of your heart."

Those frightened eyes locked on his, and the armor faltered. Her chin wobbled, her lips pinching, though her eyes pleaded for the emotion to stop. Unable to stand it any longer, Ambrose pulled her into his arms, and the sobs tore out of her.

"Don't you see what a treasure you are?" he whispered into her ear. "I never thought I would find someone with whom I would want to spend my life. I could never imagine prostrating myself so, and then you appeared, and I would do anything for you. You make me so happy. So complete."

Miss Hayward burrowed into his hold, her body shuddering under her tears.

"Don't you see that we are two of a kind? A matching set. Your kind heart is protected by those prickles of yours and mine by the careless gentleman of leisure. But I see past your mask and you past mine."

One of her arms wrapped around his middle, clutching him to her.

"Do you know that I spent a good thirty minutes choosing a carriage?" he asked. "When you and Dottie were stranded at that inn, I rushed to Mina's to get us a vehicle, and I spent half an hour agonizing over which one was the right one to guarantee you a safe and comfortable journey. No one needs me—not even my family—and for the first time, I had someone depending on me. You gave me something to care about."

"But you just want a mother for Dottie," she blubbered, the words coming out in a near incomprehensible string of syllables.

At that, Ambrose laughed—a good, long laugh that warmed him almost as much as having his Mary wrapped in his arms. "My dear Miss Hayward, if I was simply looking for a lady to fill that role, I assure you that there are plenty of suitable ladies who would cause far less of a fuss. It is you who makes me care about the world. You inspire me to do more with my life than waste it away in nothingness."

Miss Hayward's cries softened as she listened to that, and Ambrose pulled away in order to look her in the eyes.

"I do not want just anyone," he whispered. "I want you, and I will wait as long as it takes for you to believe that I am in earnest. I will not give up."

Her eyes were wide and startled, but Ambrose saw a growing hope there, too. It was as though her soul mirrored his completely, fearing so much because there was so much to lose. Too much of her heart was at risk because it was his already, as his was hers. Seeing that, Ambrose knew there was no hurdle too great to stop him from binding his life to hers.

And there it was.

Ambrose nearly missed it, but he had far too much experience with such looks to mistake it. Miss Hayward—his dear Mary—wanted to kiss him. Though he wished he could approach this sweet lady unsullied by a past of careless affection, he was grateful for the ability he had gained to read such situations.

Leaning in, Ambrose moved carefully. Tentatively. Never before had he felt nervous over a kiss, but this was no meaningless thing and the lady in his arms meant more to him than all those other moments combined. Miss Hayward's eyes widened, but she did not back away. She did not move. Did not breathe. Simply watched him with a mixture of apprehension and anticipation. It was there in her eyes—that tugging between her fears and hopes—and Ambrose's heart reached out to hers, hoping that somehow he could make her see how magnificent she was.

Their lips brushed together, a faint graze that set his pulse racing. It was barely a touch, but the power of it threatened to undo him. And it wasn't enough.

Pulling her flush against him, Ambrose kissed her, pouring the feelings he couldn't express into it. The book in her arm poked them, but Ambrose hardly noticed under the flood of emotion roused by this dear lady. It was more than he had ever thought possible for one heart to feel.

This was the woman he loved.

As loath as he was to end it, Ambrose knew it was best, although he had some difficulty getting his head to respond. But as gently as they began it, the kiss ended, though Ambrose would not release her from his hold. She stared at him with a dazed expression that was both disappointing and adorable. It was not the exact expression a gentleman wished to see after having given such a kiss, but as he felt quite befuddled himself, Ambrose took it as a good sign.

"But I am just a 'chum,'" she murmured.

Leaning in until their lips were nearly touching again, he whispered, "I assure you that I have had many chums in my life, and I have never done that to a single one of them."

And to prove his point, Ambrose kissed her once more.

Mary had thought she knew what it felt like to be kissed, but that bit of bored affection Henry had bestowed on her was nothing compared to even the slightest touch from Mr. Ashbrook. Ambrose. There was no polite Mr. or Miss at present. It was Mary and Ambrose bound together in a moment that both soothed and startled her. It filled her heart, sweeping through her and bringing new tears to her eyes, but they held no sorrow. Mary never knew she could feel so happy and so cherished. Or love so deeply.

Her heart pounded, and her hands shook as she clung to him. All too soon, it was over, leaving Mary's thoughts delightfully muddled.

Pulling away, Ambrose looked at her and gave her a wry grin. "It appears that kissing you is the only appropriate recourse when you speak such nonsense."

"Mary!" came her mother's voice in the distance.

Mary jumped, nearly tripping over Ambrose as they pulled apart. She patted at her hair and cheeks, brushing a quick touch to her lips.

"I fear I have lost track of the time," she said, clutching her book to her chest.

"I do have that effect," he said with a chuckle.

Mary scowled at the gentleman, but it was no more serious than his comment had been. Though others might think it his usual mindless banter, Mary knew it was not. She could not quantify the difference, but she felt it in her heart. This was the teasing Ambrose she adored, not the flippant libertine she despised.

She pictured pulling Ambrose into another embrace, but she fought back the impulse and the accompanying blush. "I must go."

Mary stepped away, though she felt she must say something more. With her mama calling after her, there was little time to waste, but Mary looked into Ambrose's handsome eyes and asked, "You will come tonight?"

"Nothing could keep me from it." His smile softened, filling with such tenderness that Mary could hardly breathe. All her life, she had hoped for such a look from such a man, and seeing it there brought another mist of tears to her eyes. Reaching for her hand, Ambrose lifted it to his lips, holding her gaze as he pressed a kiss to it.

"I know what it is like to live a life of doubts and fears," he whispered to her. "But never doubt that you are my heart."

Mama's call was more insistent, but Mary didn't want to leave, for some part of her worried that she would never have another moment like this again. However, her world was demanding that she return to it.

Mary gripped the book, taking a few steps away, and he gave her another of those smiles that warmed her through like a blazing fire on a winter's day, and Mary knew she could not leave things as they stood. He had just given her so much, and she needed to do something to show how much it meant to her. Ignoring rational thought and those warning voices in her head, Mary leapt forward and pressed a kiss to his cheek.

"And you are my heart," she whispered. It was a small act and five simple words, but the joy shining in Ambrose's eyes gave a lightness to her steps as she hurried home.

Chapter 25

Gloves were abominable, and elbow length gloves were the absolute worst. Having attended so few gatherings where such monstrosities were required, Mary had never grown accustomed to wearing them, but Mama had required them every night since their guests had arrived. Tugging at the tops, Mary straightened them. Again. The silly things never liked to stay up as they should, no matter what she did.

Glancing down at her skirt, she wondered if she had picked the right dress. Mary had few gowns to choose from, and this new addition to her wardrobe had seemed the logical choice. But the teal had looked so much better in the shop. Perhaps it did not complement her complexion as well as she thought. Mary tried not to fidget, but the bodice did not lay right, and the sleeves were too big. Even with some quick alterations, the readymade dress did not fit properly—yet still, it was the nicest gown she had and the only option for tonight.

"Whatever is the matter?" asked Lydia, coming to Mary's corner of the parlor and taking her sister's arm. "You look positively faint."

"It has been a busy day," she replied. Far more than she was willing to admit, even to her sister.

"Did something happen with Mr. Ashbrook?" asked Lydia.

Mary blushed, fighting to keep what little composure she had.

"Was he rude to you?" she asked. "If he was, we shan't have him for dinner, even if Sir Duncan wishes it."

Mary stifled a laugh at her sister's naive statement. What had happened with Mr. Ashbrook had been the farthest thing from rude, and even if it had, there was no amount of bad behavior that would induce the Haywards to contradict Sir Duncan's whims.

"Mr. and Mrs. Henry Cavendish," announced Gibbs.

Together, the couple entered, arms joined together with Bess's hand resting on the swell that held their unborn child. As the Cavendishes were good friends of the Haywards, both Henry and his parents had been the first guests on Mama's list for this impromptu dinner party. But Mary felt nothing at their inclusion. No twinge of jealousy or bitterness. No pain or anguish. They were simply friends of her parents and nothing more. Her heart had no room for those old hurts when it was so full of Mr. Ashbrook.

Of course, thinking such a thing made Mary panic once more. There had been declarations, but nothing explicitly said about marriage. Or had there? In truth, Mary could not recall what had been spoken rather than implied, and it felt too presumptuous to assume Mr. Ashbrook intended to offer for her at this juncture. They were courting, but that did not guarantee a wedding.

Mary's thoughts paused as she reflected on that. Mr. Ashbrook was courting her. Her lips twitched, and she bit down to keep from beaming like a fool. They were courting. She tried to school her features, but that grin kept breaking through.

With her mind so tangled up in her own thoughts, she hardly noticed when Lydia dragged her away from her quiet corner to join the others.

"We are so pleased you came tonight," Lydia said to the Cavendishes. Drawing up beside Sir Duncan, Lydia took his arm and, with her free hand, began petting it as though it were her beloved puppy, Pepper. "I've been desperate to introduce my dear Sir Duncan to the neighborhood."

Mary ignored their prattling, turning her attention to Gibbs as he entered to make another announcement. But it was only the elder Cavendishes. Mary stifled a disappointed sigh.

"Lydia, you must come and hear what Lady Whiting was saying about the Worleys' ball," said Mama, and Lydia was dutifully escorted by her fiancé to that circle, leaving Mary with Henry and Bess.

Both husband and wife fidgeted at the uncomfortable silence that followed, and Mary simply watched them. Another first for her, for she did not feel an ounce of discomfort—though she felt no inclination to speak, either.

Gibbs entered again but brought only Mr. and Mrs. Baxter, who were yet another couple that Mary had no interest in speaking with. Mama greeted her friend as though they had not seen each other in many years rather than a few days. After all, Mama's first order of business upon returning home had been to visit the lady and tell her all about the engagement.

And then Gibbs announced precisely what Mary had been waiting for.

"Mr. Ambrose Ashbrook." Gibbs said it with that proper butler air, but there was a smile in his eyes as he glanced at Mary.

Mr. Ashbrook gave the appropriate greetings to his hosts and the guests of honor before moving to Mary. The way his eyes followed her as he wove through the guests quickened her heartbeat, and Mary marveled over what she had done to deserve such adoration. And that made her think of the intimate moment they had shared together, which brought a blush to her cheeks.

The others milled about, none-the-wiser about their secret kisses, and Mary fought to keep her composure, though the heat filling her face would likely give her away if anyone bothered to notice. Mr. Ashbrook did and gave her a look that said he knew where her thoughts lay. Which only made the situation worse. Especially when he gave her a satisfied smirk and wink.

"Mary, are you quite all right?" asked Bess, and Mary's expression fell at the sight of the Cavendishes staring at her as though she were a raving Bedlamite.

"Quite fine," said Mary. Better than they knew, in fact.

Mr. Ashbrook came up beside her, and he gave her another look, this one expressing true concern, and she returned it with a look of her own that she hoped would appease him. To her astonishment, it did. The whole exchange was wordless and took mere seconds, and yet they had communicated far more than she had to any other person in the room. Looking into his eyes, Mary wondered why she had been fighting this wonderful man who understood her far better than those closest to her.

His expression softened, and peace swept over her. Mary did not doubt. She did not question. She simply knew. This was the man she was meant to marry. With their audience, Mary could not give in to the joy that overwhelmed her, which made her want to throw herself into Ambrose's arms and blubber like a ninny for the second time that day.

No matter how much she wanted to.

"Mr. Ashbrook," said Bess, dragging Mary into the conversation. "I do not believe we were ever formally introduced."

Following the prompt, Mary made the introductions, but as the gentlemen shook hands Henry burst out with, "Addled Ambrose? Is that you? It must be!"

To all appearances, Ambrose looked as relaxed as ever, but Mary felt the shift inside him. A subtle change in the air that caught Mary's breath.

Henry grinned as if the two of them were the best of friends and turned to his wife. "We went to school together in Kent. I never had the luck of knowing him personally, but Addled Ambrose was a legend among the lads. Is it true that you ran a gambling hall out of Old Grump's private parlor?"

"I fear that is an exaggeration," said Ambrose, his smile as easy as ever, though it was that false one Mary detested, and she did not bother hiding her feelings as she glowered at Henry. Though she did not know the whole of the history, only a fool would think that such a horrible moniker was acceptable.

Henry groaned as though Ambrose had delivered a killing blow. "That is devastating, for I loved the idea that you'd gotten one over on Old Grump." He turned to Bess and said, "Addled Ambrose might have been an absolute nightmare in the classroom, but he could win the shirt off any boy at school. He had the ability to read the cards so well that it bordered on the clairvoyant."

"Dear—" Bess whispered a warning to her husband, but the man would not listen.

"They claimed you never lost a hand," said Henry, knocking Ambrose on the arm. "Please tell me *that* is true."

Ambrose's smile widened into that terrible approximation of joy he used to put people at a distance, and Mary drew her arm through his, not caring if anyone thought her overly familiar with him. Their opinions were of no consequence, for she felt his strain ease at her touch.

"I have lost a few hands over the years, but I've never lost more than I earned," said Ambrose.

"Incredible luck," said Henry, gaping at the other as though he were a great hero of legend.

"Any good gambler will tell you that luck has little to do with it," said Ambrose, his smile turning more rakish than usual. "It is about reading your opponent rather than the cards in your hand—though good ones do help."

And so the conversation continued, and Mary marveled at Ambrose's performance as the pair chatted and laughed like the oldest of friends.

"I hear you make quite a killing at the tables," said Henry. "Quite lucky for you to have found such a vocation. Proved Headmaster wrong, didn't you? What did he always say?" Henry turned to Bess again. "He had some hilarious thing he used to say about our Addled Ambrose..."

This time, Mary held on to Ambrose for the sheer sake of keeping herself from slapping Henry across the face.

"Something about rocks in his head..." mumbled Henry with a furrowed brow.

Mary shot her eyes to Gibbs, giving him the signal to announce dinner. It was a full fifteen minutes too early, but she hoped Mrs. Webb and Mrs. Gibbs would forgive her impertinence. To say nothing of Mama, who was glowering at her like a fiend when Gibbs called them into the dining room. Yes, they may be missing one of their dinner guests, but Mr. Josiah Smollet was renowned for arriving late to such gatherings and had only been invited to even out the numbers. The old bachelor cared only about a decent meal, and Mary would ensure he got plenty when he arrived.

Mary clung to Ambrose's arm but found his public face still firmly affixed. "That was awful. I am so terribly sorry."

The mask slipped, showing the hurt beneath it as he asked, "Sorry that you are being courted by such a dunce?"

"I have never once thought you anything other than intelligent."

The doubt plaguing his eyes pained Mary as he asked, "Truly?"

"Not once," she said, squeezing his arm, and then added for good measure in a tone of utter sincerity, "Unctuous, yes. Nauseating, certainly. Irritating, vain..."

She was rewarded with a chuckle as they followed the others into the dining room.

"An absolute treasure," he whispered into her ear.

Chapter 26

Mary's company was the only enjoyable thing about this interminable evening, and being stuck with the gentlemen for the requisite drinks after the meal was testing the limits of Ambrose's patience. But it was the price to be paid if he wished to regain her company. That reward was the only reason he did not beg off and leave Buckthorn Manor posthaste.

Sir Duncan was the epitome of pomposity. Being a baronet gave him only a slightly elevated station from the rest of the gentry of the room, but he had the condescending swagger of a duke. Though he did hold the distinction of being less exasperating than Mr. Baxter, who spoke every word with a definitive tone that brooked no opposition, though he had not the intelligence to support it.

Mr. Hayward was a boring, bland sort of fellow. The type that left little impression and was forgotten once he was out of sight. Mostly harmless, but his obsequious manner towards Sir Duncan was nauseating.

Mr. Henry Cavendish was an unremarkable gent, quite like many of the lads at school who had much to say but little to contribute and a conceitedness that made Ambrose feel for the gentleman's wife. It was an attitude the gentleman had clearly inherited from his father.

The final guest was a mystery, for he had arrived late and spent the entire meal scoffing the food with great vigor and concentration, and was now nodding off at the far end of the table.

Ambrose could only hope that they would join the ladies soon, and then he would spend the rest of the evening beside his Mary. No matter how torturous the entertainment and irritating the rest of the company, she would make it a delight.

Having no desire to converse with these gentlemen, Ambrose was left to his own contemplations, and he was grateful for it. Mina and Simon had accosted him once he had arrived home and not allowed him a moment's peace until it was time to dress for dinner. If he wasn't so elated by the turn of events, Simon's incessant crowing over the success of his advice would have been quite irritating. And Mina had begun planning the wedding, ignoring the fact that such things should be left to Mary and that the all-important question had been neither asked nor answered.

Would Mary accept?

Ambrose wanted it all arranged quickly. This very moment, if possible. But he would not rush her. Patience was needed.

That final kiss. Her whispered words. They had been simple. Timid. Yet they meant more than any number of passionate embraces and poetic confessions because they had come from that shy soul. His dearest Mary had opened her heart to him. How long it would take to capture it completely was a mystery, but Ambrose knew it would happen.

Casting his gaze to Mr. Hayward, Ambrose wondered if he should approach her father about an official courtship. Mary was of age, so it was not strictly necessary, but it felt like the honorable thing to do. However, some niggling instinct warned him not to, so he kept his own counsel at present. There was no reason he could not wait until the wedding contracts were ready to be negotiated.

Just the thought of that made Ambrose smile. Wedding

contracts. Marriage. Family. How far his thoughts and concerns had altered from the night when that sweet little girl was dropped on his doorstep. A family of his own.

"Horses, people, it is the same," said Mr. Baxter. "Good bloodlines, good stock."

Ambrose held in a sneer. He had heard plenty of gentlemen wax poetic about such things, speaking of wives and children as if they were nothing more than chattel to be bred, raised, and sold off at a profit. Dottie's or Mary's bloodlines were a mystery, and good or bad, it made no difference to Ambrose. But once more, he held his own counsel. Such conversations from such men were meant to be undisputed lectures and not debates.

"Too true," said Mr. Hayward.

Ambrose tried to ignore the conversation, but it continued down a path too arresting to ignore.

"Precisely. Look at the nobility," said Sir Duncan. "At my family, for instance."

The devil inside Ambrose wished to pipe up and clarify that assertion. Sir Duncan had not directly claimed his family was nobility, but he heavily implied a connection when there was none. But Ambrose contented himself with a private chuckle.

"Good blood always wins out," said Mr. Baxter with a nod.

Sir Duncan shook his head. "No, bloodlines must be nurtured. A prime stallion can have a worthless foal if bred with the wrong mare. Too many fellows are lured into inferior marriages because of a hefty dowry, but they are doing a disservice to themselves and the future generations. Having a wife of inferior birth pollutes the bloodline, and it is our duty to enhance it." Sir Duncan tossed back another glass of port. "You pair the best mares with the best stallions and end up with superior foals. That is why I picked Miss Lydia. She is a lovely girl, just like her mother, and our children will be lovely, too."

Ambrose barely contained his laugh at that. Sir Duncan was presuming that his children would take solely after Lydia, who was a fine creature, but Ambrose had strong doubts that anything pretty could spring from Sir Duncan's lineage.

"Of course, I was a bit startled when I saw your eldest," said Sir Duncan, "but there can be aberrations in any bloodline. Nothing to be worried about. Miss Lydia is quite the prettiest girl that's been on the market for years, and she is well worth the risk."

And with that, any humor Ambrose felt at this absurd conversation was gone. He started to reply, but Mr. Hayward spoke first.

"Our Mary is a wonderful young lady," said Mr. Hayward. "She may not have her sister's looks, but she makes up for it abundantly. A good, steady girl who is a blessing to my wife and me. Most especially as we grow older."

The beginning of his speech had lifted Ambrose's spirits to hear, but the sentiment soured quickly. "What do you mean by that?"

Mr. Hayward blinked at Ambrose, swirling his brandy with a frown. "Every parent should have a child like Mary. Someone to stay at home and take care of us as we get older. Of course, that is a long way off, but it is wise to plan for the future."

"Yes," said the elder Mr. Cavendish. "My wife was saying so the other day. It is quite a nice arrangement for all three of you. After all, Mary will never leave you."

"And why is that?" Ambrose asked, his voice rising.

Mr. Hayward blinked once more at him. "I love my Mary as much as any father, but I cannot deny that she is plain. She has a good heart, but the best she can hope for is to marry an older widower who wants a mother for his children. And that is no life for her. She deserves better than being a drudge in a loveless home."

The hypocrisy in that statement was laughable, but Ambrose was far more fixated on the gentleman's low expectations for his daughter. He spoke as though it were fact, and the others nodded along. No wonder Mary thought it impossible for him to love her with such vitriol filling her head.

Ambrose jumped from his chair, setting his fists on the table, ready to give them the setdown they deserved when he recalled who he was speaking to: Mary's father and future brother-in-law. For all their faults, Mary loved her family, and as much as he wanted to let his temper fly, Ambrose knew it would hurt her.

"Might I be excused? I need some air," he said as he straightened, tugging at his jacket and cuffs.

Mr. Hayward waved him away, and Ambrose strode from the table. But before he reached Gibbs, who stood with the door open and ready, Mr. Henry Cavendish called after him. Ambrose closed his eyes, sighed, and donned his affable mask before turning to greet the gentleman.

"Mr. Ashbrook, a word, if you please," said Mr. Cavendish.

"As you like," he said, and the gentleman pulled him to the far corner of the dining room.

"I wish to apologize for earlier. My wife chided me about how uncouth some of my comments were earlier, and I hope I did not give offense."

That was a pleasant surprise and one that Ambrose welcomed after the last few minutes. "Think no more on it."

Mr. Cavendish smiled. "I knew it was of no consequence, but the ladies are overly sensitive to such things. It was nothing but a good-natured ribbing from our school days, yet she acted as though I had besmirched your character."

Ambrose fought to maintain his composure. That was not quite as nice as Mr. Cavendish's first statement, but Ambrose chose to focus on the better half of the conversation. "Of course."

He turned to leave, but Mr. Cavendish stopped him.

"I did wish to mention one other thing, Mr. Ashbrook."

"Certainly," he replied as amiably as ever, though Ambrose wished nothing more than to be free of this company.

"A bit of friendly advice, in fact," Mr. Cavendish said, examining his watch. Brushing his thumb across it, he returned it to his pocket. "I admire your defense of Miss Hayward, but you would do well to tread carefully around her, for she will misinterpret your overtures of friendship."

Having no idea where the conversation was headed, Ambrose remained silent and waited for it to come to its natural conclusion. Perhaps then he could sneak away to join Mary and be rid of these detestable men.

Swinging his hands around to grip them behind his back, Mr. Cavendish continued. "She has little experience with affable gentlemen and confuses camaraderie for affection. She made that mistake with me when we were younger, and it has led to some very unpleasant scenes. Both my wife and I have been made to feel her wrath over her presumption, and I would hate for you to suffer a similar fate. Miss Hayward can be quite the beast when she believes herself jilted."

Heart thumping in his ears, Ambrose stared at Henry Cavendish's smug expression. This was the selfish lout who had crushed Mary's heart. Perhaps he should have realized it sooner. Mary had likely said the fellow's name at some point during her narrative, but she had seemed so at ease around Cavendish that Ambrose had never thought to connect him to that villain.

Ambrose could only gape at the man, to which Cavendish laughed.

"I know! Quite shocking, isn't it?" he said, slapping Ambrose on the shoulder. "As if I would choose her over Bess. But Miss Hayward got it in her head that I was in love with her. Practically threw herself at me—"

Ambrose's fist flew faster than thought, connecting with Cavendish's nose a scant second before Ambrose realized what he was doing. The bone crunched under his knuckles, blood spurting from the wound. Cavendish fell backward, but Ambrose was not finished. Hauling him up, Ambrose threw another punch at the man's jaw, and then the fight truly began. Ducking that blow, Cavendish launched himself at Ambrose.

The fellow had the physique of a boxer, and his blows were powerful, but he stood no chance against Ambrose. Having been schooled by his sailor brother and tested in gaming clubs of London, Ambrose was the more skilled of the two. And he fought dirty.

Hands grabbed him from behind, but Ambrose threw them off. He was not done with his prey. This fiend had hurt Mary for his own pleasure. Abused her trust and affection. One did not toy with sweet, innocent girls. One did not raise their hopes and break their hearts. Cavendish deserved to pay for the liberties he had taken.

Ambrose got in a few more licks before he was hauled off. The fellow lay crumpled and whimpering on the floor, his face looking like a rotting plum. Kicking, Ambrose took one parting shot before he was dragged from the room.

"Get out of my house!" bellowed Mr. Hayward as the men at Ambrose's back hauled him to the front entrance.

The ladies were gathered in the hallway, all fluttering and gasping. Mary's eyes were wide and her face pale. She stepped towards Ambrose, but the older Mrs. Cavendish screamed as she caught sight of the blood streaking the floor. Ambrose held Mary's startled gaze, calling out to her, but his handlers tossed him onto the front steps—the door slamming shut behind him.

Chapter 27

Mary's heart stopped at the sight of the blood soaking Ambrose's shirt. Ladies hemmed her in on every side, though she tried to push past them. Mrs. Cavendish screamed, and Mary scowled at the hysterics. Ambrose was hurt, and she needed to help him. His eyes were worried, and he mouthed her name, though she could not hear him in all the commotion.

"Ambrose!" Mary's voice was lost in the uproar. The grooms dragged him through the entry and tossed him from the house, barring the door behind him.

Bess stepped to the dining room doorway and screamed, which sent the ladies into a greater uproar. Mrs. Cavendish swooned, caught by one of the Whitings' servants, and Mama clutched her smelling salts; Mrs. Baxter held a handkerchief to her nose, averting her eyes from the scene. Shouldering past Lady Whiting, who merely looked put out by the whole display, Mary went to the dining room and found Bess crouched beside the bloodied mess that was her husband.

As much as Mary wanted to go to Ambrose, Henry clearly needed her more, so she sent Gibbs for rags and water and knelt beside the prone figure.

"What a disgrace!" Papa shouted.

"That madman attacked poor Mr. Cavendish without prov-ocation, and the pair went at it like savages. Nearly knocked me over," said Sir Duncan, dabbing at his temple with a handker-chief. "Never seen the like before. Mr. Ashbrook is an animal!"

But Mary knew Ambrose had been provoked. She hadn't wanted to leave with the ladies. Hadn't wanted Ambrose to face Henry's cruelty alone. But Mama's dictates had forced her hand, and this was the outcome. Even a patient man like Am-brose had limits, and Mary narrowed her eyes at Henry, want-ing to give him a good kick to the ribs.

"Gibbs," she said when he returned with the rags, "send a groom for Doctor Clarke."

"Such savage behavior, Mrs. Hayward," said Lady Whiting with a sniff as she stared through her lorgnette at Mama. "I know things are far more rough and tumble out here in the country, but one does not expect to be assaulted by such vulgar-ity at a dinner party."

"Sir Duncan, Lady Whiting, I am horrified over what hap-pened," said Mama. "Mr. Ashbrook is a brute and shall never gain admittance to our house again."

"I should think not," said Sir Duncan, his lips pinching to-gether. "We are lucky to be rid of that jackanapes."

"I refuse to be in the presence of that ill-mannered lout again," said Lady Whiting with a tone that was even more pointed than the look she gave the Haywards.

"Of course not," said Mama, and Papa quickly affirmed it.

"It is no wonder, though," said Mrs. Baxter in a hushed tone, though with enough volume that Mary was certain every-one in the room would hear. "The Kingsleys are a disgrace to the neighborhood. Horrid people. And they say that Mr. Ash-brook is keeping his by-blow at their house!"

The ladies gasped like proper fools, and Mary dabbed at Henry's face with far more force than intended, eliciting a groan from him. Bess yanked the rag from Mary and took over the ministrations.

"Dottie is not his by-blow," said Mary, unwilling to let such a rumor stand. "She is his ward—"

"Nonsense," said Mrs. Baxter. "I heard it from my house-keeper, who heard it from her friend who served as the nurse-maid to that sinful creature."

"She is not a sinful creature!" Mary shot to her feet, but Lady Whiting glared at her through her lorgnette.

"Keep a civil tongue, young lady," said the matron with such acid dripping from her words that it was a miracle she did not burn herself. "You know nothing of such matters."

"I'm afraid that the shock of this incident has overwrought my daughter's nerves," said Mama, grabbing her by the arm and leading her from the room. Mary tugged at her grip, but her mother would not release her until they stood in Mary's bed-chamber.

"I understand that what Mr. Ashbrook did was very upset-ting, but you must calm yourself, Mary. You should not speak to Mrs. Baxter and Lady Whiting so harshly!"

"Mama—" said Mary, but her mother hurried away.

Going to the window, Mary stared out at the night, wishing she could see if Ambrose was still there, but from her perch, she could see neither him nor the path to Avebury Park. Sitting on the sill, she worried for his safety and well-being, about whether this evening was enough to sour his feelings for her, how they would get her parents to soften towards him, and a world of other troubles weighing on her heart.

The stars blinked in the heavens above her, and Mary watched those flickering lights, hoping and praying that some-how all would be made right.

...

Fool, fool, fool! Ambrose stormed into Avebury Park, stomping up the stairs and to his bedchamber. One senseless act and he had ruined his standing with the Haywards. But it wasn't senseless. It was sensible. Honorable. Righteous. He'd had no choice but to put that snake in his place.

Slamming his bedchamber door, Ambrose paced the floor, his blood boiling in his veins.

That cad! A gentleman did not take such liberties with innocents like Mary. He had manipulated her and then laid the blame on her doorstep. The audacity! Henry Cavendish was lucky to have gotten away with only a few bruises and a broken nose. Ambrose's knuckles stung, but the pain added to his triumph. For good or ill, he had defended Mary's honor and exacted the retribution she so justly deserved.

And gotten himself barred from her house.

Groaning, Ambrose dropped onto his bed. Though her parents' feelings were of little consequence to him, they could turn her against him. He did not regret dealing the necessary justice, but he shouldn't have done so in such a thoughtless manner. With one foolhardy action, he had fallen from the Haywards' good graces and risked his future with Mary.

Ambrose groaned doubly when he heard the knock at his door and his sister's voice calling to him. As much as he wished to ignore her, Ambrose knew better than to try. With a grunt, he answered, and she entered.

"What is this racket? I was afraid you were going to throw the doors off their hinges—" Mina gasped, her eyes widening. Hurrying to his side, she fluttered over him, poking and prodding his injuries.

Ambrose looked down and noticed how bloodstained his clothes were. Knowing that it mostly belonged to his victim, Ambrose gave a self-satisfied smirk. "It isn't mine."

Mina touched his cheek, and he winced.

"Most of it isn't," he amended.

Calling to a footman, Mina sent for a myriad of supplies and then helped Ambrose out of his jacket. Turner appeared, assisting her as she fretted over her brother.

"I am not seriously injured," said Ambrose. "He did not get more than two hits before they threw me out."

"The Haywards? Whatever for?" she asked, pausing to stand before him.

"I pummeled that bounder, Henry Cavendish. In their dining room."

Mina placed her hands on her hips and stared at him.

"The why is not important," said Ambrose.

But Mina met that with a narrow gaze.

"He besmirched Miss Hayward's honor," he grumbled, looking away as his face heated. "And now, I'm barred from their house. What if she refuses to see me because of her family?" His voice faltered, and his head fell forward, his shoulders slumping.

Mina wrapped her arm around his shoulder. "We will make this right."

"How?"

"By cozying up to the Haywards," she said. "We are throwing a ball in a week and a half. I did not invite them because they were in London when the invitation went out, but I will personally deliver one tomorrow. And when they come, Simon and I will be excessively kind, generous, and ingratiating. We will soften their hearts through their vanity, and they will lap it up."

"They shan't accept," Ambrose mumbled.

Mina shook her head with a huff. "You, dear brother, underestimate how desperate the Haywards are to parade around their baronet. They will accept, and Simon and I will make certain they fall madly in love with their daughter's beau."

Ambrose raised his head enough to look at her. "You think it will work?"

"I will make certain of it," she said with a firm pat on his knee.

...

Mary's eyelids drooped as she stared out at the garden. Another restless night and exhausting day where she was torn between crippling fatigue and insomnia. Too worn to think but too brimming with emotions to rest. Curled up in her favorite armchair, Mary balanced her newest novel against her thighs. She had not the inclination nor strength to read, but Mary could not leave that precious present alone. Just holding it made Ambrose feel near.

Ambrose.

The name did not suit the gentleman for it was far too stodgy for such a lighthearted soul, but thinking of him in such intimate terms warmed her heart in a manner that she could not resist. Her Ambrose.

"You will never believe who came to call!" Mama rushed into the library, waving a square of paper in her hand. "Mrs. Simon Kingsley practically begged us to attend their ball next week. Delivered it herself! The Kingsleys act as though they don't care about social standing, but she is positively desperate for our Sir Duncan and Lady Whiting to attend."

Mary's eyes widened. "Then you accepted?"

Cocking her head to the side, Mama replied, "Her brother may be a crass oaf, but the Kingsleys are our closest neighbor and Bristow elite. It would not do to snub them. But we must stop wasting time. We need to leave for Madame Notley's at once."

"We are buying new gowns?"

"Of course, silly girl," said Mama, patting her on the cheek. "We must look our best."

And with that, Mama hurried off to fetch her things, leaving Mary quite stunned.

A ball with Ambrose. Would he ask her for two sets? Though she wanted more than that, two would push the boundaries of propriety. But either way, Mary would dance with a true partner. Someone who wished to dance with her and not the Hayward spinster. Never had a ball set Mary in such a dither, but this was unlike any other. She would dance with her love in a brand new gown. A dream would finally become reality.

But why was she sitting here, gathering wool? Getting to her feet, Mary hurried out the door but stopped at the sound of Gibbs calling for her.

"Mrs. Kingsley left this for you and instructed me to say that she is sorry to have missed you during her visit and that you are most especially requested to attend," he said, holding out another invitation.

The paper was finer than anything Mary had felt before. Thick and sturdy, yet soft as down with the most beautiful lettering. It was so fine that Mary was afraid to touch it.

Gibbs glanced around before stepping closer. "We all are praying for you and your fellow. He is a fine gentleman."

Mary smiled, the kindness in his expression and words bringing a prickle of tears to her eyes. "I think so, too."

Gibbs checked the hall once again and then spoke in a near whisper. "I don't think you know just how fine, miss. Those men were saying such awful things. That Sir Duncan..." Gibbs scowled, his expression as angry as Mary had ever seen it. "He's no gentleman, for one should not say such things about a lady, and you are a lady. The finest."

Mary tried to form words, but she merely blinked at him as he continued.

"And then that horrid Mr. Cavendish tried warning Mr. Ashbrook off you, insulting your honor, and your Mr. Ashbrook would have nothing of it. That's why the fight started. He was doing what I wished I could have done and gave that bounder the beating he deserved," said Gibbs. He patted her hand, his own eyes growing misty. "You are a gem, and he sees that, your Mr. Ashbrook. Don't let him go."

And with that, Gibbs tottered down the hall, leaving Mary speechless. Clutching her book and invitation, she walked to her bedchamber in a daze.

Lydia spoke up for her on occasion, but mostly, Mary was left to fight her battles alone. In her experience, no one cared enough to defend her.

But Ambrose had.

Mary had heard of heroes fighting for their heroines in countless books, but she had never expected to see it play out in her own life. It was humbling and touching. Not that she cared about the violence, but that for once, someone cared enough to feel angry on her behalf. Earlier in the evening, Ambrose had greeted Henry's callous words with an ambivalent smile, but a slight against her had driven him to pummel Henry.

Stepping into her bedchamber, Mary tucked the invitation between the pages of her book and placed it beside Ambrose's bouquet. The blossoms were already fading, but they were still lovely. Burying her nose into the petals, she took a deep breath of the sweet fragrance.

Turning to fetch her bonnet, Mary froze at the sight of another posy of peonies sitting on the outer windowsill. Shoving the window open, Mary scooped up the flowers and found a note lying beneath them.

"Please come."

It was only two words and the letters were shaky and poorly wrought, but it was clear that Ambrose had written it himself. Had willingly put his affliction on display so that he might reach out to her in the only manner at his disposal. The sentiment was far more touching than the plea itself, and Mary's eyes filled with tears, spilling uncontrollably down her cheeks as she saw the gentleman in question standing in the distance, watching her with that warm smile of his.

Chapter 28

Though some might laugh at its simple design, Mary adored her gown. Mama and Lydia had pointed her towards finer embellishments and more daring cuts, but Mary would not detract from the beauty of the silk with such unnecessary additions. Even Madame Notley said it was the finest fabric she had seen in many a year, and the color was the most charming shade of sky blue that brought a touch of the color to Mary's gray eyes. Her first silk gown.

Standing before her vanity, Mary examined it. The drape was exquisite, flattering her figure in a manner she'd not thought possible. It gave the illusion that somewhere in the swaths of fabric there were curves to her thin frame. Since the dress had arrived two days ago, Mary had spent an inordinate amount of time standing thusly, picturing her entrance into the Kingsleys' ballroom—and Ambrose's expression when he saw her in it.

But Mary sighed as her eyes were drawn to her face, and she wished something could be done to flatter her features as well.

Stepping to the growing garden on her vanity table, she chose a few of the best blossoms for her hair. Mary could never discover how or when Ambrose secreted them onto her windowsill, but without fail, a bouquet greeted her every evening.

Mary slid open the drawer and pulled out *Persuasion*. How she longed to lose herself in the story. She needed a distraction from the incessant stream of callers eager to worship at the altar of the Whitings. Mama continued to fill each minute of the day with entertainment, leaving Mary in a constant panic over the need to ready elaborate meals, card parties, outings, and tea services. The whole thing left Mary drained, bored, and desperate to be rid of it all. But no matter how she wished to escape into the novel, Mary could not bring herself to begin it without Ambrose. Only a few more hours and they would be together. Glimpses from afar were not enough.

Flipping through the pages of her book, she pulled out the invitation and his note. But the bedchamber door opened and Lydia strode inside, making Mary jump before she shoved her things out of sight.

"Can you believe that in just a short time I will be presented to all of Bristow as Sir Duncan's fiancée?" her sister asked with a smile before stopping to stare at the bouquets. "Good heavens, where did you get those flowers?"

"They are from a...friend."

Lydia's eyes widened, her mouth slowly gaping open. "A gentleman friend?" she asked in a near squeal.

Blushing, Mary hemmed. "Perhaps."

Coming to her sister, Lydia took her by the hands and led her to the bed. "Tell me all," she said, sitting atop the bedspread. Mary nearly joined her but stopped herself, for she could not stand the thought of wrinkling her gorgeous gown.

"You have been different since we arrived home, but that would make perfect sense if you had caught yourself a beau. Who is he?" asked Lydia.

Running her fingers against the silk skirt, Mary glanced at the flowers and wondered if she should say. Tempers had cooled since the incident. Perhaps it was time to admit the truth. But a cold shiver ran down her spine, warning her that they would not welcome her attachment after what had happened. So Mary hesitated.

"Fine, keep your secrets," said Lydia with a good-natured scowl. "Though I shall discover it when you dance with him tonight. But in the meantime, let me help you."

Dragging her sister over to stand before the vanity mirror, Lydia released Mary's bandeau and hairpins from her bun and let her hair cascade over her shoulders.

"You have such lovely hair," said Lydia, running her fingers through it.

Mary held back a snort and rolled her eyes at her sister in the glass.

"Do not give me such looks, Mary. You have beautiful hair, but you style it so poorly. It's soft with a delicate shine that would make many a lady envious."

Fingering the locks, Lydia gave her a look that made Mary quite nervous.

"Do you trust me?"

"That depends," said Mary.

"Your hair is too thick and heavy for the length," said Lydia. "With a little trim, it would be much more manageable."

"You wish to cut my hair?"

"I wish to make you as beautiful as I know you can be. With just a few changes, you will be radiant for your mysterious beau."

Mary stared at her sister, but Lydia matched it with a look of such pleading that Mary gave in.

"You will not be sorry, Mary!" she exclaimed, giving her sister a quick peck on the cheek before fetching the scissors.

Standing before the mirror, Mary looked at herself, wondering what the transformation would bring. Her mind ran wild with the possibilities, and a smile grew on her lips as she dreamed of how lovely she would look. Of standing before Ambrose as a new woman. Of the looks of admiration she would garner as he swept her onto the dancefloor. Mary could hardly wait.

...

Never had his jacket and cravat felt so tight and out of sorts. Ambrose shifted his shoulders, tugging at his cuffs and patting at his throat as his eyes remained fixed on the ballroom entrance. He was tired of creeping around the grounds of Buckthorn Manor to steal glimpses of Mary. He wanted to be with her. Talk with her. Hold her.

"Don't fret," whispered Mina between greeting guests. "They shall come, though they will wait until most have arrived so that everyone will see their grand entrance with the baronet."

Ambrose sighed and hoped she was right. Though Gibbs had been kind in his refusals, he continued to turn Ambrose away, and it was clear that the Haywards were not budging on his banishment.

Mina nudged him. In the few seconds his attention had drifted, Mr. and Mrs. Hayward had made their entrance, with Mrs. Hayward looking far too pleased with herself. Sir Duncan led Miss Lydia, and the girl walked with the stiff haughtiness befitting the future Lady Whiting. She was a copy of her fiancé's mother, who followed behind them with her nose aloft so that everyone knew how inconsequential they were to her; those who did not properly prostrate themselves were treated with a raised brow, a glare through her lorgnette, and a sniff.

"Insufferable peacocks," muttered Simon, though he maintained a brittle smile.

Ambrose's eyes remained locked on the entrance. His breath quickened as he stared at the empty doorway, willing Mary to materialize.

"Thank you for your invitation," said Mrs. Hayward with a curtsy to Mina and Simon. "You have quite outdone yourself with the decorations. It is lovely."

Ambrose's eyes darted between them and the entrance while Mina and her guests exchanged pleasantries.

"How unfortunate that Miss Hayward is not with you," said Mina.

Simon nodded. "We were quite looking forward to visiting with her."

"I am afraid that our eldest was not feeling well," said Mr. Hayward before Mrs. Hayward added, "A bit of a headache, the poor dear."

Miss Lydia's cheeks turned scarlet, and Ambrose wondered what had happened. But as much as he wished to prod them, there was work to be done; Mary may not be in attendance, but Ambrose could not waste an opportunity to charm her family.

"I do apologize for the unpleasantness the other night," he said, extending a hand to Sir Duncan, for though Mr. Hayward was the patriarch of his family, it was clear that Sir Duncan was the one to pacify. "I was quite disappointed that we did not get our card game, but I would love to play a few hands with you tonight. My sister has provided a card room for—"

But Ambrose's easy smiles and kind overtures were dismissed when Sir Duncan stepped away without even a glance in Ambrose's direction. The Kingsleys bristled at the blatant snub, but Ambrose simply watched in silence as Sir Duncan dragged Miss Lydia and the rest of his party away.

"They will never forgive me," said Ambrose, his expression falling as he watched them mingling among the throng.

"They just need time," said Simon. "Mr. Hayward is always saying how much he admires our horses. Perhaps we can ask him over for a ride and build from there."

"But why did she not show?" asked Ambrose. "She accepted my flowers. Surely, she would have given some sign if my attentions were unwelcome."

"Perhaps she needs more time," said Mina, squeezing Ambrose's hand.

"But what am I to do?" he asked. For all his experience charming women, Mary was a bizarre mystery he feared he was no closer to solving.

"The only thing you can do," said Simon. "Find her. With her family here, there is no one to bar you." He clapped Ambrose on the shoulder and shoved him towards the door. "Now, please excuse us, for those were the last of our guests to arrive, and the next set is starting. I want to dance with my wife."

"Talk to her, Ambrose," said Mina before her husband swept her away.

Chapter 29

Sitting beneath their oak tree, Mary watched the lights of Avebury Park and wondered if she had lost all sense. She was not one to allow her daydreams to run rampant. Mary Hayward was rational. Composed. The type of lady who was grateful to avoid the banality of society and spend a quiet night alone. Mary Hayward did not weep about missing a ball. Yet she had spent the past two hours doing just that.

Leaning forward, Mary rested her head against her knees, curling into herself. When the breezes stilled, she heard faint strains of music, and it filled her mind with pictures of what should have been. The dancers swirling around them as Ambrose led her through the steps. Her feet moving in time with the lively beats. The looks they would share. The charming things he would whisper to her. A magical night.

She should go home. There was no point in sitting here, torturing herself over what she had lost.

Something fell against the back of her neck, and Mary swatted at it without looking. Another struck, and Mary looked up to see Ambrose. For a brief moment, she reveled in the sight of him in his finery but then recalled why she was hiding.

"No," she groaned, covering her face.

"What is wrong?"

But Mary shook her head. She had no way to answer without showing him, and Mary could not do that.

"Why didn't you come?" The question was quiet, hardly more than a whisper, but Mary heard the disappointment and hurt, and she could not cling to her vanity any further. Lowering her hands, she looked up at him. She hoped for the darkness to cover her shame, but the moon was full and bright.

"What did you do to yourself?" he asked as he sat beside her.

"I wanted to look my best tonight," she said. Though she had thought her tears were spent, they returned in full force. Ambrose brought an arm around her shoulders, and Mary leaned into him as she blubbered.

"Lydia begged to cut my hair, so I let her. She started chopping but couldn't get it level. One side was always a good inch shorter than the other, but she kept trying, and then it started curling, making it even shorter and more uneven. It only got worse the more she tried." Mary struggled through the words. Yet again, she was being ridiculous. It was only hair, after all, but tears kept falling as she spoke.

"There was no saving it," she cried, tugging at the jagged edges running along her jaw. "I can't even gather it up to hide it. I don't know why I let her touch it. It is not as though she has cut hair before, but I wanted to look my best and never imagined it could end up this hideous."

Ambrose wrapped one of the errant curls around his finger with a smile. "I like your curls."

Mary gave a watery chuckle. "At least I had enough sense not to try her cure for freckles. She swears by it, but I'm sure it would have made me break out in hives."

"Don't you dare get rid of your freckles. I adore them."

Huffing, Mary leveled the look she often gave when he said such ridiculous things.

"I do, my dear Mary," he said, whispering her name with such feeling that her heart thumped at the sound. Taking her by the chin, Ambrose stared into her eyes, trapping her in his gaze. "Were you to shave your head, be covered in freckles, and have a bulbous nose like old Mr. Tryck, I would still think you the most beautiful creature I've ever seen."

Though part of her wanted to laugh at those ridiculous words, Mary couldn't mock the devotion that filled each syllable. His expression held such intense honesty that she wondered if he truly meant it, and if he did, how it was possible.

"You are kind," she said, "but I am no beauty."

"You are to me." And with that, he pressed his lips to hers. It was tender and sweet. A simple thing done with a reverence that made tears trickle down her cheeks as they then leaned back against the tree to look out at Avebury Park. The moon was as bright as Mary had ever seen, casting the darkened landscape in a magical glow.

"I wanted to dance with you," he murmured, entwining their arms so that he could take hold of her hand as Mary rested her head against his shoulder.

"And I with you, but it's probably for the best that we didn't. I am a terrible dancer."

"Perhaps you need the right partner."

"Perhaps, but we would not be allowed such..." Mary paused for effect, mimicking Ambrose's wicked tone, "...close proximity in that ballroom, and I find I would rather spend my evening like this."

His shoulders jostled her as he let out a rumbling chuckle, but then he shifted, and Mary raised her head to peer at him. Mrs. Gibbs had said that no one could make her see her own value, but when Ambrose looked at her in that way, it made it far easier to believe it.

"How would you like to spend every evening like this?" he asked.

Stilling, Mary stared at him. There was so much implied in that question that her thoughts ran wild with speculation.

Reaching up to play with another of her curly locks, Ambrose rephrased his question. "Perhaps I should make that clearer. Will you marry me?"

Mary blinked. Though she'd been hoping for him to ask that all-important question, it did not diminish the surprise she felt at its sudden appearance. Mary knew her answer—had no doubts as to what it should be—but she was overcome by the sheer delight that came with hearing those words.

Though Mary wanted to make some grand, eloquent declaration, her heart was too full to speak. More tears filled her eyes as she nodded, managing to whisper a single, "Yes."

"That is all? A simple yes?" he asked, staring at her. "No argument? No denials? I was certain you would run away screaming."

Swallowing back the lump in her throat, Mary fought to say what needed to be said and free the truths that she had yet to utter. "I cannot pretend that I understand why you love me, but I am done doubting it. I love you, Ambrose Ashbrook, and I want to spend the rest of my life by your side."

His smiled warmed her through, and she kissed him. There were more hurdles to overcome, but for a few precious minutes, the world around them faded. It was just the two of them sealed together as her heart swelled from the love she found in Ambrose's embrace. Mary had imagined just such a moment many times, but none of her silly schoolgirl fantasies compared to this. There was no greater perfection to be found, and Mary would not trade this tender moment for anything.

Every lady should get engaged under a full moon.

...

Giddy was an odd word, one that Mary had never cared for. It was juvenile and silly, and she would scowl when ladies described their feelings as such. But now, Mary was decidedly giddy, and she embraced that glee coursing through her.

Ambrose held her by the hand as they stood in the Kingsleys' library. It was one of the few vacant rooms in the house, far from prying ears, and would serve their purpose to perfection.

"Are you certain about this?" he asked, pulling her into his arms once more.

As much as Mary wanted to melt into his embrace and forget about everything else, there was something far more important that needed doing. "This is our best chance."

Ambrose sighed and released her. "I know, but I fear your parents will not accept me, no matter how we stage it."

Taking his hand in hers, Mary looked into his eyes. "Sir Duncan is the issue, and tonight is the only feasible time to separate my parents from him and speak privately. With your sister's ball in full sway, Sir Duncan and Lady Whiting are either dancing or being inundated by the guests. I doubt we'll find another opportunity until after Lydia's wedding. And I don't want to wait."

His expression shifted, that delightful smile of his softening into what Mary thought of as her own personal smile. As free as he was with them, that particular one was only ever given to her. It belonged to her alone and set her heart aflutter.

"My treasure," he whispered before placing a quick kiss on her cheek. "Mina and Simon are with us. When they bring your parents, they will do what they can to help—"

But he paused when they heard her parents' voices from just outside the door.

"That was quick," said Mary.

Ambrose chuckled. "I fear my sister is desperate to get us properly bound before you have a chance to come to your senses."

Taking his arm, Mary whispered, "Never."

"What can you possibly have to tell us in private?" grumbled her papa as the library door opened.

Mary squeezed Ambrose's arm and offered a silent prayer, hoping things would be made right.

"What are you doing here?" asked Mama as she laid eyes on Mary. "I thought you were home with a headache."

"And what are you doing with that scoundrel?" added Papa with a scowl.

Simon motioned for her parents to step inside, while Mina attempted to calm them. Ambrose met Mary's gaze, asking one final time if she was certain. She stepped closer, turning them towards her parents as a united front.

"Mr. and Mrs. Hayward," said Ambrose, "Mary and I would like to speak with you—"

"How dare you take such liberties with my daughter!" said Mr. Hayward, his face growing red. "She is Miss Hayward—"

"Papa, please, calm yourself."

"Calm nothing!" he barked. "We came to this ball out of respect for Mr. and Mrs. Kingsley, but we will not be subjected to this blackguard's behavior."

"Papa!"

"Mr. Hayward, please," said Simon. "I am very sorry to know that you have such a poor opinion of my brother-in-law, but please hear him out."

"Yes," said Mina, coming to Mama's side to usher her to the sofa. But her mother would have none of it.

"I asked your daughter to marry me," said Ambrose.

At that, both Mama and Papa stilled, frozen in place as they gaped at the pair of them. Mary held her breath, clinging to Ambrose's arm as she watched their faces grow ashen.

"She has accepted, and we hope to have your blessing."

Papa drew himself up, stalking towards Mary with a fierce countenance that had her quaking. Never had she seen him in such a temper, and for a brief, terrible second, she thought he might actually strike her. But then Ambrose rested his hand on hers, and peace wrapped around her heart. She was not alone. And this was the right decision.

"Have you lost your senses?" asked Papa, his voice a low growl. His eyes bore into Mary, but she refused to be cowed. "You would engage yourself to a rascal? A libertine who nearly killed a good friend of ours during a dinner party?"

Mary had held her composure up to this moment, but that

nonsense broke her self-control. "Do not speak of him so! I will not have it!"

"How dare you speak to your papa like that," said Mama, coming around to Mary's other side. Pulling Mary's free hand into hers, she leaned close and whispered, "How can you defend him? He has the morals of a dog, keeping his by-blow under this very roof. It's disgraceful. Do you honestly want to raise his ill-begotten child?"

"I will not stand here and listen to you besmirch his character. Ambrose is honorable and good. The very best of men." Mary's throat grew tight, but she pushed through to speak the necessary words. "He is everything I could wish for in a husband, and far better than I had ever hoped to find. Without a thought, he took in that poor abandoned babe, and it will be an honor to spend my life as his wife and her mother."

At that, Mary realized Dottie's future had never been explicitly decided. Turning her eyes to Ambrose, she asked, "We are keeping her, aren't we?"

Had they been alone, Ambrose would have taken that good lady into his embrace and shown her how much her words meant to him. If he'd had any doubts before—which he did not—they would have disintegrated beneath Mary's fire. She thought herself so far below him, but Ambrose was awed and humbled to witness her impassioned defense of his honor. It was not the brutal altercation he'd had with Cavendish, but it was a fight all its own, and Mary showed unflinching courage as her parents railed against her and her choice.

And then for her to turn and ask that question with her heart in her eyes made the whole moment all the more perfect. He could never be worthy of such a lady.

"Of course," he whispered, for that was all he could manage. Mary's face lit up. Pure beauty shone through her, and he wondered how she couldn't see how lovely she was.

"Can we please sit down and discuss this before this gets

out of hand?" asked Simon.

"Yes, let me order some refreshment," added Mina.

But as Ambrose turned his attention to his sister and her husband, several things happened in rapid succession. Mrs. Hayward stepped around her daughter, wedging herself between Mary and Ambrose. Having to choose between stepping on Mary's mama and stepping away, he chose the latter, and Mr. Hayward lunged forward, yanking at his daughter. Unwilling to hurt her, Ambrose released his hold on her, and the Haywards had Mary encircled, dragging her away.

"Let go of me!" Mary pulled against their grip, but they marched to the door.

"Mr. and Mrs. Hayward, please!" said Mina, reaching for Mrs. Hayward. "I know this is shocking, but hear us out."

Mrs. Hayward sneered at Mina, shrugging her off.

"Mary!" Ambrose moved to follow, but Simon stepped in his path, putting a hand on his chest.

"It's best to leave things be for now," he said. Ambrose stepped around him, but Simon merely moved to block his path once more.

"Out of my way!"

"Tempers are high at present," said Simon, his eyes pleading with Ambrose to listen. "Pushing things will only cause more damage. Give it time."

"But..." The advice was sound but broke Ambrose's heart.

"I know," said Simon with a sad nod as Mina joined them, sliding her arm around Ambrose's shoulders. "But we will find a way."

As her parents led her along, Mary watched him, lifting a silent hand in farewell. Seeing the determination in her eyes was the only thing that kept him calm. Though fears plagued him, Ambrose knew the only recourse was to trust her. Mary was not giving up on him or their future. She loved him, and this was not the end.

Chapter 30

No one spoke once they left the library. Having left their carriage for Lydia and the Whitings, Mary and her parents made the trek from Avebury Park with nothing but the night wind rustling through the leaves to break the silence. The cool breeze felt wonderful against Mary's flushed skin, helping to cool her temper.

They arrived at Buckthorn, and Gibbs relieved them of their outerwear, though still, no one spoke. The butler watched Mary with worried eyes, and she tried to comfort him, but she had little to offer. Mama and Papa shared a look through which Mary knew they were deciding the next phase of attack, and she awaited the verdict. And then Papa left, calling for a bottle of brandy to be brought to his study. Mama moved to the stairs with a look that brooked no refusal, so Mary followed.

They made their way to Mary's bedchamber, and Mama shut the door, keeping her back to her daughter. For several long moments, she stood that way with Mary watching from her bed.

Patience. That was all Mary needed. Obviously, her parents were in no state to accept Ambrose now, but they would in time.

Once Lydia was well and truly married, her future would be irrevocably secure, and there could be no further objection. Sir Duncan and his bride would return to his estate, and she and Ambrose would be free to work on her parents. Ambrose had charm to spare. He would change their minds. As much as Mary wanted her future settled now, a few weeks were nothing if it meant a future with Ambrose.

"Why are you so determined to hurt us?" The question came so softly that Mary nearly missed it.

"Don't be silly, Mama."

"Silly?" She turned and glared at Mary. "You would marry a libertine, thus ruining Lydia's reputation and marriage, and I am being silly?"

"He is not a libertine!"

Mama held up a staying hand and sighed. "Mr. Ashbrook is unacceptable, Mary. You must see that. The man is a savage."

Mary got to her feet, brushing her skirts to calm her shaking hands. "I shan't sit and listen to you speak of him so. You do not know him so you cannot judge him."

"Dearest, please." Mama sighed again. "I do not wish to fight. There have been enough angry words tonight. Come, sit with me a moment."

Mother and daughter sat side-by-side on the bed, and she took Mary's hand in hers. "Darling, your father and I cannot approve of your choice. Do you know what that might do to Lydia's future? What Mr. Ashbrook's reputation would do to her?"

"Mama," she said with a huff. "The wedding contracts are signed and the plans are underway. Do you think Sir Duncan would damage his reputation by crying off at this juncture simply because he does not care for his future brother-in-law? He hardly notices me, and I doubt he would care about the gentleman I marry."

"Do you not see how precarious our situation is, Mary?" Mama looked positively startled at the words, as though saying them aloud gave them greater strength. Her fingers crushed Mary's hand as she continued. "Sir Duncan brings our family financial stability, and I will not risk that for Mr. Ashbrook."

"You speak as though we have no income, Mama. Even if Sir Duncan were to jilt Lydia, we need only economize a bit and all would be well."

"And live like paupers?" She spoke the word as if it were the worst thing a person could be called.

"I hardly think that anyone who keeps a carriage and several servants can be called a pauper," Mary replied with a roll of her eyes.

Mama gave another sigh and was quiet for a few moments as she brushed her fingers along Mary's hand. "Let us pretend that you are correct—that Mr. Ashbrook's suit does not offend Sir Duncan or that we are able to live without his support. That still leaves me wondering how you can choose to leave us when we need you here so desperately."

Looking at her daughter with tearful eyes, Mama pleaded with her. "Don't you see how much your father and I rely on you? What would we do without you? How can you abandon your family?"

"You speak as though we would never see each other again," said Mary. "Mr. Ashbrook and I have not discussed where we will settle, but even if we moved to another county, we would visit often. It is no different than Lydia."

"But that was our plan for her. You, on the other hand, were meant to stay with us. I thought that is what you wanted. To take care of us in our dotage." She spoke the words as though they painted a happy little future.

"For me to be your caretaker?"

"To be our daughter." Mama released Mary's hand and crossed her arms. "Really, Mary, you speak as though you are a prisoner, but you like taking care of us, organizing the household, and all that. Why would you wish to leave that? Leave us?"

Turning in her seat, Mary looked at her mother, revealing her heart in her gaze, hoping it might give a glimpse into the depths of her affection. "Because I love Mr. Ashbrook. I want to spend my life with him." But then Mary amended her statement. "I *am* going to spend my life with him."

Mama stared at her for several long seconds. She straightened, her gaze taking in the bedchamber as she slowly stood and smoothed her skirts.

"I see," she murmured, clasping her hands. Coming to stand before Mary, Mama looked at her daughter with an expression so devoid of feeling that Mary had no guess as to the thoughts churning in her mother's mind.

"It appears you have a decision to make, then." Mama swallowed and took a steadying breath. "You are of age, and you do not need our approval to marry, so it is your choice. Are you going to support your family—the people who love you and have cared for you your entire life—or are you going to abandon us and marry a man who might well be the financial ruin of this family? A man who will likely be unfaithful and bring you nothing but heartache?"

Mary gaped at those horrid words.

"If you choose to act selfishly, I will warn you," said Mama, her eyes dropping to the floor. Her chin wobbled and her shoulders slumped. Clearing her throat, she began again. "Your father and I shan't risk Mr. Ashbrook's reputation damaging this family. If you marry him, we shall cut all ties with you. We shan't see you or speak to you ever again. You will be lost to us, and we to you."

Tears filled Mary's eyes, her hand coming to her mouth as she realized what Mama was saying. Mary saw the earnestness in her mother's words and posture, leaving no doubt that should she marry Ambrose, the threat would be carried out.

"You would do that?" asked Mary.

But Mama would not speak another word. Turning, she slid through the door, closing it behind her.

Chapter 31

S taring off into the darkness with only the flickering fire and a solitary candle to light her bedchamber, Mary sat in shocked silence, unaware of the passing hours. Her parents would disown her. She'd known that her engagement would cause upheaval, but Mary had expected a minor flurry, not an avalanche. And certainly not an irrevocable choice between the life she had and the life she wanted.

What *she* wanted. The memory of Mama's words filled Mary's heart with burning shame. Was it truly so wrong to think about her own dreams and desires? Mary could not bear the thought of giving Ambrose up, but was that simply a sign of her selfishness? Did she have the right to choose her own happiness above that of her family's?

Time passed as she sat there, the candle melting into a nub, and Mary was lost.

A tentative knock came at the door, but Mary didn't answer. She was in no state to talk to anyone. However, Lydia ignored the dismissal and poked her head inside.

"I noticed the light in your room and just had to see you," said Lydia, hurrying to Mary's side. "Is it true? I overheard Mama and Papa speaking of it when I arrived home. You and

Mr. Ashbrook?"

Mary nodded.

Lydia's eyes widened as she dropped onto the bed. "What were you thinking?"

Standing, Mary rubbed her forehead as she paced. "If you knew Mr. Ashbrook, you would not ask such a question. He is impossible not to love. But I am not up to talking right now."

"Love?" snapped Lydia. "What does that have to do with it? If marriage were about love, I would not be marrying that awful Sir Duncan!"

Mary turned to stare at her sister, shocked to find her suspicions confirmed. "You don't love Sir Duncan?"

Lydia sighed, her shoulders slumping. "Could you love that pompous windbag? He's Papa's age, for goodness' sake! But that doesn't matter because this isn't about what I want."

Her eyes wandered from Mary to stare out the window. "Love is grand, but do you truly wish to live like a pauper? Sacrifice your security to marry some man who scrapes by? Even if the very sight of him makes the world brighter?" She trailed off into silence, her eyes gazing into the distance.

"Mr. Ashbrook is no pauper," said Mary, puzzled at her sister's words.

Lydia jerked her eyes to Mary and wiped at a tear trickling down her cheek. Standing, she wrapped her arms around her waist and gave her sister a sad smile. "Your heart may tell you one thing, but it does not know best. I do not love Sir Duncan, but our marriage will bless my family. With time and practice, I might feel something for him. And there will be children. That will be enough."

"You cannot be serious." The words were little more than a whisper, but listening to Lydia's stark assessment of her future startled Mary. Horrified her.

"Mama and Papa have invested everything in my future. I cannot repay them by going against their wishes." Lydia's eyes were bleak. There was nothing of the blushing bride in them. They were old and sad, and Mary wanted so much more for her dear sister. Listless, Lydia shuffled to the door and left without another word.

Mary stared after her sister, chilled at the vision of what her own future would be if she stayed. Before Ambrose, her life had been a long string of nothingness. She had accepted it then because she'd had no other option. But not anymore. Mary could not settle for a joyless existence, for she had seen how beautiful life could be.

Mama's words mixed together in Mary's mind, arranging themselves into a stark revelation. Her parents were selfish creatures. Everything in their lives was about their own wants and needs. Even their daughters were nothing more than tools for their use. And Mary would not be party to their machinations any more.

She deserved better.

...

The candle snuffed itself out around the time the sun began its slow creep up the horizon, and Mary tucked the two books Ambrose had given her into the top of her portmanteau. The covers bulged from the blossoms crushed between their pages, but Mary would not part with them. She had not the space to take the bouquets with her, but she contented herself by preserving a flower from each one.

With a snap, she shut her bag and then her trunk. Checking once more that all her things were properly packed, Mary took her portmanteau in hand and left. She knew of a place where she would be welcomed without caveats, and she would not stay another day at Buckthorn Manor.

Mary did not sneak. There was no need to. Likely, her parents thought she would bend, but they would discover soon enough how wrong they were. She only hoped their bitterness would not keep them from sending her trunk, for it was too heavy for her to carry on her own.

"Now, you'd best not be thinking you can simply slip away without a proper goodbye."

Mary jumped, teetering on the stairs. "Gibbs?"

The butler stood at the bottom, holding her bonnet and spencer in his hands. Mrs. Webb and Mrs. Gibbs came to stand beside him, their eyes bright as they watched her descend.

"We found this young fellow skulking about the grounds," said Mrs. Webb, pointing over her shoulder, and Ambrose stepped from the shadows.

Dropping her bag, Mary launched into his arms, needing to hold him and be held.

"I choose you," she whispered.

Ambrose leaned away to look at her, with a brow raised. "Good choice," he said with that mocking grin of his.

Mary smacked his arm with a playful scowl, though his teasing could not dislodge that sliver of sadness digging into her heart. Ambrose brushed a finger across her cheek, and she met his gaze. In it, she knew he saw her pain.

"They aren't going to change their minds, are they?" he asked.

When Mary shook her head, he glanced down at the portmanteau and back at her, a tinge of worry in his eyes, and she knew he was questioning her decision, though he would not ask.

"I choose you," she repeated.

"Let me get to my lass," said Mrs. Webb, nudging aside Ambrose to sweep Mary into a hug. The Gibbs came next, embracing her as they murmured their support and congratulations, giving Mary the happy words a bride wished to hear. Each brought new tears to her eyes as she realized that this would likely be her final farewell to these people who had been such an integral part of her life.

"You'd best take care of her," said Mrs. Gibbs, dabbing her eyes before hugging Ambrose.

"My father was a butcher, and he taught me well," said Mrs. Webb, wiping at her cheeks as she scowled at Ambrose. "If you hurt our Miss Mary, I can end your existence and get rid of the evidence in a trice. Mark my words, boy."

Ambrose blinked, wide-eyed at the woman, but she softened her threats with a quick hug before Gibbs gave him a stern handshake. Taking Mary's bag in one arm, Ambrose offered up his other with that smile that belonged solely to her. Together, they walked out into the dewy dawn, and Mary knew the sacrifices of today would be nothing compared to the joy that would come from a life with Ambrose.

Epilogue

Ambrose tugged at his sleeves and straightened his waist-coat, then checked his cravat. Puffing out his cheeks, he let out a slow breath and walked over to the mirror once again. All was well. Ambrose kept repeating that phrase to himself, as though the repetition might somehow make him believe it. But staring at his reflection only made him more anxious, so he resumed pacing the parlor.

"You needn't worry, Ambrose," said Graham, coming up to give him a rough pat on the shoulder. "Any woman who throws herself so enthusiastically into your embrace as Miss Hayward does is not likely to run off."

"What?" Ambrose glared at his brother. "Don't be crude."

But Graham gave a great bark of laughter, slapping his brother on the shoulder once more. "Not so fun to be on the receiving end of such a comment, is it?"

Ambrose glowered, but Mina chimed in, "Behave, boys." She gave each of her brothers a stern look before placing a kiss on her husband's cheek and heading out in search of whatever dire wedding details needed attending to.

"Is it time yet?" asked Ambrose.

"No," said Simon with a groan. "Another fifteen minutes

before we leave for the church."

"And the trunks are packed?"

"The carriage is ready to leave once the ceremony is over," said Nicholas. "Though I have no idea why you are bringing Dottie along. She is a lovely child, but after your last journey with her, it seems a mistake to bring her on your wedding trip."

The memories of those few days together brought a smile to Ambrose's lips. "Perhaps we are inviting disaster, but we both agreed that we cannot bear the thought of leaving her behind while we tour a few investment opportunities in Lancashire. We have missed too much of her life already and don't want to spend weeks apart."

Graham clapped Ambrose on the shoulder yet again. Though he did not say the words, Ambrose saw the understanding glint in his eyes, for he was in the same boat with his new wife's son, Phillip.

"I don't know how you got Mina to forgo the wedding breakfast," said Graham. "Tabby tried everything to dissuade our sister from a lavish affair, and she is positively envious that you two are able to avoid all the pomp."

"Yes, well, with the uproar the Haywards have caused, quiet is better," said Ambrose. Clasping his hands behind his back, he tapped his fingers against his knuckles, fretting once more about the decision to marry now. Perhaps if they had waited until after Lydia's wedding, her parents would have been more forgiving. But his instincts did not agree; Mary's defiance had been the death knell of any possible reconciliation.

"Calm yourself, Ambrose," said Nicholas. "She is a fine lady, and she loves you dearly."

"For some odd reason," muttered Graham with a grin. Ambrose glared at him, but it only broadened his brother's smile.

"You two are as well-suited as any couple I've met," said Simon.

Ambrose took in a breath, letting it out slowly, and took another. This was the right decision for them. As he held on to that certainty, the panic faded into a peaceful confidence.

The parlor door opened, and Tabby rushed inside, her eyebrows knitted together. "Ambrose, I think it best if you see to Mary. Her sister came to visit, and now she's upset—"

Before Tabby had finished speaking, Ambrose bolted out of the room, hurrying to where the ladies had set up camp. But he found only Louisa-Margaretta.

"Mary's in the library," she said, pointing across the hall. "She wanted to be alone."

Ambrose worried whether he should intrude on her solitude, but he shook that concern away. Though she often sought a quiet corner to get away from the madness that was his family, she never rejected his company. Stepping into the library, he saw her standing before the window with Dottie in her arms. Caught in the morning light filtering through the glass, Mary swayed as she rubbed the babe's back and hummed a soft tune. Dottie lay asleep against her shoulder, and Mary pressed a kiss to her forehead.

At his footsteps, she turned and Ambrose halted in his steps, mesmerized by the sight she made. He had thought that he understood beauty. He had spent much of his life admiring the fairer sex and had heard many a gentleman wax poetic on the subject. Empirically, he knew that others did not think so, but his eyes told him that Mary was gorgeous. Though she bemoaned her newly cropped hair, it curled at her nape in such a manner that it made him hunger to place a kiss there.

But then he noted the redness in her eyes and the tears on her cheeks.

"Miss Pert?"

The nickname drew a wry smile, though it did not chase away the sadness in her eyes. "I suppose someone told you about Lydia."

"And I came straight away to keep you from bolting," he said, coming to her side and running his hand over Dottie's head.

"You cannot be rid of me that easily," she said, but tears gathered in her eyes. Ambrose drew his arm around her, and she rested her head on his shoulder as she sniffled. "Mama and Papa won't even speak my name. Lydia thinks they will never forgive me."

There were no words he could offer to soothe that ache, so he simply held her as she spoke.

"I know they can be so awful, but they are my family and I still love them. I cannot seem to help myself." She sniffled some more as he stroked her back. "But the worst of all is that she is making the wrong decision."

"Lydia?"

Mary nodded. "She snuck away to give me her love, but she still won't listen. She is going to marry him in two days' time, and I know it's going to ruin her life, and there is nothing I can do about it."

"I know, sweetheart," he murmured, pressing a kiss to her head. They stood together for several moments, Mary clinging to him and Dottie as she shed more tears. It pained him that he could do nothing to heal this heartache. Perhaps with time things between the Haywards and their daughter would get better, but Ambrose did not hold out much hope. Regardless, it did nothing for the lady in his arms who deserved only joy on her wedding day.

"I love you, my Mary," he said, giving her the only words he could.

"I love you, too," she murmured, and Ambrose hoped he would never tire of hearing her say that.

"Thank you for not giving up on me, Ambrose." Mary lifted her head to meet his gaze, her eyes bright with tears. "No matter how I pushed you away, you never stopped fighting for us. If not for your persistence, I would be stuck in that cold and unhappy life. Thank you for loving me unconditionally."

The adoration in her gaze burned through Ambrose, and he brushed away a tear clinging to her cheek. "You act as though you are the only winner in this situation, but you have given me so much more."

As she always did when he said such things, Mary gave a

huff and rolled her eyes, resting her head on his shoulder to hide from the truth she did not fully accept. Yet. Ambrose let her silent denial go, for beneath her bluster he saw his own truth. Mary was beginning to believe him.

Running his hand along her back, Ambrose wished he could heal the damage done to her heart but contented himself with knowing that in a few minutes they would be husband and wife, and he would have many years to show her just how true his words were. Until she believed it without a single doubt.

Mary Hayward may think it was he who saved her, but it was she who saved him. Mary had given him everything, and Ambrose would do everything in his power to make certain she knew it.

Exclusive Offer

Join the M.A. Nichols VIP Reader Club at

www.ma-nichols.com

to receive up-to-date information about upcoming
books, freebies, and VIP content!

About the Author

Born and raised in Anchorage, M.A. Nichols is a lifelong Alaskan with a love of the outdoors. As a child she despised reading but through the love and persistence of her mother was taught the error of her ways and has had a deep, abiding relationship with it ever since.

She graduated with a bachelor's degree in landscape management from Brigham Young University and a master's in landscape architecture from Utah State University, neither of which has anything to do with why she became a writer, but is a fun little tidbit none-the-less. And no, she doesn't have any idea what type of plant you should put in that shady spot out by your deck. She's not that kind of landscape architect. Stop asking.

Website   Facebook   Instagram   BookBub

Made in the USA
Middletown, DE
18 July 2024

57517319R00168